Even Now

GINA ARDITO

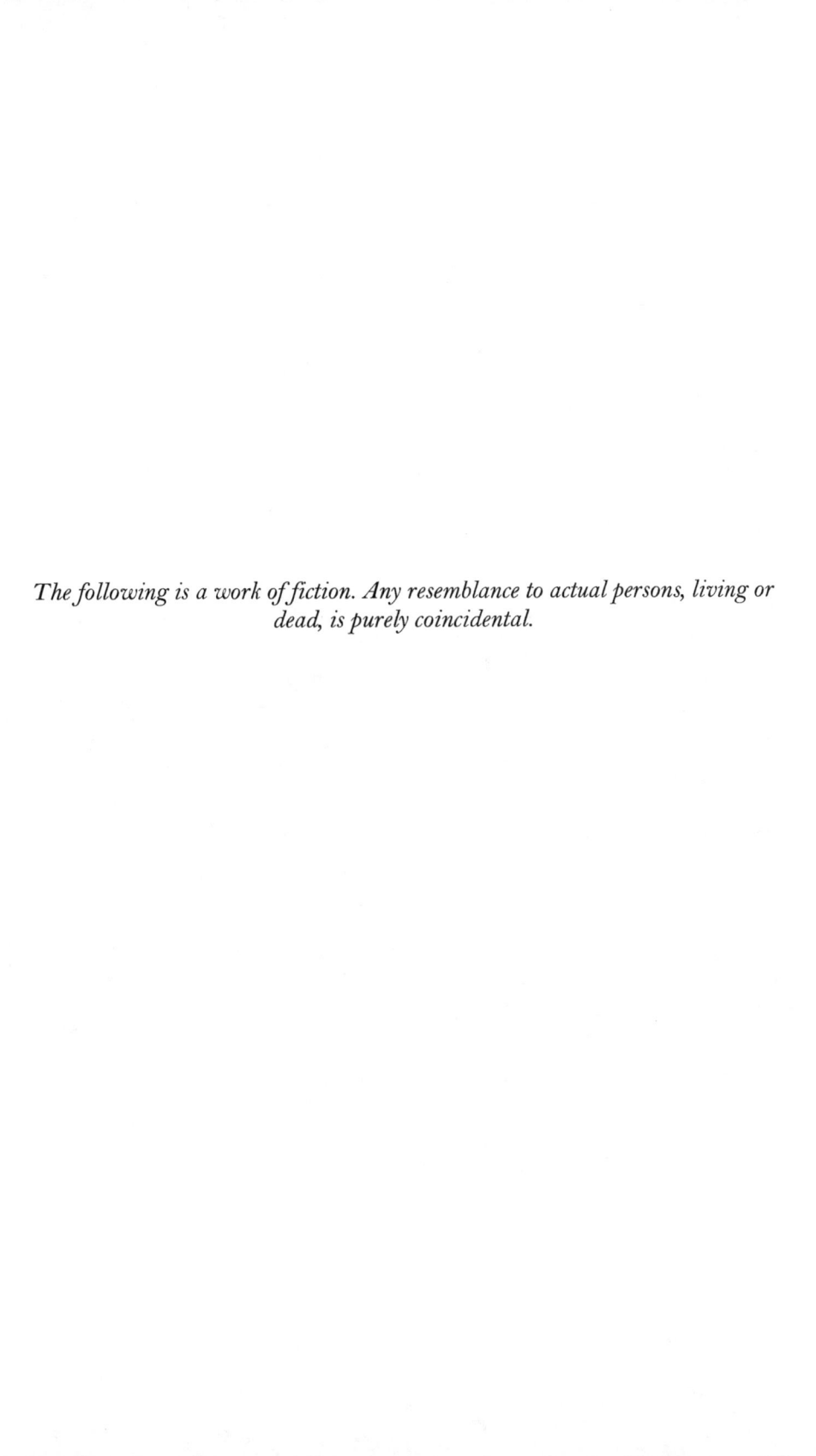

DEDICATION

For all those who work with shelter pets, adopt shelter pets, and love shelter pets.

1

FUR-EVER FRIENDS ANIMAL SHELTER
This Evening

"You think you can just walk in here with your money and your fancy red sports car and your fame, and fool me into believing you? That if you tell me you're sorry, I'll forget all about how you deserted me and I'll fall in love with you all over again?" Sniffing back tears, Leah shook her head. "It won't happen, Wy. Face it. You want us to go back to the way things were so you can feel better about us before you fly out of here for another seven years. Or would it be for good this time?"

"Neither." Wyatt took a tentative step closer, hoping, she supposed, to keep her from running out the door, though, with the difference in their strides, she'd never get past the desk before he stopped her. They both knew it. "I'm asking you to come with me. To be by my side for *all* time."

An anguished wail rose up inside her, but she clamped her lips shut. What she wouldn't have sacrificed to hear those words seven years ago. Now? Now, it was way too late. "Forget it. I've got a life here, and it doesn't include you anymore."

"So, that's it?" Wyatt demanded. "You're not even gonna consider giving us another chance to make this work?"

"No." Before he could see the hurt in her eyes, she dropped her gaze to the mountain of paperwork on her cluttered desk. "I guess that makes us even now, huh?"

❦

FUR-EVER FRIENDS ANIMAL SHELTER
Three Months Ago

Leah Stewart swallowed a huge gulp of disappointment while viewing the chaos around her. Two trees had fallen during last night's storm: the two-hundred-year-old oak and the recently planted weeping cherry. The cherry was a monument tree, meant to mark the place where long-time resident Buddy the Bull Terrier's ashes were buried. If not salvageable, the sapling was, at least, replaceable.

The fallen giant, on the other hand, now dissected her backyard, its massive trunk crushing the stockade fence at the rear of the property. The uppermost branches had missed the cat sanctuary by a few feet, but took out the power lines, a telephone pole, and the transformer box in one swoop.

"Well, that explains the power outage," she muttered to Casey, who stood beside her, slack-jawed and eyes agog.

"Now, what do we do?" His whine raised the hackles on her nape. He was a sweet kid, seventeen and willing to work for minimum wage, but God, he was a *young* seventeen. Had she ever been so naïve, so helpless, so totally out of touch with the world when she was a teen? If so, she owed her father a major league apology.

"We go back to the office and use our cell phones to contact the power company, the phone company, and the rest of the staff. Make sure everyone's okay, and see who's available to come in to help. It's probably gonna be a while before we can get a utility employee out here to assess the damage, much less to repair it. We may need to relocate some of the animals 'til then."

The nor'easter that had blown into town last night had cut a wide swath of destruction throughout their area. With all the damage residents sustained, Leah's little out-of-the-way shelter wouldn't be a priority for tree crews, utility workers, or the denizens of Town Hall. Stray animals didn't rate high on the emergency action list; they didn't vote.

Terrific. How much would it cost to fix all this? With angry dollar signs buzzing around her head, she plodded through the wasteland of mud, broken tree branches, and bits of debris to the rear door of the office, Casey on her heels.

Inside, she headed straight for the storage closet and rummaged around for the portable radio, hoping the batteries were still good.

"Where should I start?" Casey asked.

"The employees. I'll get the ball rolling on the electricity and phone." She clicked the power button on the old boom box and immediately got an earful of static. A flick of the dial landed her on a local radio station where an overenthusiastic deejay rattled off a list of towns experiencing power outages. Lots of them.

"Great," she grumbled. "Looks like we're gonna be out for a while."

This was trouble. Big trouble. Already, the temperature in the building had dropped to the point she could see her breath on each inhale and exhale. She'd have to move the animals until she had heat and electricity in here again, especially the sick ones in the infirmary. She wondered if any of the other shelters in the area had fared better. Her list of phone calls to make kept growing, while her battery life would continue shrinking. Luckily, she had her backup quick charger. Still, even that would only last so long.

"And, in other, *better*, news," the deejay intoned, "it seems the rift between Wyatt Blackthorne and his bandmates, The Ungrateful, has finally been mended. Rumor has it all the boys are back in the studio, working on the last few tracks on a brand new album, called 'Homecoming.' According to the band's website, Wyatt plans to launch their upcoming concert tour this spring with the first stop right here on Long Island where his career started."

Alone in the reception area, she stiffened, gripping her cell with the strength of a vise. Wyatt? Coming back? Surely, not to Osprey Cove. Seven years ago, he couldn't wait to leave this town—and everyone in it—behind. He hadn't returned since.

The pain, long dormant, reawakened with vengeful fangs to eat out her heart.

You're not that same dumb bunny anymore, she reminded herself. You're smarter now. Smart enough to know there was more to life than the pursuit of fame and fortune. Unlike Wyatt.

Wyatt Blackthorne had disappeared from her life at the exact time she'd needed him most. To this day, she often wondered if he'd suspected she was in trouble, and that was what sent him running without a backward glance.

"Something wrong with your phone?"

Casey's question shook her out of the past. "Huh?"

"Your phone. You're staring at it like it's dead or something."

To avoid his scrutiny, she busied herself with organizing the jumble of collars and clipboards on the front desk. "No, it's…umm…it's fine. I've got a full charge and I'm ready to go. I was just trying to figure out which area shelters might be able to help us out." Tossing memories of Wyatt the traitor into the dumpster in the back of her brain, she refocused on the problems at hand. Wyatt was old news. Old flame, old wound.

No, he wouldn't dare come back to Osprey Cove. She wasn't the only one he burned on his rocket ride to stardom.

Thirty minutes and half that many phone calls later, Leah buried her face in her hands to keep Casey from witnessing her total breakdown. The rep from the power company she'd finally reached had promised her they could send a crew to remove the tree by next week. Oh, and another crew would gladly come to reinstall the transformer box and utility pole, too. But the rep couldn't tell her when she could expect the second crew. Only after the first crew had removed the tree could she be placed on the waiting list for the second crew. Then she'd have to shell out for an electrician to connect her buildings to the new box and pole. The phone and cable companies couldn't do their jobs to get her back in contact with the public until she had electricity again.

Meanwhile, area shelters lucky enough to still have electricity and all the other modern conveniences were crammed full of lost pets and the overflow from other, larger adoption centers.

The irony of this situation? Yesterday's fundraiser, meant to help buy a generator for instances where the building might lose power, had been cancelled due to the extreme weather.

Leah glanced at the daily roster. Fourteen dogs, three of them recuperating from some medical treatment or temporarily quarantined until they'd received a clean bill of health. Eleven cats, five taking up residence with the recuperating dogs in the infirmary. In total, twenty-five prospective pets currently onsite with nowhere to go.

Well, technically, with one-where to go.

"Fire up the van," she ordered Casey. "We're gonna have to get all these pets to my house before it gets dark."

His eyes rounded. "All of them?"

"Unless you think your mom will let you take home a dozen cats...?"

"Yeah, umm...no."

"I didn't think so. Well, they have to go somewhere. I've still got power there, at least, so I can keep them until everything's back to semi-normal here. Did you reach all the employees? Everybody else is okay?"

"Uh-huh. It looks like the storm picked sides. Everyone north of Main Street is without power, anyone south had their lights flicker, but they never went out." Grabbing the van keys from the hook by the door, he headed outside.

Mother Nature sure was fickle. The shelter, powerless, sat on the north side, her home, with electricity still working, waited for her on the south. It would take a while to move everyone, but she had the room, and more importantly right now, the modern comforts they all needed.

"Hey."

At this new intrusion, Leah glanced up from the assortment of pet paraphernalia on the reception desk and into the concerned expression on Jenny Conway's face. Jenny, the shelter's assistant manager, wore pink sweats and, thank-you-to-the-caffeine-gods, carried a cardboard carryout tray that held three tall disposable coffee cups.

"I brought reinforcements," she announced, hefting the tray. She settled the coffee on the desk and handed one to Leah before peeling off her jacket. "How bad is it?"

Leah sipped the beverage, reveling in its heat and hoping to gain some liquid courage before replying, "We've got a downed tree that took out the power lines in the back. I don't know how long it's going to take to get us up and running again. The other shelters around here are dealing with their own issues. Casey and I were about to start transporting everyone to my place."

"Well, I can help a little in that respect. I've got all the comforts of home at my place so I can take some of the animals, too."

"That'd be great. Thanks so much."

"Don't thank me yet. There's a catch," Jenny replied with a smirk. "I'm taking Duchess."

Duchess was a hound mix, longtime shelter resident, and the staff's favorite because of her sweet nature. She was shy around strangers and tended to hide in the corner of her area when visitors strolled through. Often, potential pet owners assumed, wrongly, that she must have been abused in the past and that explained her reticence to connect with humans. But Duchess's true story was a common one. She'd been dropped at the town's kill shelter when her elderly owner died and no one in the deceased's family would take in Grandma's old dog. Loyal Duchess, confused and frightened, had been abandoned by everyone familiar until Leah found her and brought her to Fur-Ever Friends.

Nowadays, the staff took turns working with the old lady dog to re-socialize her. They took her in their cars when they went on errands, played with her in the yard, walked her on the street, and showed her the love she'd been missing since her owner's death.

"Fine," Leah said with an exaggerated sigh. "You get Duchess."

"Ha!" Jenny shimmied a mini-victory dance.

"But it's gonna cost you all the cats in the infirmary."

"I'm still getting the better deal." She sobered. "Wait. How many are there?"

"Two dozen."

The triumphant grin wobbled. "Two dozen? As in twenty-four?"

Leah had to hide her own triumphant grin. "Yup. Still think you drove a great bargain?"

Jenny sank into a chair, as if the number was too ponderous to bear while standing, then replied, "Yeah. Come to think of it. I do."

"Good. Because there are only eleven cats, five in the infirmary."

"Oh, thank God," she uttered and dropped her head to her folded arms on the desktop. Leah found her first laugh of the day, and Jenny raised her narrowed-eye gaze. "I shoulda told the guy at the bagel shop to put decaf in your cup."

"You wouldn't dare!" To be on the safe side, Leah took another sip, this time testing the taste on her tongue for that familiar zing.

"No." Jenny smirked. "I wouldn't. I'm not as mean as you."

"No one's as mean as I am," Leah remarked, raising her cup in a mock toast.

"True. That's why we appease you with the sacred dark bean juice."

"You got that right."

The two friends shared a sip and a smile before Jenny sobered once again. "How'd everybody else fare? Have you heard from them?"

"I had Casey call the staff. Everyone's okay. South of Main seems to be relatively unscathed, but the north side got hit hard."

Casey chose that moment to slip in through the back door. "Oh, good. The coffee's here. Which one's mine?"

Jenny held up the last cup, and he took it gratefully. "Awesome." After peeling back the piece of lid and taking a healthy swallow, he turned to Leah. "Van's all fired up. Where do you want to start?"

"The infirmary. Jenny's gonna take the cats. I'll take the dogs."

Hours later, exhausted, dirty, and with the last five dogs in hand, she pushed open the door to her temporary pet shelter: an updated, detached garage she'd renovated for emergencies just like this one. A cacophony of barks and yips erupted.

"Okay, guys, settle down. It's been a busy day." One by one, she wrangled the final five into their crates. The last one, Murphy, the diabetic pug, barked twice to signal it was time for his insulin shot then swiped his wet tongue over her cheek. Not because he loved getting his shots, but because he couldn't resist the peanut butter treat he got after each one. "Gimme ten minutes, Murph. I got another patient that needs me more right now."

After checking the locks were all secure, Leah left the garage and walked across the lawn to the back door of the center hall colonial she called home.

Giselle sat at the kitchen table, sipping a cup of tea. "Everything okay? The troops all settled in?" Her heavy Jamaican accent gave the questions a musical quality.

"For the most part." Closing the door by leaning against it, Leah let out an exhausted sigh. "I just need to give Murphy his insulin shot."

"I'll make a deal with you," Giselle said, rising. "You take care of that cranky guy upstairs and I'll take care of the pooch in the garage."

Leah grimaced. "Bad day?"

"No more than usual. He's been waiting for you, though."

Of course he was. Dad hadn't left the house since Mom's funeral. Leah was his only link to the outside world. "Go on home," she replied. "You've had enough excitement for one day."

Her neighbor cocked her head and stared at Leah. Her caramel eyes, sharp and ageless, missed nothing. "You sure? You haven't exactly spent the day sipping cocoa, either."

"I'll take care of Dad *and* Murphy. I appreciate you keeping an eye on my father for me."

Giselle shrugged. "Wasn't really necessary. He's had an old friend visitin' since about three. I think that's why he's so amped up for you to get home tonight, so you could say hello. Anyway, I washed your dishes and vacuumed the living room while I waited for you."

A flush burned her cheeks. "You didn't have to do that. You could've just gone home."

"You asked me to stay 'til you got the animals taken care of. I stayed."

"But you didn't have to clean my house. That wasn't part of the deal. Once his friend got here, you could've left. Who is it anyway? One of his VFW poker buddies?"

A grin wide and predatory as a shark's stretched Giselle's frosted mauve lips. "Oh, honey, I don't think so. This man's much too young. Young and tasty."

"How young?" More importantly, how tasty? Her gaze flew to the ceiling as if she might see who loitered in her father's bedroom upstairs. What stranger was in her house? Or was it a stranger at all? What if it was someone from the past, the same someone mentioned on the radio today? A shiver of unease ran through her. "It wouldn't happen to be Wyatt, would it?"

"That it would, sweetcakes." His too familiar voice, along with the hated nickname he'd pinned on her in tenth grade, slithered from behind her.

She whirled, and there he stood, at the bottom of the staircase cutting between the den and the kitchen. Well, crap. Years later, her luck still hadn't changed. Wyatt Blackthorne had always had those steely good looks that made her heart trip its rhythm. Vivid blue eyes peered out at the world from under soot-colored curls. His tall and rangy body held a certain appeal Leah couldn't describe, but she, along with hundreds of other women since his first album released, suffered under the effects of that subtle, sexy allure.

Seven years had elapsed, and Wyatt hadn't changed—no new wrinkles, not a gray hair, no pot belly. If anything, he looked...*yummier*, that polish of stardom shining up all his natural attributes.

Too bad the same couldn't be said for her. Oh, she had no wrinkles, gray hair or pot belly, either. But she certainly didn't have that raw sensuality he wore so well. After the day she just endured, she looked and smelled like something the cat dragged in. Literally. Leah didn't need a mirror to know her face was streaked with grime and sweat, her hair flew in a dozen different directions around her head, and she wore more dog hair than fabric.

"Well?" he drawled as he glided closer to where she stood, stunned. "Won't you at least give me a kiss hello?"

She shook off the awe he'd cast over her and stumbled to the back door. "Actually, I've got something better to do. I gotta plunge a syringe into a stray dog's butt. Bye, Wyatt. You can let yourself out."

♋

Sweet Leah. Wyatt Blackthorne leaned against the doorjamb and grinned as she fled out the back door. She still had the face that had haunted him for nearly a decade, a cutting wit, and the ability to put him in his place. God, he'd missed her!

After he first left Osprey Cove, he'd written a song about the way she made him feel, pouring out all his love and regrets about leaving her behind. His manager had made him change the title, "Sweet Leah" to "Sweet Kira," claiming the more exotic name would create a better buzz with the public. Maybe Cooper was right about the sales, but with the change, the song lost meaning for him. The lyrics had originally been his way of apologizing to *Leah*, not to some faceless, anonymous Kira. He hadn't wronged anyone named Kira. Over the years, lots of things lost meaning for him. This trip home was all about recapturing what he'd lost—Leah, most of all.

"I take it you two have a checkered history," the woman who'd let him in earlier remarked dryly. Her golden eyes, like a tiger's, glinted with mischief as she studied him while rinsing out her teacup.

"You could say that."

"I *did* say that." Cackling, she placed the cup in the dishwasher's top rack. "You were upstairs a long time. Trying to milk the old man for information about her before she came home?"

He could have lied. The intensity in this woman's steady gaze almost dared him to try. "Something like that," was the best he could do. He'd spent the afternoon and half the evening with her father, apologizing for not attending Mrs. Stewart's funeral last April, offering his condolences, and…yes…feeling out Mr. Stewart on how Leah might react when she learned of his return to Osprey Cove. "I'm Wyatt, by the way."

"I know who you are." Her eyes narrowed to slits as she turned to lean her rump against the counter. "But you don't remember *me*, do you?"

He stepped into the room to study her under the light. Should he remember her? He'd met so many people over the years, fans mostly, and they all asked, "Remember me?" He could usually get away with something bland like, "You bet I do. You were at my show, right?" And they'd squeal in delight before filling in all the details: what show, what year, where they sat, their favorite songs, and something banal they might have done or said that was supposed to instantly connect him with their memory.

You looked right at me when you sang "Take My Heart Again." That was always my favorite song.

You tossed your guitar pick into the audience, and I caught it.

You signed my t-shirt.

I was backstage and gave you a bottle of water when you finished your set.

His stock answer wasn't going to work with this woman. She, based on the suspicious set to her expression, was not a fan of his.

"No," he admitted. "I can't say I do."

"Uh-huh. Figures. Now that you hit the big time, you forgot about all the people who helped you when you needed 'em."

Funny. He would've said that ever since he hit the big time, all these people came out of his past to take credit for his hard work, his risks, his dedication. The one person who never got in touch was Leah. Ironically, she was the only one he wanted to hear from, the only one who truly had made a difference in his life. He folded his arms over his chest and glared at the woman who glared back with equal scrutiny.

"I'll give you a hint," she said. "Coifs and Cuts."

He recognized the name of the old recording studio in the back of the hair salon, but the woman…

Wait.

"Giselle?"

She nodded, her lips breaking into a knowing smile, and she pushed away from the counter to move closer to him. The scent of jasmine wandered in the air when she stood toe-to-toe with him. "Ah, so you do remember me. And all the times I slipped you and your friends in through the back door after hours so Jean-Claude wouldn't charge you for the studio time."

She'd done that and more. She let him sleep in the storage room in the salon whenever his father was on one of his vicious benders. The hideaway began as temporary when he was in high school, then became more permanent when he attended college. Giselle had been one of his havens in stormy times. How could he not remember her?

"I'm...sorry," he said, glancing at his feet. "I should've known who you were instan—"

"Bah. I'm not surprised you don't remember what I look like. You always had your head down when I saw you. Like a whipped dog, you were. Who could blame you with what that vicious man put you through? Water under the bridge now, though. You've come home a big star." She waved a hand at him, and the dozen golden bangles surrounding her wrist jingled. "Think it'll matter to her?"

A snippet of a lyric whispered in his ear. *Music flies from her fingertips.*

He'd have to play with that when he got back to the motel. But, first, he'd have to compose another apology for Sweet Leah. "I sure hope so."

2

After seeing to Murphy's treatment, Leah purposely stayed in the garage for nearly thirty minutes, giving Wyatt time to realize she wasn't coming back. In an attempt to regain her sense of balance, she leaned against the wall near the cages until she could get the tremors in her limbs under control. Wyatt. Her brain struggled to compute his surprise appearance in her house. Meanwhile, her heart cracked in a dozen places—old places where his abrupt departure years ago had broken and healed over time. Wyatt. Back. Here.

"What do you think he wants, guys?" she asked the dogs.

In reply, Murphy wagged his tail, Bowie jumped up on the latched cage door, and Hermione scratched her ear. The rest of her four-legged tenants couldn't be bothered to respond in any way.

"You're all a big help."

"Maybe he wants another chance," a low voice said from the doorway.

She gasped when she spotted his silhouette. "Stop doing that!"

Hearing her distress, the dogs broke into a cacophony of barks and yips.

"Doing what?" Wyatt drawled as he strode inside.

His smug smile raised the fine hairs on her flesh, and she folded her arms on her chest to hug herself warm. "Sneaking up on me."

"You didn't come back to the house." He flipped the grin to a disappointed frown. "I was waiting for you."

Manipulative jerk. "What for?"

"I missed you, Leah. It's been a long time."

"Funny. Since my address and phone number haven't changed since I was born, I can only assume this bout of nostalgia is a temporary condition for you." She pushed off the wall and strode to the cages to double-check the locks. While fumbling with the latches, she prayed he would see her ploy as disinterest in his very existence. "Don't worry. I imagine once you've crept away in the middle of the night, you'll forget all about me. It worked so well for you last time."

"How about we start with today and work our way backwards? How are you? You look great."

His voice came from behind her, too close for her peace of mind, and she dug up the bitterness she'd buried in her heart for so long.

She whirled to face him. "Really? You think that tired line will weave some spell on me? The woman you left behind? You skipped town without saying a word. Worse, you stole my work when you left." She thumped a fist on her chest. "*My work. My very soul.* I only found out when I heard *Take My Heart Again* on the radio, a hit by new music sensation, Wyatt Blackthorne. Just one problem, bucko. The song wasn't written *by* you. I wrote it."

"I never said it was written by me, and I doubt you'd find anyone who'd say I ever claimed I wrote it. It was performed by me. You got credit as the lyricist. I made sure you received every dime of royalties you deserved. You get checks every quarter."

Checks she always let Jenny open and deposit, since she couldn't bear the reminder every three months.

"Uh-huh. My friends here," she swept an arm around the garage, encompassing the crates of barking dogs, "are extremely grateful for your compensation."

He toyed with the latch on one of the cages, and the metallic click skittered up her spine. "Your father told me you bought the local shelter. I'm sorry about your mom, by the way."

"Yeah," she bit out. "I could tell by the bounty of flowers and sympathy messages you sent at the time. Why, we were practically drowning in your touching tribute." Acid roiled in her stomach. She didn't want to talk about her mom. Or the past.

All the confidence on his face melted away, and he had the grace to look away from her. "I was in Europe at the time."

"Right. Where there are no phones, no contact with the outside world. Perfectly understandable." She didn't want to talk about *anything* with him.

He held his hands out in supplication. "I didn't know, Leah. You have to believe me. I would've come home if I'd known."

"Uh-huh," she said again, her voice tight with still-unleashed fury. "So…what? You just found out a week ago? Yesterday? How long did you wait, Wyatt, after you heard, before you came home?"

He paused for a full minute, as if considering an argument, but shook his head instead. "Let's not do this. Please. I'm here now. And I'm sorry. Really." He took a step closer. "I loved her as much as I loved—"

She held up a hand. "Don't! Don't you dare say 'as much as I loved you.'"

"Why not? It's the truth."

"It's a lie. Either that or you never really cared about either of us. I can handle knowing you never gave a flea about me, that you were simply using me to get out of Osprey Cove—I figured that out years ago. But my mom." Her voice broke. "My mother loved you. She never wanted to believe you'd abandoned us—me. Every time she heard *Sweet Kira*, she swore the words were actually your apology to me."

He shook his head, a humorless smile twisting his lips. "Leave it to your mom to see right through me. She always could. I did write that song for you."

She snorted. He wouldn't dare use her late mother to manipulate her. "Nice try."

"I swear. My manager made me change the name from Leah to Kira."

Apparently, he wasn't above trying the mother manipulation tactic after all. Didn't mean she had to fall for it, though. "Right. Because 'Kira' would translate into more record sales than 'Leah.'"

He held up his right hand. "I swear. My manager made me change the name. He really did think Kira would sell better."

"Proving, yet again, if that's true, that you sold your integrity for the promise of a gold record and a pile of cash."

"Enough." Two quick strides ate up the ground between them, and he took her by the shoulders, his steel blue eyes hypnotic in their intensity. "I'm sorry. Okay? I'd say it a million times if it would make a difference."

Leveling a glare at him, she jerked out of his hold. "You could say it a million and one times, and I still wouldn't believe you."

Hermione let out a yip, which launched the entire canine choir into a symphony of barks and howls. She shushed them into a quieter song before Wyatt spoke again.

"Then there's nothing else to say, is there?"

Despite the sharp and jagged pain in her chest, she sucked in a deep breath. "At last, we agree on something."

"Goodnight, Leah."

"Bye, Wyatt. Have a safe—"

His lips stole the rest of her statement, crushed against hers in a fevered kiss. He'd mastered the art since their last meeting, and part of her suffered a pang of jealousy at all the lucky women who'd taken control of his education. Another part sent up a silent message of gratitude for their tutelage.

Wait. What was she doing? Even allowing him this much leverage to use against her would destroy her resolve. With her palms flattened to his chest, she shoved him backward, severing their connection.

"Maybe now would be a good time to tell you I'm engaged." Oh, please, she should've stapled her mouth shut before the lie escaped. Too late now. His fault, really. His kiss had left her dizzy and unsteady.

"Is that so?" His eyes narrowed. "Funny your father never mentioned it."

"Did you ask him?" she ventured.

"Well, no, not in so many words."

She gave a shrug she hoped came off as non-committal, though inside, her skeleton sagged in relief. "You know Dad. Everything is black and white with the old engineer. You want an answer to a specific question, ask it. He's not good with hints or hidden agendas."

He nodded toward her left hand and smirked. "I notice you're not wearing a ring, either."

"At the shelter?" Quirking her brow at him, she gave herself silent kudos for coming up with a sensible lie so quickly. "It's way too dirty on a good day with all the water and more…unpleasant messes. Today was even worse, thanks to yesterday's storm. I spent the better part of the day trying to remove a fallen tree from the yard." Well, calling to have someone remove it was close enough, right?

"So, who's the lucky guy?"

"No one you know."

"Oh, come on, Leah." The knowing grin he flashed made her blood pound in her veins. "You can do better than that."

"His name's Julian," she blurted. "He's a rising star at an architectural firm in Manhattan, and he's everything I ever dreamed of: considerate, generous, smart, and witty." He also happened to be the fictional hero in the current romance novel on her nightstand. Still, she knew enough about him to create a flesh-and-blood man from the pages. "He's currently in San Francisco, working on a special project." An orphanage or children's hospital. Something noble and selfless. "We met at a fundraiser for the shelter a few years ago."

"Does Julian have a last name?"

"Lannier." She provided the name so quickly and smoothly, he blinked, which told her he was beginning to believe her.

"I'll look forward to meeting him when he gets back. Goodnight, Leah." This time, he didn't wait for her to respond before leaving the garage with the same silent footfalls he'd used to enter.

Leah stared at the empty space, too stunned at their conversation to move. She'd won this round. So why did her victory leave a bitter taste in her mouth?

♏

Engaged? To some twit named Julian?

At first, Wyatt was sure she'd lied about the guy. While he hadn't come right out and asked Mr. Stewart if his daughter was involved with anyone, their conversation danced around the subject enough. He would've expected the old man to reveal the existence of a fiancé, if there was one. And Leah had seemed so flustered when he first pointed out that fact to her.

Then again, she had a valid explanation why she wasn't wearing a ring, and she hadn't skipped a beat when he'd asked for the mystery man's name. The details about Julian Lannier flowed from her as if the facts sat firmly on her tongue. The Leah of old would have stuttered and stammered her way through a series of lies, giving herself away with sideways glances and bright red blushes. This Leah came across as polished and knowledgeable about her subject. So, either she was telling the truth, or she'd learned the art of deception in the last several years.

After climbing into his rental car, he drove back to his motel, taking the long way around closed-off streets where chainsaws buzzed through fallen trees and electrical workers dealt carefully with destroyed power lines. He could've driven a more direct route, but the idea of viewing his childhood home—no matter who lived there now— pitched his stomach. No good memories lingered there, if they'd ever existed at all.

For this trip, the local motor inn was as good a stomping ground as any for him and his mates. It was situated on the lucky side of town, power-wise, and allowed all the band members to be in close proximity for last minute jam sessions or writing jags.

When he walked inside, his roommate and best friend, bass player Chaz Norris, sat on the sofa, feet propped on the coffee table, icy beer in hand, his gaze glued to the big screen television tuned to a soccer match. "How'd it go?"

"She hates me," Wyatt replied without preamble.

Chaz swigged his beer. "We kinda figured she did, didn't we?"

He leaned against the door to close it and sighed his frustration. "No. *You* figured that. And I'm guessing the rest of the guys have a running bet on it."

"Yup. Five hundred bucks goes to the one who comes closest on when she finally forgives you. The least amount of time is Kenny's one month. Everyone else thinks it's gonna take longer."

"What's your bet?"

Another swig, followed by a swipe with his forearm across his mouth. "Me? My money's on never."

"Thanks." He sank into the chair opposite Chaz. "That's hopeful."

"Has nothing to do with hope. I mean, I don't know Leah, but I do know you. Let's face it. There was a time, not so long ago, *the whole band* hated you. You used to be a nice guy. Then you started getting all full of yourself, thinking you were the sole reason for our success. Lucky for you, you wised up and apologized, but we only *really* got over your attitude when you agreed to renegotiate our contracts. Apologies are nice, but money talks and b.s. walks, as they say. We all got our pride to maintain." He pointed the bottle at Wyatt. "I'm betting Leah's hurt goes much deeper than her pride, and she's nursed that hurt a lot longer. I doubt she's going to let you off the hook for money *or* a pretty apology."

Wyatt frowned. "You don't know that."

Another swig, another swipe, this time followed by a snort. "You don't know women like I do. They can hold a grudge for centuries past death. It's gonna take something extraordinary to win her back."

Wyatt swallowed the bitterness burning his throat. "I think she's engaged to some other guy, too."

"I'm gonna win the pool," Chaz sing-songed.

"Could you at least show a little sympathy for me here?"

"Why? You're feeling sorry for yourself enough for ten guys. You don't need more sympathy. What you need is to either move on, or find a way to win her back. Which way you wanna go?"

He'd tried moving on. He'd left everyone and everything behind when Cooper dangled the golden carrot under his nose. In his moment of desperation, he'd made a ridiculous promise and agreed to use the bus ticket, to take nothing but his guitar, and get out of town before sunrise. He'd hoped that after a time, Leah would contact him, tell him to come to her. A few months, tops, he'd figured.

Months turned into years without a word, not even when his business attorney had started sending her royalty checks. Still, he'd waited patiently, expecting someone to tell him his long wait had ended and he could, at last, come home. When word didn't come, he resigned himself to create a new life for himself, a life where there were always songs to write, shows to play, new cities to visit. The longer he went without hearing from her, the more resentment brewed and bubbled in his gut, spewing into his personal life. He focused solely on the fame, the money, always striving for more in the hope she'd become so jealous about his success she'd break down and contact him.

Eventually, his arrogance and greed got to be too much for everyone around him to stomach. One by one, his bandmates walked away from his obnoxious presence—including Chaz. The music in his soul dried up, leaving him empty of lyrics and melodies. Once again, Cooper dangled bait for him, this time the solo tour in Europe, and

Wyatt welcomed the opportunity to get away from the States. The nights became a blur, with shows in ten countries in twenty-five days, until he heard about Leah's mother passing. *Now*, he thought. Now, Leah would contact him. She never did.

That was when he woke up. He reached out to his former bandmates, made atonements for acting like a callous jerk, and they decided to put together a new album to celebrate their reunion. The title, "Homecoming," was the last impetus he needed to do just that: to come home, to find out once and for all if Leah still harbored the slightest love for him.

He plucked a stray thread on the chair arm, keeping his fingers busy and his gaze on the upholstery. "I'd give up every dime I've made in the last seven years if I could spend that time with Leah instead of without her."

Chaz snorted. "Aww, now, that touches my heart."

"Scoff all you want. She was the best part of me, and I let her go without a second glance. I need her back. I never should have left her behind."

"So, why did you?"

He shook his head, his lips tight to avoid spilling his secrets. Leah needed to know the truth first—if she'd open up long enough to hear him out.

Chaz rose from the sofa with a groan, tossed out his empty bottle, and strolled to the mini-fridge. "Okay, okay. Don't tell me. I'll help you anyway. But if this escapade goes south—and it probably will—don't blame me. First, what do you know about the new guy?"

"His name's Julian. He's an architect out of Manhattan, currently working on a project in San Francisco."

Chaz clapped. "Okay, that's good. Distance works in our favor. Do you know how long he'll be gone?"

"No."

"All right. We'll work with a narrow time frame to begin with. If the dude stays away longer than we anticipate, benefit for us."

"And if he comes back tomorrow…?"

He opened the fridge door and pulled out two more beer bottles. "We have to move faster. I can't guarantee stellar results either way, though we might at least convince her to rethink the engagement if we've got a minimum of a few days' head start."

Wyatt took the bottle Chaz offered and twisted off the top. "That's good. I can work with that. What do we do first?"

"Steady, Wy. We start where every battle begins, with reconnaissance. Who are her friends? What do they think about the guy? How about her dad? Other family members? Coworkers? Can we draw any of them onto our side?"

Wyatt took a long pull off the bottle and shook his head. "I'm not sure. Her father's her only family. I would've thought, considering the circumstances, he would've mentioned the guy when I talked to him, but I don't know."

"Circumstances? What circumstances?"

"Nothing," he said, hoping to cover his gaffe, and quickly refocused the conversation. "Just in general. I mean, Leah didn't hesitate to mention her fiancé to me. Why would her father? Then again, I get the feeling he's not a hundred percent in this world anymore. Maybe he forgot about the guy or maybe he doesn't like him and hopes I can win Leah back. Either way, I won't manipulate her dad to our side. It wouldn't be right. Besides, there's been too much manipulation between all of us. As for her friends, I wouldn't begin to know who they are or how to contact them. I lost touch with everyone in this town when I..." Shame stole his ability to continue.

"...when you slipped away in the middle of the night, telling no one where you were headed or why," Chaz finished for him.

Wyatt nodded. That night, he'd been so desperate to escape he'd never considered the feelings of those he'd left behind. Not even Leah. Over the years, he'd often wondered. If he'd seen her when he'd gone to her that night, if he'd told *her* what he'd done, if he'd never heard about the promise he wound up making, would she have come up with a better solution for his dilemma? Would she have said to hell with the consequences and come with him? He'd never know.

Chaz held up his beer in salute. "To 'Operation Win Back Leah.' May victory be ours."

Wyatt lifted his bottle toward Chaz's. The musical clink of the bottles raised in salute left a hollow echo in his heart. He didn't want to wage a war with some other guy to win her back. He'd always imagined the day he came home, she'd be waiting for him, she'd throw herself into his arms and rain kisses on him—the way she always did in their youth.

And even when she hadn't reacted the way he hoped to his surprise appearance at her house, she *had* responded to his kiss with the same innocent ardor he'd always loved about her. He loved her. He'd always loved her, would go to his grave with her name on his lips.

The existence of Julian Lannier, fiancé, was a complication he hadn't expected that would now have to be dealt with.

3

The next morning at the shelter, while she and Jen took advantage of the electricity downtime to get some general office straightening done, Leah also used the opportunity to confess her stupidity with Wyatt. She finished with the comment about telling him she was engaged.

"Now, I've got to make that happen."

Jenny stared at her in wide-eyed shock. "Are you crazy? How are we supposed to create a fiancé from scratch?"

Leah straightened the pile of blank adoption applications and bounced them on the desk to even out the edges. "It's not that big a deal. Wyatt won't stay here long. I've already told him my fiancé is away on business. In the meantime, we let a few people know that, if he asks, I'm engaged to Julian Lannier."

"Wait. Why does that name sound familiar? Who is he?"

"The sexy architect in 'Building a Dream.'"

"Ohmigod, yes! I remember now. Gee, Lee, you couldn't even come up with your own fictional guy? You had to pluck one out of a romance novel?"

"I panicked. It flew out of my mouth before I could stop it."

Jen twisted her lips in a moue. "I find that hard to believe. You don't panic. And you certainly don't lie on the fly. You don't lie, period. What'd he say that made you react to such an extreme?"

"Nothing." She played with the staple remover, squeezing it shut and releasing it to spring open again, over and over.

Jenny grabbed the makeshift toy from her fingers. "Why the lie, Leah? You could've told him to get lost and thrown him out."

"I did that."

"And…?"

Without the remover, her fingers still clenched and unclenched. "And nothing. He wouldn't leave. I told him to go, that I wasn't interested in hearing anything he had to say."

"There had to be more than that. You're not easily intimidated. What else happened?"

"Nothing."

"Spill it, Lee."

"He kissed me!" she blurted.

Jenny cocked her head, a smile lighting up her features. "Did he? I'd ask how it was, but based on the pink in your cheeks, and the lie you told him, I can guess he was superb."

No sense in avoiding the truth. She sighed, losing herself in the memory of the delicious sensations he'd evoked. "And then some."

"No kidding?" Jenny placed the staple remover in its place on the desk. "Then I don't get it. He's single, you're single. He's hot. You're hot for him. Why the fake fiancé?"

"Because I don't dare trust him. You know what he did, Jen. What he took from me."

"You've always overreacted to that. Yeah, he took the song, but he gave you writing credit, and you've benefited from the royalties."

"That's not the point! *Take My Heart Again* was mine! It was private. I didn't plan to share it with anyone else but…"

"But Wyatt," Jenny finished for her. "You love him."

"Yeah. But I can't trust him. Do you have any idea how much that scares me?" She swiped the staple remover from the desk and squeezed it in erratic fashion. "Let's face it. His solo album didn't sell so well."

She could almost see the lightbulb illuminate in Jenny's brain. "Ah. You think he's come back to steal another song from you to relaunch his comeback."

The staple remover's claws opened and shut in staccato rhythm. "Why else? Do you know what this tour is called? 'Homecoming.' That's no accident. He's come back to Osprey Cove because he thinks he can romance a new song out of me. Once he realizes I'm not that same dumb, trusting girl, he'll leave again."

"You could've told him you don't have any more songs for him." Leah didn't have to reply. Her gaze flew about the room landing on nothing long enough to focus. Her best friend for the last six years, Jenny probably read the emotions playing on her face. Sure enough, she added, "But you're still writing them, aren't you?"

Leah nodded.

"I thought you gave up music when he left."

"I gave up playing my sax and making music," she clarified. "But the words get crammed inside my head so I have to put them on paper to get them out."

"How many?"

"I dunno." She shrugged. "About fifty or sixty, I guess."

Jenny's jaw gaped. "Fifty or sixty songs?!"

A rush of heat bathed Leah's cheeks, and she glanced down at the boxes of paper clips she'd reorganized in her desk drawer. "They're not songs, per se. They're just words on a page. My words. My feelings. My thoughts. But if Wyatt finds out I have them, he'll put them to melody and commercialize my life for his worldwide audience."

"You don't have to share them with him."

She shook her head. "Wyatt's a very charming guy. He's always been able to get me to do things I shouldn't."

"Oh, yeah?" Jenny placed her chin on her fist. "Do tell."

"I'd rather not."

Not now, not ever. Her surprise pregnancy and subsequent miscarriage remained unknown to everyone but her. The only other person who'd shared her secret, Mom, had carried the pathetic tale to her grave. Even Dad never found out Wyatt had abandoned not one, but *two* Stewarts the night he left. She always wondered if Wyatt had disappeared because he suspected the truth or for some other reason that had nothing to do with their pending pregnancy. Regardless, she refused to confront him about the past now. Dumb, wildly in love, twenty-one-year-old Leah Stewart had grown into a mature, not-gonna-fall-for-it adult who knew how to keep secrets and carry on when the world inside her had collapsed into a barren wasteland. Besides, what good would it do? Neither of them could change what happened.

"Anyway," she said, shaking off the bitter thoughts, "that was a long time ago. I'm not about to let him get close enough to take advantage of me again."

"Enter Julian Lannier, fake fiancé."

She glanced up again, her gaze steady and her expression fixed into firm determination. "Exactly. I'll do whatever I have to, if it will keep Wyatt as far away as possible."

Jenny looked at her quizzically. "You think the existence of Julian will be enough to dissuade him?"

"Of course. If he thinks I'm engaged to someone else, he won't try to romance me. That's not Wyatt's style. He'll move on, and I'll never see him again."

Her voice cracked on the last word, and Jenny pounced like a kitten on a laser dot. "Because that's what you want, right?"

"Yes, that's precisely what I want." She hoped she'd placed enough emphasis on the statement to make it sound credible.

"Uh-huh." Jenny held up one of their promotional pens. "One problem, though."

"What's that?"

"There's no way he's going to believe you if you don't at least *try* to believe it yourself."

♏

Inside the red rental sports car, Wyatt and Chaz watched the shelter from across the street. Red. Why hadn't he insisted on a sedate, non-descript gray? Oh, right. Because he'd hoped to wow Leah with his celebrity status and show off to the old townspeople. Gray wouldn't have cut it. Of course, Leah had been infuriated and disgusted with him instead. And no one else he'd come across so far seemed the slightest bit impressed with the bad-boy-made-good. This whole trip had become one gigantic mistake. For God's sake, Leah was engaged! Why was he even here? He should pack up his stuff, pack up the band, and get out of Osprey Cove before he did something stupid.

"This is ridiculous," he grumbled, tapping his fingers on the steering wheel. "What good is hovering out here like a deranged stalker?"

"I told you," Chaz retorted. "Reconnaissance."

Great. Any minute now, some Neighborhood Watch member would call the local police, and he'd be even more infamous in this town. He should have requested the gray car. "Let's get outta here." Squirming in the driver's seat, he reached for the keys still dangling in the ignition.

"No, wait!" Chaz gripped his wrist.

The shelter's main entrance door opened, and muffled feminine voices flitted on the chilly autumn air.

"Duck!" Chaz ordered, and they slinked down low in their seats so as not to be visible to the approaching women.

Wyatt moved a little too fast and slammed his knee against the steering column. "Ow!"

"Ssssh!"

He glared at Chaz and rubbed the offended area. The pain was forgotten when Leah's laughter reached through the closed car windows. The familiar sound tickled his senses, drawing him back to long ago days when she'd wrap her arms around his waist and giggle while he nibbled her neck.

"Whoa." Chaz's murmur shook him back to the present. "Which one's Leah?"

Wyatt dared a quick glance up. "The blonde in the blue jacket."

"Oh, thank God. Who's the brunette?"

"I'm not sure."

"I say we follow *her*."

"The brunette? Why? I thought we were tracking Leah."

"We are. But I'm betting that brunette can give us info on Leah we won't get by following her or talking to her again. She'll have all her walls up. You want details on the boyfriend, the brunette's the key. I feel it."

"Uh-huh." Wyatt shot his friend a smirk. "That your brain talking or your libido?"

He grinned and winked. "Both, my friend, both."

They waited until the women started their cars and drove off before following the brunette, staying a few car lengths behind her at all times. When her compact pulled into the parking lot of the local police station, Wyatt's heart sank.

"She's onto us."

And she was furious! She climbed out of her car, hands on her hips. "Come on out, creepers. You can explain to the cops why you feel the need to follow a lone female driver."

"Dang," Chaz remarked as he stared out through the windshield. "I think I'm in love."

"Personally," Wyatt drawled, "I think we're in trouble."

"Well?" she shouted at them. "In ten seconds, I'm walking into that precinct and bringing out every policeman I can find."

The threat spurred Wyatt into action. If she kept yelling, she'd draw a crowd. He scrambled to get out of the car, his hands in the air. "Wait! You've got it all wrong, I swear."

"So much for subterfuge," Chaz mumbled as he followed Wyatt out of the car, his hands upraised as well.

The woman's eyes narrowed, her posture relaxed, and she pointed at Wyatt. "Don't I know you?"

No sense in denying it. "Wyatt Blackthorne."

A light of understanding lit up her face, and she smirked. "Ah. I suppose your following me has something to do with Leah then?"

"My idea," Chaz interjected, approaching her with an outstretched hand. "I'm Chaz Norris."

"Back off," she snapped. "I've got pepper spray in my pocket, and I'm not afraid to use it."

He took a step back, but his trademark grin never faltered. "Feisty. I like that in my women."

She frowned at him, but directed her comment to Wyatt. "Could you put your Neanderthal ape back in the car, please?"

Chaz chuckled. "Neanderthal ape. I think she means me."

"Of course I mean you. You see any other shaggy-haired knuckle-draggers in the area?"

He wagged a finger at her. "Now, that's not fair. Knuckle-draggers like me deserve some respect, too. We're handy to have around. Since our arms are too long for our bodies, we can help you by getting stuff off high shelves. And on cold days like today, we can start a fire—we Neanderthals have always been good with fire."

Her lips twitched, but remained set in a grim line. Her eyes, however, danced with delight. "And can I use your hair as a mop in an emergency?"

"Just not at the shelter. Please, not at the shelter."

The laughter erupted from her in one loud trill, breaking the tension in all of them. When she finally stopped, she wiped her eyes and straightened. "Okay, Wyatt Blackthorne and friend. What do you want?"

"Just to talk," Chaz answered before Wyatt could. "Swear to God."

Ignoring Chaz, she pinned her scrutiny on Wyatt. "About Leah."

There was no question in her statement but he nodded all the same.

"Fine. A big music star like you, driving a snazzy car like that can afford to buy me a hot meal while we talk. Since I just spent the afternoon in an office with no heat, I'm in the mood for a good cup of chowder. I take it you know where Annie's Diner is?"

"If it's still in the same spot it's been in since 1895, then yes. I know where Annie's is."

"Good. I'll see you there in fifteen minutes. Use your celebrity for something worthwhile. Call ahead and get us a table. I don't have a lot of time. I've got a houseful of cats to get back to."

"Aw, honey, you're way too young and pretty to be a crazy cat lady."

Wyatt cringed at Chaz's less-than-smooth compliment.

To her credit, though, she didn't take offense. With a snort of disbelief and the whisper of a grin, she asked Wyatt, "Is he always such an idiot?"

"Only around a beautiful woman," Chaz interjected. "I can't help it. All the blood leaves my brain to pump harder around my heart."

"Uh-huh. Whatever. Not that I owe you an explanation, but I took all the shelter's cats to my house since I've got power and the shelter doesn't. Leah took the dogs; I got the cats."

That explained the dogs in the garage Wyatt had seen yesterday. He'd wondered at the time but, caught up in trying to get Leah to talk to him, hadn't bothered to ask. "The shelter doesn't have power?"

"Nope. Leah was hoping to buy a generator before the first major storm hit the area." She held up her right hand with her thumb and index finger squeezed together. "Missed it by that much. Anyway, 'til we're up and running again, the shelter residents have been temporarily relocated."

"An angel of mercy as well as beauty," Chaz enthused.

Wyatt had to struggle to keep his eyes from rolling up to his brain of their own accord.

The woman had no such restraint. After silently letting Chaz know he sounded ridiculous with an exaggerated eye roll, she opened her car door and climbed inside. "Fifteen minutes, boys. If you're a minute late, I'm gone. I got things to do and no time for nonsense."

As she reached to close the door, Chaz called out to her. "Hey! What's your name? Or should I just call you 'Beautiful Angel'?"

"Jenny. Conway." She slammed the door, started the car, and drove out of the parking lot.

"Jenny Conway," Chaz murmured, watching her car turn onto the road. "I never thought I'd say this, but thank God you've got lady problems, Wy."

"Oh?"

"Yup. I'm gonna have fun romancing that sweetheart while helping you."

Terrific. This plan had gone from bad to worse.

4

Leah balanced the dinner tray on one hand and knocked on her father's bedroom door with the other. After counting to ten to give him time to prepare for her entrance, she opened the door and walked inside.

Dad sat at his drafting table, a souvenir from his years at work, which he'd brought home when he retired. He glanced up at Leah and smiled while rolling up the large sheet of schematics he'd been working on. "There's my girl! How was your day?"

"Cold. Jenny and I only went in to the shelter for a few hours to do some minor maintenance. Even so, I don't know if I'll ever regain feeling in my fingers." She set the tray on the nightstand and sat on the edge of the bed, on Mom's side, placing her hands in her lap. "How's the project going?"

Ever since Mom died from a brain aneurysm only two months after being declared in remission from bladder cancer, Dad had dedicated all his energies and knowledge to devising some kind of gadget that would predict if a blood clot might rupture, which, he hoped, would eventually lead to new technologies that would allow medical personnel to intervene before it was too late.

"Coming along."

He gave the same answer whenever she asked the question. The fact he had no background in biomedical engineering didn't deter him. He used the internet, a local librarian, and a retired podiatrist friend for research—clearly establishing a timeline of "probably never" to see this dream realized. Still, the work brought him peace in some odd way, so she let him doodle and calculate to his heart's delight.

One of these days, Leah would love to slip in when he wasn't around and get a peek at what he'd come up with so far. The little girl in her, who still looked up to her daddy as a superhero, hoped she'd see a bunch of real charts, graphics and scientific formulas. But her adult side, accustomed to disappointment in her heroes, feared she'd find nothing but cartoon ducks and tic-tac-toe games.

Of course, he never left this room now anyway, so the point was moot. Always claiming he felt Mom's presence strongest here, he hadn't changed a thing since the day the ambulance came. All her mother's clothing still hung in the closet, her jewelry sat in the chest on her dresser, even the shoes she'd removed that last night remained at the side of the bed. At least Dad allowed Leah to make the bed every day, but he wouldn't let her change the pillowcases on her mother's side, believing Mom's scent still lingered there. He didn't know, though, whenever he was deeply involved in his project and paying no attention to her, Leah discreetly sprayed the pillows with Mom's favorite cologne.

Maybe it was wrong to perpetuate her father's dreams, but he'd always indulged hers: playing Prince Charming to her Cinderella when she was five, putting up with her band practicing in the garage during her rock and roll teen years, standing by her when she'd used the royalty money from the song Wyatt stole to buy the shelter instead of finishing school. Through it all, Dad never complained, never told her she couldn't. She owed him the same courtesy.

"What's for dinner tonight?" he asked.

"Chicken and dumplings."

He rose and stretched, arching his back then rolling his shoulders to loosen the kinks acquired from hours slouched over his figures and research papers. "Your mother's recipe?"

"Of course."

"Good girl." He rolled his drafting chair to the nightstand, sat, and proceeded to eat. "Mmm. Delicious. Just like your mom's."

Her father's highest praise was to compare anything she did to her mother's version. If she styled her hair a certain way or wore a particular color, he'd remark how much she resembled Mom. His eyes would take on a certain luster, and she always knew, at that moment, he was lost somewhere in the past in his mind, remembering times when her mother was still with them. Theirs had been a love-for-all-time match, something she'd always aspired to achieve, as well.

Between bites, her father said, "Guess who came by to see me yesterday."

The romantic fantasy building in her head crashed and burned. She grimaced. "I already know who. Wyatt."

"You saw him?"

"I saw him. He came out to the garage when I was treating Murphy last night."

"And...?"

"And," she replied, folding her arms over her chest, "with luck, he's already packed his bags and vamoosed out of town, never to be seen again."

Dad, a dumpling speared on the fork in his hand, quirked a brow and pointed his morsel at her. "Your choice or his?"

"Both."

"Funny. Wyatt seemed awfully anxious to see you when I talked to him. I would've bet he planned to stick around a bit longer this go-round."

"Yeah, sure. Because he needs another song and figured he'd charm a new one out of the dumb bunny who gave him his first big hit."

Dad chewed the dumpling thoughtfully and swallowed. "I didn't get that impression at all."

"Of course not. This is Wyatt we're talking about, Dad. Remember? The man's a born manipulator. You never trusted him. You used to always say all he had going for him was his silver tongue."

"Well, yes, that's true but—"

"You said he was no good, that he'd never amount to anything, that I could do so much better. Wyatt was one of the main reasons you wanted me to go away to school instead of staying home and attending a local university. You were hoping *physical* distance would put emotional distance between us."

"Aw, now, sweetheart. What did you expect from an overprotective father? Most of what I said was bluster."

She shifted her weight to one side and folded her arms over her chest. "Excuse me?"

"You were *fourteen* when you started dating him." He shook his head. "Much too young to fall in love so hard. You thought the sun rose and set on your Wyatt. He was your one and only for years. I looked at him the way a dad looks at the man who's captured his little girl's heart. *You* saw Prince Charming. *I* saw a kid from a violent home who had a rebellious streak, no job, and no real future. As Prince Charmings went, he was a real fixer-upper. He scared the hell out of me. Every time I saw you two together, I worried you'd come home and announce you were pregnant and marrying him."

Leah stifled the sharp gasp that rose to her lips.

"Your mom and I wanted you to have a bit more life experience before someone captured your heart. You needed to learn how to be independent and find your true passion in life first. Not your passion for a man, but what drove you to succeed, what fulfilled you when you were hollowed out, what gave you joy. The more you insisted Wyatt was your soulmate, the more your mom and I feared you'd hitch yourself to him without knowing yourself first. After Wyatt left, we actually breathed a sigh of relief for a day or two. Until you discovered you were pregnant. Then we worried for a whole 'nother reason."

This time, the gasp escaped. "Mom told you?"

"Of course she did." He pointed the fork at her, his eyes misty. "We didn't keep secrets from each other, Leah. That's no way to nurture love. Your mom and I shared everything."

"She never told me you knew."

"She didn't want you to worry, though I don't know why you should've. She may have carried you those nine months, but you were no less my daughter from the minute you were born. *You* should've told me."

A block of unshed tears clogged her throat, and she swallowed hard before nodding.

"Besides," he continued, "how long did you think you would've been able to keep me from finding out my little girl was going to have a baby of her own? Especially since we live in the same house?"

Reflecting on it now, Leah was forced to admit she hadn't given that question much thought. Stupid, really. "I don't know. I think I wanted—*needed* some time to get used to the idea first. Then I miscarried, and I just assumed you only knew about the cyst. I had no idea Mom told you the baby exacerbated the cyst and the cyst endangered the baby."

"You should've come to both of us, Leah. From the start."

She stared at the carpet, studying the worn nap. "I didn't want you to be disappointed in me."

"Well, now, I admit I probably wouldn't have been thrilled at first, but I like to think I would've come around in short order. You could never truly disappoint me. You're the best thing that ever happened to your mom and me. Always have been. All either of us ever wanted was for you to find your life's passion and be happy."

"I *am* happy."

He sipped from his water glass before answering. "I know you are, most of the time. You found your passion in that shelter, and that's great. But, sweetheart, you'll never be truly happy until you make peace with Wyatt."

She stiffened. "What are you talking about?"

"You know exactly what I'm talking about. Did you ever tell him about the baby?"

"He left before I even knew I was pregnant."

"He still deserves to know the truth."

"Why? He didn't stick around. He didn't even say goodbye. And since I miscarried anyway, what can possibly come from telling him, except harsh feelings?"

"You already have the harsh feelings. It's why you claim you can't forgive him for stealing your song. It's not the song you blame him for. It's that lost baby and the fact he wasn't here for you when you needed him most. I told you. It's never good to try to nurture love with a secret between you—especially a secret like yours."

She shot to her feet and planted her hands on her hips. "I don't love Wyatt."

"You sure?"

"I did love him. A long time ago. When I was a dumb kid who didn't know any better. Turns out, you were right all along, Daddy. Wyatt Blackthorne is no good for me. He never was. Luckily, I have no doubt he'll soon turn around and go back to wherever he's been for the last seven years, if he hasn't already. So there's no need for me to tell him anything."

♋

Annie's Diner was *the* tourist spot in Osprey Cove. Owned by the same family for more than a hundred years, the eatery was known as a favorite stop for such notables as Teddy Roosevelt, F. Scott and Zelda Fitzgerald, and the Marx Brothers. Other politicians and celebrities had come and gone through its Romanesque revival doors over the years, and each one had left an autographed photo which now graced the "Wall of Fame." A visitor could spend hours looking over each one.

The current "Annie" was, in actuality, Frank Donovan, the original Annie's great-great grandson and a fixture inside these iconic walls since his days as a busboy in the seventies. All the Donovans began their apprenticeship here at age thirteen, bussing tables, washing dishes, mopping floors, and learning the day-to-day activities of the family business.

When Wyatt walked in with Chaz, Frank's daughter, Vanessa, greeted him with an effusive, "Wyatt!" followed by a boa constrictor hug and a kiss on the cheek.

"Hey, Vanessa. How've you been? I see you got promoted since I was last in here."

She laughed. "Yeah. Now my daughter's a waitress and I'm in charge of the front door." She leaned toward his shoulder to whisper, "To be honest, I'd rather be serving tables. It's freezing up here all winter and hot as Hades all summer."

"Gee, I'm sorry about that," he said.

She waved him off. "Nah. It's all good. I just don't get the opportunity to kvetch much. Who'd listen?"

They shared a laugh, and he introduced her to Chaz before asking for a table for three.

She grabbed three menus from the maître d' station. "You got it." She led them to a booth in the glass-enclosed privacy room, once known as the smoking section in that limbo time of the eighties when smoking was still allowed in public, but in a separate area. "Figured you wouldn't want to be accosted while you're eating."

"Thanks, Vanessa. I appreciate it."

"No problem," she said with a wink. "You know us. We know how to treat our *special* guests."

Special. As in celebrity. He assumed that meant he'd be signing a photo for the wall now. Wow. Weird.

"Okay." She handed them each a menu then held up the third. "That's two. Who's joining ya?"

"Jenny Conway."

She nodded. "I'll send her over soon as she arrives. You wanna wait before ordering drinks or should I have Kaitlyn come by now?"

"We'll wait," Chaz said, a little too eagerly and with too broad a grin.

While Vanessa headed back to her station near the door, Wyatt gave Chaz a disgruntled look. "You gotta stop the lovesick act, man."

"It's not an act. I'm crazy about this girl. Who said you're the only one who can be struck by Cupid's arrow? You don't own the copyright on love, you know."

"The difference is I've loved Leah most of my life," he retorted.

"Umm…" a voice interrupted. "I think I'll go to the ladies room first."

Terrific. Jenny had arrived in time to hear his declaration. He sighed. "No. It's okay. I mean, unless you have to…umm…"

"No!" she replied, her cheeks pink, whether from cold or embarrassment he couldn't discern.

"Good." Chaz slid closer to the wall. "Come sit. We waited to order. Didn't want to be rude, you know? Not that we ever are. We're good guys. Honest. Wyatt can vouch for me. Oh, wait. You don't really know Wyatt, either, though, do you? Would it mean anything if I vouched for him and he vouched for me?"

Wyatt had never seen Chaz in such a state. The man babbled like a drunken fool and stared starry-eyed at Jenny as she slid onto the bench seat beside him.

Maybe he really was, at the least, infatuated with her? It couldn't be love. They'd only spoken for five minutes. Still, when he thought back to the first time he met Leah, he could honestly admit to experiencing a similar intense interest after their initial conversation.

It was their freshman year of high school. They'd been paired up in biology class lab by their chauvinistic teacher who'd assigned boy/girl partners for the frog dissection. Apparently, Mr. Kincaid didn't think girls had the guts to handle…well, *guts*. Cocky as he was in those

31

days, Wyatt had picked up the scalpel and, with an arrogant tone, announced he'd be the one to make the incision. Leah quirked a brow and folded her arms over her chest, clearly annoyed, but she didn't say a word.

He pressed the blade into the flesh, and almost instantly, some weird-smelling liquid squirted up and hit him in the face. He jumped back, dropping the scalpel, and scrubbed his hands over his eyes, until Leah's soft laughter burned his ears.

"Serves you right for being a jerk." She retrieved the scalpel and finished the job with a perfect, precise cut. Glancing up at him with a knowing smile twitching her bubble-gum-pink lips, she added, "There. I guess we're even now."

He'd fallen for her at that moment. Oh, sure, at the time, he'd just found Leah interesting, but that interest, over time, had transformed into something deeper. Maybe Chaz had arrived at the same place with Jenny, but took a shortcut to get there. Who was he to judge?

"If you expect me to intervene with Leah on your behalf," Jenny said, drawing Wyatt back into the present conversation, "you're wasting your time and money. I don't know anything about what went on with you two, and I don't want to know."

Chaz patted her arm. "Oh, no, nothing like that. We're not asking you to take sides. Wyatt just wants to make sure she's happy. That's all. Is this new guy...what's his name?"

"Julian?" she provided. "What about him?"

Wyatt's heart plummeted. If Jenny could let his name slide from her lips so easily, he must be a fixture among Leah's circle. So much for hoping this guy wasn't real. "What's he like? Is he good to her? How'd they meet? How long has she known him?"

Her lips clamped shut, and she shook her head. "Mmm-mmm. I'm not saying anything more than Leah's happy with her life now and doesn't need someone to come in and screw it up. Let's leave the topic at that."

Before he could deny her subtle accusation regarding his motives, their waitress appeared. She bore such a close resemblance to Vanessa, Wyatt had no trouble recognizing Kaitlyn Donovan, even before reading her nametag.

"Hi there," she said. "Can I start you all off with something to drink while you're looking over the menu?"

"I don't need the menu, Kaitlyn," Jenny replied. "I want a cup— no, make that a bowl—of your New England clam chowder with extra oyster crackers and coffee with whole milk."

"Well done," Chaz said then told the waitress, "I'll have the same."

"Three," Wyatt said.

"You got it," she replied, giving the words the same inflection her mother had earlier, and gathered up the unopened menus.

Once she was out of earshot, Wyatt brought the conversation back around to Leah. "What makes you think I want to screw up Leah's life?"

She rested her arms on the table and leveled a steady gaze his way. "Leah's loyal. Like Boy Scout loyal. Marine Corps loyal. So if you and she haven't spoken in a long time, I'd say it's your fault, not hers."

Wyatt squirmed in the vinyl seat. "I screwed up. I know that. But it was a complicated situation, and I had very valid reasons for leaving."

"I'm sure you did, but like I said, I don't want to hear them. If Leah had the slightest desire to take you back, you'd be with her right now instead of trying to pump me for information."

He flushed. God, the woman was blunt.

"So, we can either talk about something else, or I can have Kaitlyn pack up my meal to go and I'll head on home."

"We don't need to talk about Leah. Or Wyatt, for that matter," Chaz said with a twinge too much eagerness in his tone. "None of our business, right?"

"Thanks," Wyatt grumbled. "I appreciate that."

Chaz ignored him. "Tell us about you. Where are you from originally?"

She gave him a look that communicated boredom. "A little town you've never heard of in Wisconsin."

"No kidding." Chaz sat up higher in his seat, his eyes alight. "I'm from Wisconsin."

"Uh-huh. Cute." She nudged him with an elbow. "Quit sucking up to me. You stink at it."

"No, seriously, I am!" He turned to Wyatt. "Tell her."

Wyatt nodded. "He is."

She cocked her head to one side, brows arched in quizzical fashion. "Oh yeah? Whereabouts?"

"Hopkinsville."

Now, she straightened and flashed a beaming smile that illuminated the entire diner. "I'm from Warren!"

"That's like twenty minutes away from where I grew up."

"I know, right? This is crazy. So, do you know...?" She snapped her fingers, jogging her memory. "...what's the name of the place in town that all the singers perform at?"

"Bluestopia?"

"That's it!"

"Yeah, sure. I played there a bunch of times."

"Did you really? Ohmigod, that is so cool. I sneaked in once when I was seventeen to see Bobby Billings play there..."

Wyatt watched their interaction, forgotten on the other side of the booth. "Umm, I think I'll tell Kaitlyn to pack up *my* meal to go." He slid off the seat, but the couple was so deep in conversation, they didn't seem to notice.

"No kidding. You know I played bass on a coupla cuts on his new album."

"Chaz?" Wyatt received no answer so he said the name again, this time loud enough to draw attention from other patrons. "Chaz!"

"Huh? What?" When he finally looked up at Wyatt, Chaz's cheeks were flushed but his brow puckered in confusion. "Wait. Where you going?"

"Back to the motel. You want me to leave you the car?"

"No, that's okay," Jenny said as she slid closer to Chaz and wrapped her arm around his. "I'll be happy to drop him off later."

"Right," he replied with a sigh. "Jenny, nice to meet you. Chaz, I'll see you later."

"*Much* later, *amigo*," Chaz said while Jenny canoodled closer and flashed Wyatt a smirk.

Terrific. Wyatt was now back to square one.

5

The following day, Leah was stunned when Jenny not only didn't complain about working in a building with no heat, she'd stopped at the local bakery on her way into work and picked up a box of doughnuts to go with their coffees.

Casey, of course, gobbled up three in one breath. "These are awesome. Thanks."

Jenny slapped the lid closed before he could reach for a fourth. "Now that you've received sustenance, young one, go outside and burn off some of that sugar. You can either hose down the outdoor kennels, or cut up the large branches and haul them to the curb."

Casey's face took on a look of horror fit for a slasher movie. "Are you crazy? It's freezing out there. I'm not hosing down the kennels."

"It's a balmy fifty-five degrees, Case. Not ten below." She cocked her head. "But if you don't want to do the kennels, it's lumberjack duty for you. Get cracking."

"I shoulda known the doughnuts were a trick," he muttered. "My mom always told me there was no such thing as a free lunch. Didn't realize that meant no free breakfast, either."

Both Jenny and Leah waited until he trudged out to the yard before bursting into giggles.

"'No free breakfast.' Someone should embroider that on a sampler." Jenny lifted the lid on the pastry box and pulled out a chocolate honey-dipped doughnut. "Here. Your favorite."

Leah took the treat, but didn't succumb to the sweet lure. Instead, she studied her friend, eyes narrowed in suspicion. "What's up with you today? You're like Suzy Sunshine."

Her face suffused with bright pink color from nose to hairline, and her smile glowed. "I met a guy yesterday."

"You did? Where?"

The smile evaporated, and she held up her hands in surrender.

"Don't get mad."

A chilling premonition crept up Leah's spine. "Why would I be mad?"

"He's Wyatt's bass player. And for what it's worth, I think you're wrong about Wyatt."

The impact of Jenny's comment hit her right between the eyes, and she sank into her office chair behind the mountain of paperwork on her desk, the doughnut forgotten. She blew out an exasperated breath. "Not you, too."

"Too? Who else?"

"My father." To close the discussion, she picked up the shelter's business insurance contract and waved the thousand or so pages. "I swear I'd need a gaggle of lawyers and a year to wade through all this legal gobbledy-gook."

Jenny strode to Leah's desk and leaned on the edge to view the contract. "What are you looking for?"

"You know, the usual stuff." She raked her fingers through her hair to stem some of her frustration. "Why do insurance companies have to make everything so complicated? Why can't they just include a page with the breakdown of deductible, payout amounts, and the phone numbers I need to call to file, instead of having me swim through page after page of the 'party of the first part' stuff?"

While she ranted, Jenny took the contract from her and flipped all the pages until she reached the front cover.

"Hey!" Leah extended her hand. "Give that back."

"I will. In a minute."

"Stop! Look what you're doing. You lost the page I was on. Now I'm going to have to start all over…"

With exaggerated motions, Jenny peeled up the first page and folded it behind the rest then laid the pile in the center of Leah's desk and placed her index finger on the top line. "Is this what you're looking for?"

The words, "Summary of Coverage" met Leah's gaze, and her cheeks flamed with embarrassment. "Oh. Right. There it is. Thanks."

"God, you're tense. What's up with you today? Is it Wyatt?"

"No, it's not Wyatt." Fabulous. In the last fourteen hours, she'd come up against two people determined to pick away at the scab on her heart. She'd lost the first battle, but she sure as shinola didn't plan to lose this time. "I'm trying to figure out how I can get this place up and running again, so if you could put your love life on hold for a few hours and focus on helping me with that, I'd be really grateful."

Jenny's eyes rounded. "Wow." She headed back to her own desk. "Okay. Sure. What do you need, boss-lady?" The words were clipped, curt, and layered in hurt.

Ashamed of her rudeness to her best friend, she dipped her head. "I'm sorry. I didn't mean that the way it came out. I'm genuinely happy for you, though I will warn you to be careful around anyone connected to Wyatt. Musicians, you know, aren't known for their loyalty to the ladies left behind."

"Yeah, okay. I get it. I'm sorry, too. Don't worry. I'm a big girl, and my eyes are wide open. And as far as you and Wyatt, what's between you two is just that: between you two. It's none of my business."

"How did you meet this bass player anyway?"

Sinking into her seat, Jenny slapped a hand on her desktop. "Okay, promise me you won't get mad first."

"Oh, for God's sake, Jen! Spit it out."

"Right. Wyatt and Chaz followed me home from the shelter yesterday."

"They what?" Of all the lowdown, dirty...

"Stay calm, okay? It's not as bad as it sounds. Chaz said they hung around here, parked in the street most of the day yesterday. When we left, he saw me and was struck by how lovely I was." She flipped a curl of hair from her shoulder, and Leah would've sworn she was preening at the lame line. "He decided he needed to know more about me, so he convinced Wyatt to tail me instead of you. Isn't that romantic?"

She twisted her lips in disgust. "No, it's creepy and stalkerish. If I were you, I'd consider a restraining order." She might have to do the same if Wyatt planned to continue hanging around here, parked in the street most of the day.

Jenny shook her head. "You had to be there. I'm not doing our interlude justice."

Interlude? Since when was a guy following her home an interlude? This was so unlike level-headed, feet-firmly-on-the-ground Jennifer Conway. She hoped she wouldn't have to stage an intervention.

Jenny must have read the doubt on Leah's face because she added, "Believe me, I gave them hell when I first realized they were following me. I mean, they scared me to death. I actually pulled into the police station and confronted them in the parking lot. But then I found out it was Wyatt, and I knew they were following me for details about you, so I told them to meet me at Annie's and buy me dinner."

Leah's stomach flip-flopped like a landed flounder. Details? What kind of details? "Did they show up?"

"Yup. But don't worry. I didn't tell them much."

"What did you tell him—*them*?"

Jenny shrugged. "Wyatt basically wanted to know about you and Julian. Were you happy? Where'd you two meet? How long you knew each other. That kinda stuff. I wasn't sure how true you stayed to the book, so I played 'loyal friend' and said that yes, you were happy, and I wasn't going to discuss anything more about your love life. He backed off right away. In fact, he didn't even stick around to eat with us. Took his meal to go and went back to the motel."

Leah released the breath she didn't realize she held. "Okay. Good." Maybe now, he'd believe she was serious about someone else and leave town again. This time, forever.

Jenny picked up a pencil and tapped it against her desk. "I think you're wrong about him, though. I don't think he's here to steal another song from you. I mean, let's face it. Even if his last album didn't do so well, he's still a big name in the music business. You don't think he can get someone in the industry to write songs for him?"

"Of course he can. He obviously did, since he's released six albums in the last seven years. But the point is, none of those other songs would have hit as big as they did, if not for the first single from his first album—the song he stole from *me*." She thumped her chest on the last word.

"I dunno, Lee. It seems like a lot of inconvenience on his part just to get a song or two out of you. He could've called."

"He wouldn't dare. Not after all these years."

Jenny tossed the pencil on top of her desk. "So…what? You think it's easier for him to show up and confront you face-to-face?"

"For him, yes. He knows it's easier for me to say no over the phone. In person, I'm too much of a pushover."

"You? The woman who single-handedly convinced the Osprey Cove Historical Society to allow us to host our Tails and Sales fundraiser in the arboretum for *free*?"

She waved a hand in dismissal. "That's different. That was for the shelter."

When it came to her animals, she'd arm wrestle the devil himself if it meant another dog or cat wouldn't be put down for no other reason than the lack of an owner. For herself, though, Wyatt was her own personal devil, a man who could smooth-talk her into giving up her soul.

No!

"No what?"

She hadn't realized she'd spoken the denial aloud, and with so much force, until she noticed Jenny's concerned expression.

"Nothing," she murmured. "I was…umm…" She pushed her hair back off her face and tucked it behind her ears. "I was thinking about something else."

"You know what?" Jenny rose from her seat and walked toward

where Leah sat. "You've got a lot on your plate right now. Why don't you let me handle the insurance?"

"You don't mind?"

"Of course not. Oh! And I may have found an electrician for us. Remember the Jorgensens? They adopted Maxie?"

She remembered Maxie, an eight-year-old, buff-colored shih-tzu with big brown eyes that could make the steeliest heart melt and a temperament to match. She always remembered the animals. The people? Not as often. "Uh-huh."

"Mrs. Jorgensen's brother is an electrician."

"How do you know that?"

"He was their family reference on their adoption application. I took a chance, called them, and they're happy to ask him to come help us out. In fact, while he's here, they said he might want to see some of the dogs we have for adoption. He was so impressed with their experience here, he's thinking of adopting one for himself. I thought, maybe, we might try matching him with Duchess. That'd be a win-win, right?"

She looked at Jenny with a sense of wonder. "You're amazing."

"Thanks. I learned it from you. So now all you need is an animal lover at the power company who's willing to bump you up the list for tree removal and pole repair, and we're back in business."

Jenny made the process sound so simple. Might as well say, "When I'm a millionaire, I'll buy an airline and travel around the world. I already have the luggage. All I have to do now is get the million dollars." Okay, not really. But it sure felt that way.

So, take smaller bites. Let's try a page from Jenny's book. Who do we know with clout in the power company?

She got up from her desk and pulled out the top drawer of the file cabinet. She'd made so many contacts over the years. There had to be someone.

"Leah," Jenny said. "Eat your doughnut first. Five minutes isn't gonna make a difference, and you need a little sweetening if you plan to ask for a favor."

♋

This time, Wyatt played the odds and showed up at the shelter around six o'clock, near closing time. And he refused to hover outside the gate like a deranged fan the way he had yesterday. No, he parked and strode inside with all the self-confidence years of onstage performances had instilled in him.

As he opened the door, a set of sleigh bells attached to the doorknob jangled, heralding his entrance.

"Sorry, we're clo—" Jenny looked up from the counter-style desk in the receptionist area, and her demeanor went from business to pleasure in the blink of an eye. "Oh. Wyatt. Hi. Is Chaz with you?" She stood on tiptoe to peer past his shoulders.

"No. Sorry. He's back at the motel. He said you could go see him there. If you want."

"Oh. Umm…okay. Thanks."

He nodded. "Sure." He'd warned Chaz not to play games with this one. If he really wanted a serious relationship with Jenny, he would have to pursue her with serious intent: dinners, flowers, listening, paying attention to her wants and needs more than his own.

Sadly, like most of the guys in the band, Chaz was accustomed to ladies chasing him and had forgotten how to go after what he wanted. Too many years of different romantic trysts in different towns with different women had made them all lazy. Wyatt knew firsthand that the right woman, the one who'd stay by her man's side through thick and thin, who'd challenge him and love him and make him crazy for her every day for the rest of their lives, didn't tolerate a neglectful lover. She wanted to know she was valued, that her man held her in the highest esteem. If he was fool enough to forget that—or let *her* forget—she'd be gone, never to return.

He was living proof.

Which brought him back to his reason for his appearance here. "Is…she…umm…Leah. Is Leah in?"

"Uh-huh. She's in the back office. Give her a few minutes. She's on the phone."

"Okay. I'll wait." While Jenny returned to work, he strolled around the reception area, looking through all the photographs posted on the walls.

It was like viewing a slide show of Leah's life after he left. The first photo showed a group of people outside the front door of the shelter, Leah standing beside an older man who held an enormous pair of scissors, poised to cut a large red ribbon wrapped around the building's front porch. *Opening Day, September 1, 2010.*

Next. Leah and the gentleman who'd held the scissors in the previous photo, standing with a family of five: mom, dad, and three kids, and a cute brown and black dog. *First adoption. Licorice goes home with the Quinns. September 9, 2010.*

From there, he gazed at photo after photo of happy adopters with their new pets. Some featured Leah, others captured Jenny's grinning face, and still others showed several shelter employees celebrating with the new family additions. Most of the photos depicted dogs, but there were dozens of cats, as well. Aside from the adoption pictures, there were also snapshots taken at different events: adopt-a-thons, pet fairs, and one or two fancy-looking fundraisers with Leah all dressed up. Dressed up or dressed down, though, didn't make a difference to Wyatt. She was still the most beautiful woman he'd ever seen.

And he'd let her go.

"Is Julian in any of these pictures?" The question came out of his mouth before he could engage his brain. He mentally slapped himself for the sheer desperation he'd framed the words in.

Jenny looked up at him again, a red pen near her mouth. "Huh? Oh! Right. Julian. I'm not sure. Maybe."

Maybe. Not exactly the answer he'd hoped for. He studied the more formal shots carefully, searching for a man with a possessive eye or arm on Leah, found several possible candidates, but no definites.

He shivered. "It's freezing in here."

Jenny shrugged. "No heat. No heat, no power, no phone service. The shelter got hit pretty hard by the storm the other night. Leah's trying to get help right now."

"What's the problem?" he said with a frown. "Isn't the town responsible to get you up and running again?"

"Sure. As long as we don't mind waiting 'til Christmas. The shelter's not exactly a priority for them."

"If I know Leah, she'll have a dozen people here in an hour," he boasted. "She's always lived a charmed life."

"Wow. You don't know her at all, do you?" Jenny frowned. "No wonder she doesn't want to see you."

"Yet, he showed up anyway," Leah said from the doorway. She strode toward him, her steps eating up the distance between them. "Shouldn't you be loitering outside, Wyatt? Waiting for me to leave so you can follow me home?"

Jenny cleared her throat. "I…er…think I should go now. Casey left over an hour ago. Leah, I'll see you tomorrow morning. Wyatt, would you tell Chaz…?" She stopped, shook her head, and grabbed her coat off the chair back. "Never mind. Don't tell him anything. Jerk."

She stormed past them both while shoving her arms into her coat sleeves and disappeared out the door.

"I couldn't agree more," Leah said, her arms folded over her chest. "Goodbye, Wyatt."

"I didn't come here to start trouble," he assured her. "I thought I could take you out to dinner. Just…" he added, his hands held up, "as friends."

"I can't. I have to cook dinner for my father, take care of the dogs in my garage, and I'm still trying to get *someone* to come over to remove the tree from my yard. I don't have scads of free time on my hands to hang around outside someone's place of work so I can follow her home."

He took her by the arms, and she stiffened, but he wouldn't let go. "Okay, look, I'm sorry. You're right. It was a crummy thing to do."

"Then why do it?"

"I wanted to talk to you. I still want to talk to you. Someplace where we could be civil to one another."

"Like in your car outside my shelter?"

"That was Chaz's idea. I shouldn't have listened to him. I was an idiot. Come on, Leah, give me a break. Please? Dinner. That's all I'm asking for. One lousy dinner. Then you can go back to your life, unhindered by me and all the reasons you hate me."

Her posture relaxed, while her expression remained stern and unsure. "Okay. Let me check on things at home first. I'll meet you at the Aerie at eight o'clock."

"I'll pick you up."

She jerked out of his grasp. "I'll *meet* you there."

"I'd like to see your father again anyway. Don't be silly, Leah. It's not like you don't know me. You've driven in a car with me lots of times." Okay, that didn't come out right. He took a deep breath and tried again. "I just want some time alone with you—even if it's a simple car ride."

He watched the emotions play over her face as she shifted from one foot to the other, studying him. He could almost see her weighing the options. At last, she scooped up her jacket and thrust her arms into the sleeves. Her reply was barely audible over the sound of her zipping up.

"Okay."

6

Okay.

Why on earth had she said okay? Not just to dinner, but to allowing him to drive, as well? Now she had no escape hatch. The entire time Leah showered and changed, she mentally chastised herself for her weakness where Wyatt was concerned. As she sat before the mirror doing her hair and makeup, she gave her image a much-needed pep talk.

"You can do this. You're not the same person he left all those years ago. You can sit across from him and not let him know how much he hurt you." She ran her brush through her hair and caught sight of her left hand—her *very naked* left hand. Dang. He'd definitely expect her to wear her engagement ring, especially on a date with another man. Now, what? She couldn't exactly run out and buy one for herself.

Mom. Mom's jewelry still sat in the box in her father's room. Leah wondered if any piece in there could serve as an engagement ring. It didn't have to be a diamond. She had never been the diamond type, and Wyatt knew that.

Years ago, when Grandma passed, Mom had reset her mother's freshwater pearl ring into a cocktail piece with a delicate white gold setting and three clear sapphires on each side. It wouldn't pass a jeweler's loupe inspection, but to Wyatt's untrained eye, it *should* look enough like an engagement piece to get her through the night and keep the pretense alive.

Dressed and ready, she headed to her father's room and knocked on the door. When she went inside, he whirled from his desk, gave her a long whistle, and said, "You look nice. Where you going?"

"The Aerie with Wyatt." She looked down at her black slacks and cream-colored sweater. Too much? The restaurant was on the upscale side, so she couldn't exactly show up in jeans and a tattered t-shirt. She'd chosen the place because she wanted Wyatt to know she wasn't a fast food drive-thru girl anymore. Curse her pride because, on second thought, that option would have been quick and efficient—like yanking off a Band-Aid. Oh, well. Too late now. He'd be here any second. "Can I borrow Mom's pearl ring?" She made her way over to the dresser before her father had time to think about it, much less answer.

"Wyatt, huh? Are you ready for that?"

She opened the top storage area where the ring sat, among a nest of earrings and loose pendants, and frowned. "No. Which is why we're only having dinner and some non-combustible conversation."

His brow furrowed. "You *are* going to tell him, aren't you?"

"Not tonight, no. But…eventually." Maybe. *Unless I can convince him to leave town first.* She slipped the piece onto her left ring finger, held it up to study the potential. Not bad at all. The fit was a little tight, but she could probably get away with it for an hour or two without risking a loss of circulation to her extremities.

"The ring's in the—. Oh, you found it."

"Uh-huh. Thanks, Dad. Do you need anything before I go out?" She almost wished he'd tell her not to go, tell her he wanted help with his project, but of course, he waved her off.

"No. Go have fun. You work too hard."

The doorbell rang, ending any possibility she could convince him he desperately needed her before Wyatt showed up.

"You do, too, Dad. Take the night off for a change." She kissed his forehead. "Why don't you call the guys and get a poker game together?"

He shook his head, and his mouth formed a grim downturn. "They don't want to come here anymore. They say they get bored always coming up here. They want to play at other houses."

She couldn't blame them. They probably wanted a place where they could spread out, eat pizza, drink beer, and not have to sit on the edge of a bed or worry they were dissolving Emily Stewart's lingering scent with their overabundance of sweaty testosterone. "You *could* do that, you know. Go to someone else's house. I promise everything would be safe here 'til you got back."

"Nope." He turned back to his table and picked up his drafting pencil. "I need to stay here. Work on the project."

Sighing, she wished him a good night and headed downstairs. She opened the door to Wyatt, who looked too darn tasty in a pale blue dress shirt and sport coat over a pair of charcoal gray slacks. She definitely should have opted for the drive-thru.

"Looking good, Leah," he said and slid a kiss across her cheek.

Something in the way he spoke, the way he moved, as if he'd said the exact same cheesy line and made that same smooth pass a thousand times, turned her to ice. "Yeah, thanks. You ready?" She grabbed her purse and jacket and pulled the door closed.

"I…umm…thought I was going to say hi to your dad."

"He's got his poker buddies over," she lied. "Let's go." She tossed her jacket over her shoulder and strode down the steps to the walkway that would lead to his ostentatious red sports car. When she reached the curb, she opened the door.

"Let me get that for you," he offered.

"No need. I've got it." She slid into the seat and pulled the door closed with finality. While he strode around to the driver's side, she buckled up, placed her hands in her lap—pearl ring up—and stared straight out at the street.

He got in and started the engine. "The Aerie, huh? You know, I looked up the place on the web. They have a pretty extensive menu. You eat there often?"

She didn't avert her gaze from the windshield. "Now and then." More like once, for a fundraiser. In her mind, extensive also translated to expensive, way out of her budget. But it was the type of place Julian would take his fiancée, so…

Neither spoke for the longest time, their silence punctuated by the roar of the engine as Wyatt accelerated on the highway. Leah's nerves mirrored the car's horsepower. How on earth could she sit across from him and maintain an amiable discussion when all she wanted to do was tell him to go away, get out of her town, and never come back? It had taken her forever to get over his departure. She had finally made peace with the past. Now, he was back and stirring up all her memories of heartache and loss to rise to the surface again.

The traffic light outside the restaurant turned red as they approached, and he braked to a halt.

"Oh, hey!" He lifted her hand. "That's the ring, huh?"

She feigned disinterest, as if accustomed to wearing it. "Hmm? Oh, yes."

"Is that a pearl?" She nodded, and he added, "I would've thought the guy would spring for a real rock."

She pulled her hand away. "I don't need 'a real rock.' Big diamonds don't impress me, and Julian knows that. For your information, the pearl is a symbol of deep, abiding love in the gem world." She was pulling that fact straight out of thin air, but she'd bet her shelter and every pet in it that he had no clue about symbols in the gem world. If there even were symbols in the gem world.

The light changed to green, and he turned into the valet parking area as her cell rang.

"Oops, sorry." She searched through her purse and pulled out the phone. A quick glance at the screen sent all thoughts of dinner and sitting across from Wyatt from her mind. "I…umm…think I'm about to cancel our plans tonight."

"Oh?"

She held up a finger and pressed the button to connect the call. "This is Leah."

"Leah, hi, Gabe Porter. We need you here. Now." Gabe Porter was an animal law enforcement officer, the liaison between the town's kill shelter and the ASPCA. If he was calling her, it meant she was about to go back to work—in the worst conditions imaginable.

"It's okay. What've we got?"

"Dogs. About thirty of them, some in desperate need of vet care. They've been living in their own filth, no food or water for at least a week, best we can tell. No shelter from the elements. The town's already overrun with lost pets, thanks to the storm the other night. You're our next call."

Dang. If she didn't take them, they'd be put down. God knew what these poor creatures had already survived. To die never knowing the true love of a good owner was so unfair. But since her shelter was still without power, and her garage was already crammed full with her own animals, she couldn't possibly find a place for this group. Unless…

"Gabe, I'd love to help, but I'm in a bit of a situation myself. The storm knocked down a tree on my property and pulled down the power lines. I've got no heat, no hot water, and no electricity."

He paused for a long moment, and she held her breath. Gabe had more clout than she did. If anyone could make a miracle happen for her, it was him.

"I can probably set you up with a generator temporarily and call the town tomorrow morning. See if I can light a fire under the power company for you. Would that make a difference?"

"Yeah, it would." Halleluia!

"Great. How soon can you get here?"

"How soon can you get that generator to my shelter?"

"Within the hour."

"Give me time to grab the van. What's the location?" He rattled off an address about fifteen minutes' drive from her shelter. "ETA, less than thirty. I'll have Jenny meet the generator," she said and hung up then turned to Wyatt. "I'm sorry. I've got an emergency. Can you drop me off at the shelter?"

"Everything all right?"

"Yes and no. I'm fine, but the animals I'm about to retrieve…" She shivered. "They're going to be in pretty bad shape from neglect and starvation."

"I'll go with you. Maybe I can help."

"No, honestly. You're much too dressed up for this kind of work." He cast a meaningful glance at her suede jacket and dress slacks.

"And you're not?"

"I'll put on a Tyvek suit."

"Got an extra?"

"Sure. Of course. We have several. But, Wyatt, I don't—"

"You can say yes and I'll turn around right now, or you can continue to argue with me and we'll sit here all night."

Why in the world would he want to—? Oh, wait. He probably thought she'd planned Gabe's phone call to weasel out of their dinner date. Well, he was in for a rude awakening.

This time, she secretly reveled in allowing the word to leave her mouth. "Okay."

♋

Wyatt had never seen anything so pathetic and revolting. On the outside, the house looked fairly normal, if unkempt. When he stepped into the backyard, however, under the dozen floodlights set up around the grounds, a scene of misery played out. Dogs, many of them so thin their bones poked out of their skin, shivered and cringed, too weak to bark. They were chained to trees, to outbuildings, to fence posts, given only enough lead to turn around or lie down. Flies buzzed around their ears and eyes. The smell of rotting flesh permeated the air.

Leah, in her hooded white coverall suit, facemask in place over her nose and mouth, spoke with a man garbed in a similar outfit about the condition of the animals.

"We've already transported the seriously ill and injured to the clinic," the man said. "The remaining ones here are yours."

From what Wyatt had overheard, the investigation had started a week ago, after numerous complaints from neighbors about the sheer number of dogs chained in the yard, especially in the hours immediately before and after the nor'easter had blown through town. Law enforcement had attempted to contact the resident to no avail. After obtaining a search warrant, they entered the premises and discovered the deplorable conditions of more than thirty dogs.

"Crime lab's processed the scene, and there's an arrest warrant out for the homeowner. No sign of him yet."

"I'm sorry," Wyatt interjected. "Did you say 'crime lab'?"

"Yes, sir," the man replied. "Aggravated cruelty to animals is a felony in the state of New York. Therefore, this site has been deemed a crime scene and will be treated as such." He turned to Leah. "New recruit?"

"Old friend," she said. "He happened to be with me when I got the call and volunteered to help."

"Well, make sure he knows what he's doing." From the back door of the house, a police officer called, "Director Porter? We need you inside, sir."

"Right!" the man shouted back. "Thanks, Leah, for coming out here tonight." He glanced at Wyatt again. "I'm pretty sure this isn't what you had planned for the evening."

"I'm pretty sure these animals hadn't planned to wind up here, either," she replied.

With a curt nod, the man strode away.

"From this moment on," she told Wyatt, "you do exactly what I say. You don't move unless I tell you to. No questions asked, okay?"

He offered her a crisp salute. "Got it."

"I'm serious, Wyatt. You heard Gabe. This is a crime scene. And I don't want this monster getting off on a technicality because you touched something you shouldn't have. Stay with me, and do exactly what I tell you. No deviation."

He held up his hands in surrender. "I swear, Leah. You say, I do. No argument."

For the next several hours, he followed her lead and rediscovered her compassion, her deep sense of justice, and her strength in the face of the cruelest adversities. Despite the smell and the filth, she knelt time and again to look into the eyes of the suffering, to stroke their matted fur, and soothe their fears. Once she'd calmed a frightened beast, she'd loop the leash around its neck and lead it to the van, where she'd gently place it in one of the numerous crates inside.

It was well past midnight when the last animal sat, suspicious eyes glaring, in the last crate, and she locked the back door of the van. "Okay. Let's go."

She hopped into the driver's seat and started the engine.

Pushing the hood of his Tyvek suit off his head, he studied her as she pulled out into traffic. She'd also removed the hood and mask, and her makeup ran in sweaty streaks down her face. Yet, while the work and the misery had exhausted him, Leah gave off waves of frenetic energy.

"Okay, kids," she said loud enough to carry to the van's rear, "the tough part's almost over. Hang in there with me a little longer." When she pulled into the parking lot at the shelter, lights illuminated the building. "Woo-hoo! Way to go, Gabe!" She'd barely thrown the gear into park before she leaped out and raced to the back of the van again.

Wyatt, dirty and dog-tired—no pun intended—took a bit longer to ease out of the passenger seat. Outside, a dozen figures in Tyvek suits clustered around the grounds, waiting to participate.

"Who are all these people?" Leah asked him.

"The Ungrateful."

She didn't immediately place the name, and her brow puckered in lines of confusion.

"Chaz called them." Jenny strode forward out of the throng and pointed at the man beside her. "They're his bandmates and road people."

Wyatt quirked a brow at Chaz. Technically, he thought, they were *his* bandmates and road people—Chaz included. He bit his tongue. After years of receiving most of the accolades from studio execs and audiences, he'd let the praise go to his head and begun treating the rest of the group as if they were less than him, expendable. When they'd turned their backs on him, he'd learned *he* was the one who was less than. After his solo album tanked, he'd crawled back to the members of the Ungrateful, humbled and ashamed. Nowadays, he valued each of them as individuals and for the talent they contributed to the group's success. They were a team.

Leah, meanwhile, turned to the bass player, her smile lighting up the night brighter than the flood lamps, and pulled off her gloves to shake his hand. "You must be Chaz. Thank you. This is...*incredible.* Thank you, all of you! I'm touched. Really."

Wyatt's jaw dropped. He'd gone with her to that pit of despair, worked next to her for the last four hours, and hadn't received a handshake, a thank you, *or* a smile. All he got were orders like, "Don't touch that," "Don't move," and "For God's sake, don't you know better than to put your face so close to a terrified animal you don't know?"

"It's nothing," Chaz replied in his boy-next-door Midwestern twang. "The fellas and I are used to hauling heavy stuff. When Jenny told me what was going on and why, we all leaped at the chance to help out. Heck, we love animals, too."

"Where do we start?" Roscoe Barrymore, one of the band's roadies, asked.

"The crates deeper in the cab have the animals that can go straight into kennels after a bath," she announced. "For now, we start right here with the ones who need special attention."

Wyatt had never considered there was a method to the way Leah had inspected and chosen the animals in the yard. Oh, sure, he'd seen her examine each one carefully. Some, she'd immediately bring to the van. Others, she'd walk away from, only to return later for them. At the time he'd detected no real order to the routine of take the brown one, ignore the white one. Now, however, he realized her random choices were actually a form of triage.

"Okay, listen up," she told the crowd, her voice hoarse from exhaustion. He wondered how she still managed to stay on her feet. The work they'd completed already had been heart- and back-breaking. "Jenny and I will take the dogs out of the crates. They'll be removed one by one and passed over. As we take each one out, you guys will help us walk them in the yard. Bear in mind, they're scared and confused right now. Slow steps. Be gentle, speak softly, and don't put any part of yourself you don't want to lose close to their mouths. As we get them calmed down, they'll each go into the tub. I have tranqs, but I'd prefer not to use them unless absolutely necessary. So please, everyone, be careful. And be patient. This is going to take hours, so if anyone wants to leave, let me know."

She waited, expecting someone he supposed, to say, "On second thought, I got a thing in town…"

No one did.

Wyatt tapped her shoulder. "Where do you want me?"

She didn't answer right away, and he sensed she chose her words carefully. "Honestly, Wyatt? You should probably go back to your motel room. You've done enough tonight. You must be pretty drained by now."

He shook his head. "You stay. I stay."

"I stay because I have to. This is part of my job. It's not yours."

Chaz stepped between them. "Let him stay, Leah. We're musicians. We're used to late nights."

Wyatt wanted to tell his friend he didn't need an intervention or referral, but Leah shifted her focus from one man to the other as if weighing the pros and cons of letting him stay. Jeez. How far had he fallen in her eyes? Apparently, to subterranean levels.

At last, she frowned and slipped her mask back into place. "All right, fine. Let's get started."

7

Shortly after twelve noon, Leah placed the very last dog in her new temporary home, too tired to amass enough breath to sigh. Using her last stores of energy, she pulled off her face mask. "On the positive side," she said to Jenny, "I finagled us a generator."

"And all it cost us was blood, sweat, and a sleepless night." She peeled off her gloves and flexed her fingers. "God, it feels good to have air in my pores again." Leah followed suit, stripping off the gloves, and Jenny gasped. "Ohmigod, where'd you get that?"

"Shoot," she replied as she stared at the pearl and white sapphire ring on her finger. "I forgot I had this on. Wyatt made some kind of crack about my not having an engagement ring, so...I..."

Jenny clucked her tongue and whispered low, "Oh, for God's sake! You got yourself an engagement ring? Aren't you taking this too far?"

"Sssh!" Panicked, she looked around to make sure Wyatt was nowhere in sight.

"Relax." She flipped her hand in dismissal. "He's outside with Chaz and the others. Leah, have you lost your mind?" That same hand now became some kind of baton, bouncing in rhythm with each syllable Jenny uttered. "You do know all he has to do is talk to someone who knows you, someone besides me, and he'll learn there is no Julian."

Despite the warning voice in her brain that agreed with Jenny's assessment, she shook her head. "He won't. Besides, he'll be gone in a few days, and it won't matter."

Jenny pursed her lips in obvious doubt. "Uh-huh, sure."

As if summoned by their conversation, Wyatt appeared in the doorway between reception and the kennel area, still masked, gloved, and garbed in Tyvek. He pushed off the hood and removed his gloves. "How we doing?"

"Good," Leah replied. "We're all done. You guys can go. Make sure you tell your friends how grateful I am, and if any of them decides he wants a pet from the shelter, it's on the house."

Jenny smirked. "That's my boss. No sleep for more than thirty hours, and she's still marketing."

"It's what I do," she said with a shrug. "God, I'm beat! I may sleep 'til Christmas. Let's close up shop for today. If Gabe delivers on his promise, we'll have the power company here by the end of the week and can be up and running as a real business again soon."

"Good. Then I can get the cats out of my house and hook up that electrician guy with Duchess." She held up crossed fingers.

Wyatt stripped out of the Tyvek suit and rolled it into a ball. "What do I do with this?"

Jenny took the bundle from him. "I'll take care of it." She grabbed Leah's and her own as well and left the area, closing the door behind her with a firm click.

When they were alone, Wyatt held out his hand. "C'mon. I'll take you home."

"Oh, I'm staying here," she said.

"You just said you could sleep 'til Christmas."

She swept her arm across the various kennels. "I know, but I need to start working with these guys. Plus, now that I've got the generator and a little electricity, I want to catch up on stuff I wasn't able to do before."

He frowned. "You've been awake a day and a half. The work can wait another day. You should get some sleep."

"I will. I've got a cot in my office."

His voice rose. "You need a bed, not a cot."

The tone and paternal attitude snapped her last nerve. "Since when do you know what I need? I'm a big girl, Wyatt. I take care of myself, this place, my father, the house I grew up in, and a hundred other priorities on a regular basis. I've been taking care of most of this stuff for a long time now. Some, since the day you left seven years ago. What makes you think you can come back here after all this time and have some say in what I do or where I do it?" Her scathing rebuke left her lips so fast she didn't have time to consider the outcome.

The shocked look on his face, though, made the experience worthwhile. He didn't speak for a long minute, but she wouldn't back down. Instead, she leveled a steady gaze at him, and folded her arms over her chest.

"Defiant to the end," he said at last. "Fair enough. Would you, at least, like me to check in on your father for you?"

She maintained her brook-no-argument posture. "Thanks, but that's not necessary. I called Giselle earlier this morning. She'll stay with him, make sure he eats, keep him company and take care of the dogs 'til I get there later tonight. I really don't need you, you know.

Oddly enough, I never have."

He winced and sucked in a breath. "I get it. I hurt you all those years ago. Now, it's your turn to hurt me. Are we even now?"

Not by a longshot. Not unless he could lose a part of himself he never realized he wanted until it was gone. And she wasn't referring to his appendix.

"It has nothing to do with hurting you, Wy. I think, deep down, I always knew you'd leave Osprey Cove. You were so unhappy here. I admit, though, I thought we were a package deal. When I realized you'd left without me, I was devastated—for lots of reasons you know and a few you don't. Eventually, I toughened up. I realized I had to move on without you. I had no other choice. Did you expect me to sit around and wait for you? For seven years?"

His expression was wooden, from exhaustion or emotion she couldn't decipher. "Of course not."

"Then what *did* you expect, Wyatt? I had to go on with my life. You obviously had. I mean, look at you. You're a big success now, right? Be honest. You assumed you could come back here, show off for the town—show off for me—and expect us all to bow down to the famous Wyatt Blackthorne. Well, guess what? We don't care. We all went on with our lives, all made new plans. Maybe we didn't hit it big the way you did, but maybe that's because we stayed here and took care of our responsi-*bilities*." Her voice broke on the last word, and she turned her back to him. "Go home, Wyatt. I've got work to do and you're getting in my way."

His sigh pierced her heart, but she remained stoic, resolute. He could not, would not, get under her shields again.

"Will you at least promise me you'll get some rest?" His tone was low and full of sorrow. "I do care what happens to you, Leah. I always did."

A lump rose in her throat, and she swallowed hard. "Bye, Wyatt. Thanks for your help last night."

Tears pricking her eyes, she stiffened her spine and kept her gaze pinned to the setter mix she'd only finished tending a few minutes before. Luckier than her counterparts, this brownish-red pup must not have been on the property too long. She suffered from flea infestation, dehydration, and a few minor scrapes from lying up against the broken chain link fence. She'd be the easiest to rehabilitate and prepare for possible adoption. Leah decided to call her Penny because her coat, when cleaned, had the color of gleaming copper. This little girl would land on her feet; she'd make sure of it. Penny might even make a good therapy dog—she had the perfect temperament. Even during her bath, she remained gentle, occasionally licking Leah's hand to show her gratitude at being rescued.

Now, Leah's mind buzzed with words, screaming for release, and she headed to her office, unaware of whether or not Wyatt stayed where he was. She just plain didn't care anymore.

To prevent any interruptions, she locked the door behind her before taking a seat at her desk. Assured she was alone, she reached into the lowest drawer and riffled through the hanging folders until she found the one labeled, "Quarterly Projections." Inside the pocket, camouflaged by Excel spreadsheets with random years and numbers, she found her five-by-seven-inch pink journal. She had a dozen of them. Some were filled up and locked away. Others still had space for her to write out the emotions tumbling inside her. She always kept one journal in her bedroom and one in her office for times like this.

In these books, she put down in words, her thoughts, her dreams, her fears. Her lyrics. Pen in hand, she flipped to the first clean page and wrote one for all she'd experienced in the last few hours.

> *Pretty girl, pain in her eyes,*
> *Looking for someone to love you.*
> *We found each other in misery*
> *And made our dreams come true.*

> *You wanted a home, safe and warm.*
> *I needed someone to hold.*
> *Now, all we have is time*
> *And promising days to unfold.*

And, of course, she needed to pour out her anger at Wyatt.

> *Why'd you have to come back*
> *When I finally learned to live without you?*
> *When the memory of your smile*
> *Has faded from my view?*

> *Why'd you have to come back*
> *When all I want is to forget you?*
> *When the pain of what we once were*
> *No longer cuts me in two?*

She studied those lines with a jaundiced mind. No. Not right. Try again. She flipped to a new page, her imagination seeing the smug look on Wyatt's face when he'd told her she needed sleep, the way he tried to play responsible adult, like she'd spent the last seven years dithering around, never able to make a decision without a big strong man to help her. Anger swelled, and using her pen as her weapon, she wrote at a feverish pace.

You look down from your perfect tower
So sure you'll never fall
But I'm the one who had the power
Your love was mine once, after all.

My heart's no longer made of glass
Not broken shards on the ground.
I still have dreams that are made to last
Don't bother to come 'round.

That entry was much closer to what she felt about the night's events. While it didn't matter if the words were perfect, since no one else would ever read them, she had to fully capture her mood, if she had any hope of minimizing the emotional rollercoaster she rode.

A wave of nostalgia washed over her, and she flipped through the pages until she found the one she wrote seven years ago, on the worst night of her life.

So small and frail, no way you could survive.
I held you for so short a time
I barely knew you were mine.

The rest of the words blurred into blue blobs, indistinguishable and incomprehensible. Familiar pain doubled her in half. Tears slid down her cheeks, hot and wet. Boy or girl? She never knew. She clutched her abdomen, feeling the ghost inside even now, after all this time. Before her tears landed on the pages and smeared the ink, she closed the book and replaced it in its secure nest. She stumbled to the cot in the corner of the office and curled up, hugging her knees to her chest.

She slept. In her dreams, a dark-haired child with electric blue eyes sat on a swing beneath a summer sky and called to her, "Higher, Mommy! Higher! Faster!"

♋

Wyatt returned to the shelter shortly after six that evening with a heavy white shopping bag in his hand. No cars sat in the parking lot, but the lights in the kennel area were on, as dusk fell. The generator's steady hum provided the only noise. As he drew closer to the building, one dog's sudden barking broke the stillness, followed by another, then another.

Good thing he hadn't planned to sneak up on Leah; she had a full symphony of guardians in there.

The front door opened before he reached the first step, and she peered at him through the storm door's screen. The circles under her eyes were darker, more pronounced, and her lashes cast extra shadows on her cheekbones. She needed a full night's sleep—in a real bed, not some foldaway canvas contraption. "Wyatt? What are you doing here?"

With a wide grin, he held up the shopping bag. "You owe me dinner. I knew I wouldn't convince you to try again tonight, so I had the Aerie set us up with takeout."

"Aerie doesn't do takeout."

"You'd be surprised what people will do when you have a recognizable name."

She frowned. Whoops. He hadn't meant to throw his celebrity in her face, but her disgusted look suggested that was exactly how she took his statement.

"Uh-huh." Using the flat of her hand, she pushed the screen door open. "Come in then, I guess."

He stepped inside, vowing not to let her mood ruin his. He'd waited too long for this conversation, had rehearsed what he'd say a thousand times. While her speech this afternoon had given him pause, he chalked it up to major league burnout. They were all tired from the all-nighter. After leaving the shelter earlier, he'd gone back to his motel room and fallen face-first into the mattress, only coming up for air several hours later. When he did, Chaz still snored from the couch. "Did you sleep at all?"

"I caught a nap for an hour or two. I'm fine."

He wouldn't bet on it. She looked…brittle. As if an unkind word or deed would snap her into pieces. Careful to tread lightly, he hefted the bag again. "You have a place where we can set this up?"

"The kitchen. In the back."

He followed her down the narrow hall to a cramped room where a scarred old Formica table took center stage, surrounded by four mismatched metal chairs. On a laminate counter sat an old drip coffeemaker and a miniature microwave. To the right of the counter stood a cheapie white refrigerator, the door dented in two spots. The windows looked out over the yard where the generator roared. The dimmest slice of sunlight came through the dirty glass to illuminate the dismal atmosphere. Not exactly the ambience he hoped for, but he'd make do.

"I hope they provided all the condiments and stuff." She

rummaged through drawers as if looking for something, but he sensed she used the action to avoid looking at him. "I had to clean out the fridge, thanks to the power outage. I might have some salt and pepper packets laying around, but—"

He placed the bag on the table, and the surface wobbled under the weight. "I'm pretty sure they took care of everything. Except…" He removed the business card stapled to the top of the bag and folded it a few times. After jiggling the table to discover where it was off-balance, he slid the card under the offensive leg and jiggled the table again. Everything stayed smooth and even. "There we are. Much better."

She took a seat and folded her hands beneath her chin. "Why are you here, Wyatt?"

"I told you. Dinner."

"That's not what I meant and you know it. Why did you come back to Osprey Cove? Why now?"

Not now, he told himself. Now was not the time to tell her the truth. He pulled up a chair and sat across from her. "Oh, well, for you to understand that, you'd have to know why I left in the first place."

"I already know why you left. You got a solo record deal. You were going to be a big star, and you couldn't wait to shake this town and everyone in it off your tail."

He should've let her bitterness slide, but her facts were skewed. Shaking his head, he pulled out the first covered dish and placed it on the table in front of her. "It wasn't supposed to be that way. I wanted you to come with me."

"Not enough."

The argument sprang to his lips, but he bit back the angry words. Instead, he removed the second plate and dug around in the bag for the plastic silverware and napkins. Looking up, he frowned. "I forgot something to drink."

She shrugged. "I've got semi-cold bottled water, if you're not picky."

"That's fine." While she opened the refrigerator door to grab the waters, he fussed with their place settings, silent. Once she sat again, he lifted the lids to reveal two salads full of greens and assorted colorful vegetables, topped with sliced pears and goat cheese crumbles, and drizzled with fuchsia-colored raspberry dressing. "Nice. No wonder you like this place."

"If you like the salad, wait 'til you try the entrees. I've never had a bad meal there. What did you order, anyway?"

"It's a surprise. You'll see soon enough."

"Uh-huh." Worry lines creased the area between her eyebrows as she picked at her salad. He'd forgotten she hated surprises, always had. Leah was a planner, a plotter, a list-maker. Whether it was details for a school assignment, a date, or their future together, she had itemized steps in a notebook somewhere.

Hoping to inspire her to eat, he speared a baby lettuce leaf and pear piece, slid the fork into his mouth, chewed and swallowed. "Delicious. Don't you think so?"

Her fork never made it close to her lips as she danced the tines through the bed of greens. "Mmm-hmm. Perfect."

"The strawberries are a nice touch," he added.

She nodded without missing a beat. "Yes. Nice and ripe."

"They're pears," he remarked.

"Oh." Frowning, she put the fork down. "Look, Wyatt, this is stupid. I'm sorry, but I'm just not up for scintillating conversation and lavish dinners right now."

"I'm not asking for scintillating. Casual conversation will do. Let's talk about stuff that should be easy for you."

"Like what?"

"Like you." He gestured at the walls around him with his fork. "This shelter. How'd you wind up owning it? I thought you planned to go to veterinary school."

Her frown deepened, but she picked up the fork. "Plans change."

"What happened?"

"I missed a semester due to…" She rearranged the lettuce in her dish again. "…a medical issue. Then Mom got sick, and I opted to stay home to be near her."

"A medical issue? What kind of medical issue?" Who else had been sick besides her mother ? Her? With what? How sick?

She waved off his concern with the empty fork. "It wasn't as extended a condition as we originally thought, but I missed registration because of it. By the time the next registration period rolled around, Mom had been diagnosed with bladder cancer, which changed everything. For all of us. Then, just when we thought it was all going to work out…" Her gaze dropped to the salad, the sentence left hanging.

He opted to redirect the topic, rather than make her discuss the tragedy of her mother's death. "And that's when you bought the shelter?"

She gave a mirthless laugh. "No. I started out here as a handler three days a week. I cleaned out the kennels, walked the dogs, showed pets to prospective adopters, filled out paperwork, and verified references. After about a year, I trained as a vet tech and eventually worked my way up to assistant manager. A few years after that, when Mr. Brooks decided he wanted to retire, I bought him out."

"Do you regret it? Not going to vet school, I mean."

"No. This is where I belong. These animals, and the ones that'll come afterward, they need me. And I need them. I'll never be rich and famous; I certainly won't ever be able to convince the Aerie to provide a takeout meal based on my name." She flashed a withering glare. "But I love what I do. Even the rough nights like last night are rewarding in their own way. I make a difference to a living being who might otherwise suffer or die." She pushed the salad to the side, stirred but not eaten.

"Should we move on to the entrees?"

"Sure." Her eyelids dropped, slowly opened again. She was clearly exhausted.

"Maybe this wasn't such a good idea after all. How about I take you home?"

"But…" She gestured at the bag on the corner of the table. "The dinner."

He waved her off. "Forget it. It's just some pasta." In black truffle oil. With fresh lobster meat. A hundred and fifty dollars a plate, *without* the exorbitant tip he'd added for takeout service. "We can try again another time." He gathered up the salad dishes and tossed them into the bag. "Come on. I'll take you home."

She shook her head. "No need. I'll drive myself."

"Don't be ridiculous. You can barely keep your eyes open."

"It's two miles. I can make it two miles."

He smirked. "Still afraid to be in a car with me?"

The challenge proved too much for her to deny. Slapping a hand on the table, she shot to her feet. "Fine. Let me get my coat."

He watched her stalk away from him. Exhaustion might have banked her fires, but the occasional spark still burned bright. He wondered if her fiancé knew how to ignite that light inside her.

8

Despite her exhaustion, Leah couldn't sleep. Her conversation with Wyatt paraded through her head on a continuous loop, reviving memories best left dead and buried. Not in the car. No. The minute he started the engine, she tilted her head back, closed her eyes, and the next thing she knew he was shaking her awake outside her house. Thank God she didn't talk in her sleep!

Why wouldn't he leave already? The more time he spent here, the more the pain resurfaced to slice her heart. Well, she'd have to reinforce her armor until he finally got the hint.

In the morning, bleary-eyed and restless, she gathered the dogs up in two groups of seven and walked each septet around the block. A few of her neighbors gawked at the cluster of dogs dragging her down the street, but most were used to the sight after all these years. Afterward, she prepared breakfast for her father and spent a few minutes with him, discussing the events from the other night and steering clear of any more talk of Wyatt.

"What's on the agenda today?" he asked.

"I'm taking the angel crew to the St. Ignatius Nursing Home this morning. Since it's just me today, I'll only take three of them. I don't think I could handle all five by myself. Then, back to the shelter to start rehabbing the newcomers. If Jenny doesn't hear from the power company before I get there, I'll call Gabe Porter this afternoon and give him a nudge. I can't keep working with forty percent power from a borrowed generator and I can't keep our guests in the garage forever, either. Ideally, I'd like to have them back at the shelter by next week. After that, if there's time, I'll try to set up a new date for the fundraiser with the caterers and vendors. I should be home again around six-thirty."

Clucking his tongue, he pointed a draft pencil at her. "You work too hard. You look drained."

Thanks for the boost to my ego. "Just this week. Soon as the electricity's on again, things'll go back to normal." She kissed his head. "Be good, Dad. I'll see you tonight. If you need anything, call Giselle."

"Will do, sweetheart. Don't worry. Your mom and I will be just fine up here."

She left him to his project and his memories and returned to the garage where she gathered up three of the angel crew, five dogs who served as "visitors" at the local senior citizen facilities. "C'mon, boys and girls. Let's go charm the old folks."

With her canine passengers, Clover; Hermione; and Scrabble, safely seated in the back of the SUV, she drove the short distance to the senior citizens' center. Wrangling them out of the vehicle was a lot easier than herding them in. By now, they knew the routine. She swore they looked forward to these visits. God knew the residents did.

She grabbed her bag of tricks in one hand, the multi-leash in the other, and they bounded out in unison, lined up in size order from Scrabble, the golden retriever to Hermione, the Maltese mix. "Let's go, kids. Showtime!"

She led them inside and met the program coordinator who waited at the front desk. "Hi, Charlotte. How's everybody today?"

The steely-haired woman in the blue suit greeted them with a smile and a heavy Scots accent. "Terrific. Looking forward to your visit as always." She bent to pet the dogs. "Hello, beasties. Welcome back."

With a cluck of her tongue and a snap of the leashes, Leah escorted the pooches into the living room where a cluster of elderly residents sat in cushy chairs, watching television or chatting quietly.

"Good morning, ladies and gentlemen," she said with an animated smile. "It's Fur-Ever Friday, and I've brought some old friends to visit."

A hum of "Aaaw," and soft applause filled the room.

She removed the leashes. Scrabble immediately padded to the corner recliner and sat at the feet of an old man, waiting patiently to be noticed. The man chuckled and patted the golden on his head. "Hello again, Scrabble. Did you bring a toy with you today?"

Leah strode to his chair and handed over the dog's favorite twisted rope. "Here you go. But go easy on him, Mr. Phipps. Last time you two played, poor Scrabble was tuckered out for two days afterward."

The old man winked at her. "To tell the truth, so was I."

Laughing, Leah meandered toward where Clover, the terrier mix, stood on her hind legs, tail wagging with enthusiasm, in front of two elderly ladies.

"Look at her, Millie!" one lady said to the other, sliding her cat glasses down her nose and peering over the frame. "Isn't she darling? She reminds me of my old dog, Lulu."

The other woman folded her arms over her sunken chest and frowned at Leah. "Why don't you ever bring cats?"

"I'm allergic to cats," the first woman said. "You know that."

"You're not allergic, Bea. You just don't like cats."

"It's both. I'm allergic *and* I don't like them."

"Maybe I can bring a kitten to your room for a personal visit," Leah suggested. Millie Lippman's glaucoma-foggy eyes lit up. "But I'll have to check with Charlotte first. Okay?"

"Okay," she replied, but her expression had gone glum.

"What do you prefer?" Leah pressed in an effort to cheer her. "Long-haired? Short-haired? Any color you like best?"

"Black," Millie said. "Or gray. Green eyes. Don't care about the length of its hair. I just want something that'll sit in my lap and purr for a little while. Do you know that they say a cat's purr can lower a person's blood pressure? I'd rather sit with a cat on my lap than take those horse pills Dr. Birnblatt is always pushing on me."

"I'll see what I can do."

Bea Stein patted Leah's hand, her blue eyes twinkling. "You're a sweetheart." She leaned closer to whisper, "You know, my grandson is single. He's thirty-four, an architect. He's so handsome."

Gee, if his name was Julian, she might have hit the jackpot.

"Myron lives outside of Boston," she continued.

The shooting stars in Leah's eyes screeched to a halt, and she sucked back a wince. Ooh, so close, but then again, no. Okay, so maybe it was short-sighted to dismiss a man, sight unseen, due to his name. But somehow, she couldn't see Wyatt ever becoming jealous over a "Myron," no matter how handsome and successful. Nor could she see a Myron able to carry off pretending his name was Julian—even for a day or two.

"Thanks," she told Mrs. Stein. "I'll think about it."

"Give me your phone number, dear," the woman insisted. "I'll make sure he gets it."

"Umm...maybe later." She reached into her bag and pulled out a squeaky rubber frog. "Here. This is Clover's favorite toy. Just squeeze it, and give her a command like 'Sit," then watch what she does. Like this." She squeezed the frog's belly repeatedly, emitting an ear-piercing series of squeals. "Clover, lie down." The dog dropped to her belly, paws splayed.

Both women laughed, and Leah handed the toy to Mrs. Stein before moving on to check on Hermione.

No need really. The white Maltese lay in front of Mr. Benjamin's wheelchair, her head draped across his foot, her black eyes staring up at him with adoration.

Charlotte stood in the doorway, back propped against the wall, an indulgent smile on her craggy face. "It's magic," she whispered to Leah as she approached. "Every single time."

"Thanks." She took a moment to drink in the calming effect of the animals, and the happy expressions on the residents' faces. "I'm really proud of this program."

"So am I. We do good work together."

She nodded. "That reminds me. Mrs. Lippman made a request that I bring in a cat. I thought I'd do it privately, in her room. Unless you think other residents might like a kitten or two to pet and play with, as well?"

Charlotte shrugged. "I don't see what harm it would do. Bring them next time."

"Well, Mrs. Stein said she's allergic."

"She's not allergic; she just hates cats."

"Yeah, that's what I thought."

The two burst into low laughter.

♋

When he walked into the studio, Leah sat on a stool with headphones covering her ears. On the stand in front of her, the microphone perched low, mid-waist, while she played a tune on her saxophone. The mournful sound she created wrapped around his heart and squeezed. She really knew how to wring every drop of emotion out of her instrument—and out of him.

As if sensing his presence, she stopped in mid-note, removing the reed from her lips and the headphones from her ears. "Wyatt! When did you get here?"

"Just now. New song?"

Nodding, she clutched the saxophone to her chest like a delicious secret. "But you can't hear it until it's finished."

"I've already heard part of it." He strode into the studio, and she climbed off the stool, leaving her headphones on the seat. He bent, she stood on tiptoe, and their lips met in the middle of their height difference.

"That's all you're going to hear for now." She grabbed her case from a nearby table and stowed the sax inside, then snapped the locks with finality. "I don't want you to hear the rest 'til I'm ready."

"When do you think that'll be?"

"Christmas." She flipped a blond tress over her shoulder. "Maybe."

"Christmas? That's five months away."

"Now you know how I felt when I had to wait to hear the results of your road test until the day you drove up to my house in your car. This makes us even now."

"How do you figure that? I only made you wait a week."

"Well, it felt like five months."

Grabbing her by the hips and ignoring her outraged squeal, he ran his fingers around her ribs to tickle her. "I'll get even with you my way—"

"Earth to Wyatt! Hello? Wyatt! You with us?"

At the sound of his keyboard player's shout, Wyatt jerked back to the present. "Huh?"

Kenny Banks rolled his eyes. "Did you like the riff or not?"

Riff? He blinked. Oh, right. They weren't in the back of Coifs and Cuts, and he wasn't sixteen years old anymore. He was almost thirty, tired, and sitting in a real recording studio instead of some hair salon's packing-foam-lined storage room. "I'm not sure," he bluffed. "Play it again."

"Oh, for the love of…" Chaz gave an exaggerated sigh and flapped his arms at his sides. "Get your head in the game, Wy. If we don't have these last few songs perfected for the new album, Cooper's gonna skin us and then give our slot to some newcomer band. This was your idea, to 'come home' to finish *Homecoming*. You said it would inspire you. You never said you'd spend your time daydreaming about the girl who got away." He stroked his chin and nodded at the keyboard player. "Hey. I like that. *The Girl Who Got Away*. Kenny, play that riff again."

When Kenny complied, Chaz sang off-key. "'She's the girl who got away. She'll always make me pay. I'm doing penance night and day, for the girl who got away…'"

While the others all hooted with laughter, Wyatt grimaced. "Funny."

"Actually," Chaz retorted, "it's pathetic."

"What do you know, Chaz?"

Chaz palmed his forehead. "Dude, you *left* her. What'd you think? That you'd come back ten years later and pick up where you left off?"

"Seven years," Wyatt corrected, "not ten."

"Like it matters." An exasperated Chaz blew air through pursed lips. "You're clinging to some dumb fantasy that Leah's gonna forget what you did, forget she's engaged to someone else, and come running back to you. Tell me something, Wy. If she *did* come running back, ditched the fiancé and declared her undying love for you, how long would you hang around before you skedaddled out of town in the middle of the night again?"

Wyatt balled his hands into fists, prepared to "I thought you were on my side."

"I was—until I met her. I hate to tell you this, but she's too good for you."

Around the studio, all heads nodded in agreement.

"Gee," Wyatt retorted. "Thanks, guys."

"Don't take it personally," Angelo, their drummer, said. "She's too good for any of us. A woman like that, who spends her time rescuing abused animals, she needs a superhero by her side."

"I've seen your laundry," Kenny quipped. "Not a red cape anywhere."

Was Julian a superhero? Wyatt kicked the thought to the curb. "Whatever. Can we get back to work, please?"

"If you can stop obsessing long enough to pay attention," Chaz replied. "Sure."

"I'm not obsessing. I *have* been paying attention," he retorted while resettling his guitar. "Just because I asked to hear the riff again doesn't mean I hadn't heard it the first time. Did it ever occur to you I had a reason for asking what I did? Like maybe I wanted to layer something on top?" He turned to their keyboard player. "Okay, Kenny. Let's hear that riff once more. See what we can do with it."

This time, while Kenny tickled the chords, he strummed along, bridging the notes on his guitar.

With a curt nod, Chaz picked up the tune and added a solid bass line. Angelo tapped the skins, and a song was born. When they finished, they smiled at each other.

"Major," Chaz exclaimed, his highest praise. "Now, all we need are lyrics."

Wyatt wouldn't admit it aloud—not now anyway—but Chaz had lit a fuse with his Girl Who Got Away idea. Oh, sure, the lyrics would need to be upgraded, but the thought was right. And God knew, he had the ideal inspiration for such a song.

"Let's put this track down, and I can play with the lyrics on my own. One more time, boys."

Each played his part again, performing a cohesive melody, and grinning with the knowledge they'd broken through. The song itself was ideal, a memorable tune that would get listeners humming along. It just waited for the right words to bring the musical magic to life. When they finished, Chaz and Kenny fist-bumped each other. Angelo slapped his cymbals.

"Woot! That's got definite 'single' potential," Kenny remarked.

"If," Chaz added, "Wy here can come up with the right poetry to create the perfect tapestry. What kind of lyrics you thinking about?"

Wyatt shook his head. "Not sure yet."

"It should definitely be a sad song," Chaz replied. "Something that'll make women misty-eyed, and get men thinking 'bout how they screwed up that perfect relationship, right?"

"Yeah, I think so."

"I told you, dude. 'The Girl Who Got Away.'"

"Maybe."

"Okay, guys." Chaz clapped his hands. "Let's get some lunch. I'm starved."

The others immediately began packing up equipment, but Wyatt remained where he stood, plucking strings and playing with words in his head.

"You coming?" Chaz asked.

He shook his head. "You guys go ahead. I'm gonna see if Leah wants to grab something."

Chaz clapped a hand on his shoulder. "You know, for such a rock star heartthrob, you actually know nothing about women."

Wyatt arched a brow. "And you're an expert?"

"At least I know when I've burned a bridge. You keep thinking she's gonna let you back in her life. And you suckered me into playing a role in this small-town melodrama of yours. But that's not even the worst part."

"Oh, really? What's the worst part?"

"The worst part is, you're not only *not* a superhero, you could almost play the villain. She wrote a song that was supposed to be for your ears only. *Take My Heart Again.*"

Kenny whirled to where the two men stood arguing, and his jaw dropped. "Seriously? She wrote that?"

"Take a look at the credit sheets, boys," Chaz replied, drawing Angelo into the mix, as well. "'Music and lyrics by L. Stewart.' That L stands for Leah. According to Leah, our questionable hero took the song she wrote *as their wedding song* a few years back and then skipped town in the middle of the night with it. Used it to launch his whole career. Now, more than ten years after she first wrote it," he flashed a look of distaste at Wyatt, "he's come back home to the girl he left behind. Is it any wonder our fair Leah thinks he's here to try to romance a new number one hit out from under her?"

Wyatt's knees wobbled, and he leaned against the wall. "Is that what she thinks?"

Chaz must have realized he'd gone too far, because he shrugged and the animosity left his tone and his expression when he spoke again. "That's what Jenny told me, yeah. And I gotta admit, dude, it makes a whole lotta sense to me. *You* kept insisting we call the new album, *Homecoming. You* were the one who said we had to come here so you could gain 'inspiration' for the last four songs. And then *you* went looking for Leah, and when you found out she was engaged, you convinced me to help you win her back. After Jenny told me what you did last time, I got to thinking. Why? Why this sudden obsession with the Girl Who Got Away? If you had really loved her to begin with, you wouldn't have forgotten about her all this time. You ran away from here years ago, leaving her behind, never getting in contact with her, for a reason. Call it theft, call it survival—"

His spine stiffened to steel as half a dozen faces accused him with pleated brows and narrowed eyes.. "It was neither of those."

"Then what was it, Einstein?"

Wyatt looked down at the floor. "I can't tell you." Not until Leah knew the truth. He owed her that much.

9

Rather than bringing them back home, Leah took the three angels to the shelter.

"Hey," Jenny greeted her with a broad smile and grabbed the multi-leash to take the dogs in hand. "Good news. Power company's here."

"Oh, thank God," she replied on a relieved sigh. "What'd they say?"

"They said Mr. Porter insisted this place was their priority today. The tree's all chopped up and gone, the pole and transformer are being replaced as we speak, and the wires should be connected within the hour. Even though they're using their own electrician, I called Mr. McLaughlin anyway."

"Mr. McLaughlin?" The name didn't ring any bells for her.

"Yeah. The electrician I mentioned for Duchess? Mrs. Jorgensen's brother?" At Leah's blank look, Jenny mimed knocking on her forehead. "Hello? We just talked about this two days ago."

We did? She shook her head. Days were melding together like three types of chocolate bars in a hot saucepan, none of them standing out with any distinction. "I'll just take your word for it."

Jenny gave her a calculated stare. "How much sleep have you had since the storm?"

She waved off her friend's concern. "I'm fine." When Jenny cocked a brow, she added a hasty, "Oh, don't get me wrong. I'll be a lot better once everything's back to normal, but, honestly. I'm okay."

"Uh-huh. Come on, guys. Let's get you settled." With the dogs straining against their harnesses to lead the way, Jenny disappeared through the kennel entrance door.

Leah strode into the backyard to meet with the workers from the power company. Two men stood beneath the new pole while a third manned the truck in her yard and a fourth worked from the truck's attached bucket launched high above the treetops.

"Hi," she said, hand outstretched. "Leah Stewart. I'm the owner of the shelter. Thanks so much for getting to us so quickly." Lie, but, after all these years, she'd learned how to play the political game.

"Ms. Stewart, I'm Jerry Bradford." He shook her hand, then indicated the others, one by one. "Happy to help you out here. You know, my neighbor adopted one of your dogs."

"Really? Who?"

"The Reids?"

Nope. Not a clue. "Right. The Reids."

Apparently, she hadn't pulled off remembering the Reids as well as she hoped because Mr. Bradford added a prompt. "They adopted Pixel."

"Pixel! The little terrier mix." Now, she couldn't contain her delight at the memory of one of her precious pups. "He was such a scamp. How's he doing?"

"Great. The kids love him. He's definitely a big part of their lives now."

"Yeah, he needed a family around him. A family and a big yard to run out his excess energy. I'm glad to hear it's working out so well. Can I get you anything? Coffee? Water?"

"No, thanks, we're good."

"Okay, then, I'll let you get back to it. If you need anything, holler."

"Will do, miss."

The wind picked up as she walked away, and she dared a glance over her shoulder at the man in the bucket several stories up. She shivered at the danger of anyone so high above the ground, working with megavolts of electricity. These guys didn't get enough credit for their heroism. They worked around dangerous equipment, often under the worst conditions and far above or below ground.

Once in her office, she placed a call to another hero, Gabe Porter, to thank him and arrange for him to send someone to pick up the borrowed generator.

"Keep it," he said. "The county's upgrading their equipment. No one will miss one old generator."

A tingle of excitement rippled through her. "Are you sure?"

"Absolutely."

Wow. This was a stroke of luck. If she didn't have to hold her fundraiser for a generator, she could start putting money toward her pet project: a spay/neuter van that could travel to lower-income areas to perform no-cost pet neutering. The amount of money required was astronomical, and more than one fundraiser would be necessary, but the payoff in the end would far outweigh the price and efforts involved.

Now, she could get a head start.

"Gabe, thank you. You have no idea how much this means to me," she gushed. "I'm very grateful for your help."

"That goes double for you, you know. You've come to the rescue—no pun intended—for Animal Control and the ASPCA so many times in the last few years. I don't know how many pets would have been lost without you and your shelter."

His open praise made her squirm, and she opted to drop out of the conversation. "I'm sure you're busy, so I'll let you go. I just wanted to express my appreciation for your generosity and for getting the power turned on here."

"You're very welcome," he replied. "Maybe we could get together one night. Have dinner?"

The sudden knock on her door preceded the quick but gentle refusal she kept in her dating arsenal. She looked up as Wyatt intruded into her office. She frowned at him. Really? When would he get the hint he wasn't wanted here? Ignoring him, she focused on her conversation and the invitation extended to her.

Of all the rotten timing. If she said no and went into enough detail about why she didn't want to date him, Wyatt would wonder why Gabe would ask her out if he knew she was engaged. Although she wasn't the slightest bit interested in a romance with Gabe, or any man for that matter, she'd have to say yes and let him down easy later.

She kept her tone even, business-like. "Umm...that would be nice. When?"

"Tomorrow night?"

Yikes. A Saturday night date was a big deal—and something she hadn't considered he'd ask for. Now what? She sucked in a breath. "Ooh, I'm sorry. I'm afraid I can't." Glancing again at Wyatt, who leaned against her wall, showing no indication of granting her any privacy, she added, "I...umm...currently have someone in my office. Can I get back to you about this on Monday?"

"Oh!" He sounded as flustered on his end as she was on hers. "Sure. I'm sorry. I didn't mean to—"

"No, it's fine. I'll call you Monday. Thanks again." She hung up and swiveled her chair to glare at Wyatt. "Is there a reason you couldn't wait in the reception area?"

He shrugged. "Nobody there. I saw the guys working in the back so I knew you were here somewhere. This was the second place I looked."

Folding her arms on her desktop, she cocked her head to study him. "Why?"

"What do you mean why? If you're not in the reception area, you're probably either in the kennels or back here in your office." He pointed to the foldaway cot against the back wall. "Don't tell me that's where you slept yesterday."

She refused to discuss her sleeping arrangements with him. "I meant, why were you looking for me?"

He planted his hands on the opposite end of her desk and leaned forward. "I thought we could go to lunch. The rest of the band is over at Annie's, but I had a sudden craving for fried mussels from that clam bar by the docks. It's still there, right? Remember how we used to love that place? I figured you might want to split a basket with me."

What was behind his constant attempts to feed her? "It's still there. New owners, but they haven't changed the menu."

He jerked his head toward her desk. "Who was on the phone?"

And why was he so nosy about her private life? "A business associate."

"Oh, because for a minute there, you got all flustered like you had a date. I thought it might have been your fiancé. But then when you said goodbye, you were kinda cool. It's an odd juxtaposition."

"Thank you for the assessment. I'll take it under consideration for all my future phone calls." She picked up a pen and a folder from the pile on her desk, flipped it open and pulled out a handful of forms. "As for lunch, I'm busy. I've got a shelter to run, so if you'll excuse me..."

Instead of taking the hint and leaving, he swiveled until his perfect, jean-clad butt perched on the edge of her desk. He leaned even closer now, his eyes piercing hers as if he could read her thoughts through her retinas. "Come with me, Leah. It'll be quiet there, and I think we need to talk."

She tightened her hands enough to crumple the papers' edges, fighting the urge to squirm or blink or give anything away. "Funny," she remarked. "I can't imagine what we could possibly have to say to each other that we haven't already covered."

"Are you kidding? We haven't talked in seven years."

"So what? It's not like we need to catch up on anything. We're two open books. You left and became a famous music star. I stayed, bought this shelter, got engaged. What else is there? You want to see a scrapbook or something? Sorry, I didn't bother to keep one on the off-chance you might come back to town, looking for a stroll down Memory Lane." She shook her head. "We're not the same kids we once were. We grew up, and we're both happy with the directions our lives took. I doubt we have anything in common anymore. End of story."

"Not 'end of story.' There's stuff you don't know. And probably stuff I don't know. We need to talk about what happened when I left."

"No, we don't." No way did she plan to share the 'stuff' he didn't know. Regardless of what she'd promised her father, she had no intention of reliving the worst week of her life again. Ever. "The past is over," she said, leveling a steady gaze at him. "We can't change what happened to either of us. None of it matters now. You don't have to keep doing penance for leaving. Was I angry? Hurt? Scared? At the time, yes. But I turned out just fine in the end. And so did you. Isn't that enough? I don't know why you decided to come back to Osprey Cove now, but whatever you're looking for has nothing to do with me or what we once meant to each other. That was a long time ago, a lifetime ago. Make peace with yourself and move on. There's no reason for you to stay here."

In an attempt to dismiss him, she stared at the words on the page, seeing nothing but shapes she couldn't comprehend. *Just go*, she tried to communicate without speaking. *Don't talk to me, don't ask questions. Just go.*

"So, no lunch then?"

"No lunch. No lunch, no dinner, no midnight snacks. No more surprise visits, no need to talk. I wish you lots more success in your music career. Be happy with what you've become, Wyatt. *I* am." When he still didn't move, she laced her tone with frost. "Now, if you'll excuse me, I have work to do."

He stood there, watching her, but she refused to look up again. After a minute or two, he sighed. "You may not think there's a reason for us to talk, but I'm staying in town, Leah. Not just for a few weeks. I plan to stay for good this time."

She stiffened, biting the inside of her cheek until she regathered her composure. No way. He had to be bluffing. No way he'd opt to live in the very same town he couldn't wait to flee a decade ago. Too many skeletons rattled in the closets here. Which gave her an idea…

Glancing up again, she feigned a casual air. "Well, that's great. Have you driven by your old house yet? The new owners have made some major changes to the exterior. I bet you'd barely recognize it."

He blanched, and they both knew she had him. "Yeah…I…er…I should probably go check it out."

"Definitely." To hide her smile and hurry him along, she returned her focus to the papers in the folder. "I'll see you around, Wyatt."

A minute or two passed, but at long last, he emitted another weighty sigh and said, "For what it's worth, I'm not here to 'romance another song out of you.' I don't know who told you that, but it's not true."

Her smile faltered, but she wouldn't look up. "I believe you," she managed to lie with perfect grace.

He offered her a curt nod and left her office as quickly as he'd appeared.

Assured she was alone, she locked her door and grabbed her

journal from its hiding place. The words screamed to get out of her head, and she poured them onto the paper in frantic fashion.

> *You railed against injustice,*
> *Challenged society,*
> *Wrestled with your demons,*
> *But you never fought for me.*
>
> *I thought I was your everything,*
> *That we were meant to be.*
> *But when the chips were falling down,*
> *You never fought for me.*
>
> *Now that I'm lost and a stranger to myself*
> *A hollowed out shell of what I once was*
> *You've come back into my life as if you never went away.*
> *You bring back painful memories*
> *Of what we once meant to each other,*
> *Of a love that disappeared too soon and a life too fragile to stay.*
>
> *I would have followed you anywhere*
> *Over the mountains, across the sea,*
> *But we were different people then*
> *And you never fought for me.*

Satisfied, she stowed the journal in her secret spot and picked up the phone. Time to reschedule and reorganize this month's fundraiser.

♋

Well, that didn't go as well as he'd hoped. He left her office, heard the definitive click of the lock behind him, and realized he'd lost this round. No problem. He could regroup. He had plenty of time. In the hall, he bumped into Jenny, who barreled out of the kennel entrance.

"Oops. Sorry. When did you get here?"

"A few minutes ago." No need for him to reveal that Leah had pretty much thrown him out. "Can I ask you something?"

"Umm..." She glanced past him to the workers outside, then stared at him, her expression hard. "You've got sixty seconds. We've got a lot of work to catch up on."

He scowled. "Leah said the same thing. Do you two stick to the same script for everyone, or is this just for me?"

Fire flared in her sherry-colored eyes. "Okay, first of all, when Leah says she's busy, she's not kidding. She not only runs this place, she's in charge of raising funds to keep us going, and she works with both the local Animal Control Center and the ASPCA. She sponsors a free trap and neuter initiative and organizes a youthful offender rehabilitation program where petty criminals volunteer as part of their community service sentences. Every Friday, she brings some of the dogs to a senior citizen center where the residents interact with the pets. She's dedicated to this town and these animals one hundred percent. And on top of that, she's gotta deal with her dad, who hasn't been all there since her mom died." She twirled her finger near her temple. "When we say we're busy, we're *biz*-zee. No one more than Leah. That woman works twenty-four/seven, three-sixty-five."

"Doesn't leave much time for her fiancé, does it?"

Her jaw dropped, but she snapped her mouth shut and shook her head. "No, it doesn't, but since he doesn't hover over her every day, they make it work." She pushed past him, headed for the back door. "Your sixty seconds are up." She slapped the handle with the flat of her hand to swing the door open and spun to face him once more. "I love Leah like a sister. And I like Chaz. A lot. Which is why I'm going to say one more thing. I have no idea what happened between you and Leah. I don't ask and she doesn't tell. But whatever it was, you hurt her deep. That woman has a heart as vast as the ocean, and somehow you managed to burn whatever bridge connected you to that heart. Short of giving up a kidney for a dog on dialysis, I doubt there's anything you could do to rebuild your relationship with her. You'd probably be better off packing up your stuff and going back to Hollywood or Nashville or wherever you've been the last ten years."

"Seven years," he corrected automatically.

"Like it matters." With a grim salute, she left him there, agape and ashamed.

Dismissed not once but twice, he drove back to his motel, all thoughts of lunch forgotten. With what Leah and Jenny had said to him, he had plenty to chew on and digest.

Alone in the silence of his suite, he tried to write lyrics for their new song, but found himself, as he'd been for over a year now, hopelessly blocked. He was missing something, some vital information that eluded him.

Leah's challenge rang in his ears. *Have you driven by your old house yet?* No, he hadn't. Nor had he gone to visit the old man. Because he couldn't face that part of his past.

But, his conscience chided him, if you can't confront all of your past, how will you ever move forward with any success?

74

Leaving his guitar on the couch in the mini-living-area, he grabbed his coat and car keys again. He'd waited far too long for this meeting. The time had come to see his father.

St. Ignatius Nursing Home was clean, quiet, and had a sterling reputation for taking excellent care of the elderly and infirm. No doubt about it, this place was far better than the old monster deserved. Monster or no, though, Ezra Blackthorne was his father and would get the best care money could buy, for as long as the money or the man held out.

After the nurse at the desk directed him to the right room, Wyatt trudged down the hall, his lips set in a grim line. When he caught sight of his blurry reflection in the brass elevator doors, he straightened his shoulders. Old habits died hard, but he was no longer the scrawny teen forced to shrink to duck the flurry of fists for the slightest infraction. Now, he stood tall and sure.

He crept into the room, not out of fear, but due to concern the old man might be asleep.

"Well, look who's finally decided to grace me with his presence."

He shouldn't have worried; the devil never closed his eyes.

Ezra sat propped up against several pillows, alert and as hateful as always. While his body had about as much meat as a chicken wing and his complexion held a yellowish tinge, the man himself could still strike dread in his son with the tone of his voice.

The room was sparse, the walls oatmeal-gray, without the slightest burst of color, except for the television above his bed, which blared some sports channel where two commentators shouted over each other about last night's best plays. Even the mounted corkboard, where other residents might display cards from loved ones or drawings from grandchildren, held nothing but the monthly meal menu. Proof positive the old man hadn't lost his power to alienate everyone around him.

"What happened?" his father continued in the same snide voice Wyatt remembered from his childhood. "Couldn't cut it on your own anymore? Now, you've come crawling back 'cuz you need a loan? Joke's on you, prissy boy. You're too late. The money from the sale of the house is long gone."

Apparently, Dad was as loveable as ever. This promised to be a short visit. Wyatt stifled the urge to sigh or lash out. Enough bad humor laced the air in this room without him adding to it. "I have plenty of money. In fact, I don't need anything from you."

"Then what do you want?"

"I came to see you."

"What for? I got nothing to say to you, except I don't want you around. You were never worth much. Always thought you were better than everyone else with your dumb guitar and long hair. Couldn't even catch a ball. Useless punk. I warned you you'd never amount to much."

"I'm doing fine, Dad." He bit back the snarky, "Who do you think is paying for you to stay here?" in favor of, "How are you feeling?"

"What do you care? I coulda died, and you wouldn't know squat. Have you ever called? Visited before now? Nope. Not a word. Whaddya want, Wyatt? And don't give me any bull about missing me. We both know that ain't true. The only person you ever cared about was that tramp you thought you were in love with. What was her name? Leila? Lorna?"

Fisting his hands, he studied the pasty-complexioned man with the beady black eyes lying in a hospital bed that dwarfed his once-enormous frame. The old man still had a razor for a tongue, and he could slice his son a thousand different ways, but Leah was off-limits. Her name wouldn't cross his lips.

"Let's catch up," he said instead and pulled the chair from the corner closer to his father's bed.

10

With the power fully restored, Leah and Jenny transferred the rest of the animals from their homes, back to the shelter. At eight o'clock that night, after they collapsed onto the bench in the reception area, she told Jenny to go home. "Sleep in tomorrow. You've earned it. I'll have the full staff back, so we should be good 'til midday."

"What about you?" Jenny asked. "When are you leaving?"

"Right now. Same as you." She rose to stretch her arms and lower back, then yawned. "I'm wiped."

"I'm not surprised. You've had a lot on your plate lately. Speaking of which, what happened with you and Wyatt today?"

"Nothing. He showed up to take me to lunch. I turned him down. Speaking of which," she added with a tired smirk, "did I tell you Gabe Porter asked me out?"

Jenny's eyes rounded like a bug's. "He did? What'd you say? No, wait. Back up. First, how did he ask? What did he say, and then what did *you* say?"

"We talked about the generator and a few other things. Then, he asked if we could get together for dinner one night. Since Wyatt was standing in my office at the time, I said I'd get back to him on Monday."

"What do you plan to say on Monday?"

"Don't worry. I'll let him down gently. I still need him to help us out here. The last thing I want is for him to hold a grudge over a simple rejection."

Frowning, Jenny shrugged into her coat. "You know, I'm beginning to think the real Julian Lannier could show up here and attempt to sweep you off your feet, and you'd turn *him* down, too."

Leah didn't take offense. Jenny was probably right. Instead, she grabbed her own coat from the rack near the door. "What's your point?"

"I'm worried about you." She slung her purse over her shoulder with enough emphasis to punctuate her statement. "In the six years I've worked here, I've yet to see you go on a date. What gives?"

"Nothing gives," Leah replied. "I just haven't met anyone I'm interested in dating."

"I guess I can see that. If my last boyfriend was Wyatt Blackthorne, I'd have trouble coming up with an improvement, too."

On an exaggerated sigh, Leah shook her head. She refused to be dragged into another conversation about him. "Goodnight, Jenny. Remember what I said. I don't want to see you until after twelve tomorrow."

"Great." She winked and gave Leah a quick nudge. "Maybe I can get Chaz to take me out to breakfast."

"You do that. Just leave me out of the conversation."

Jenny clucked her tongue. "Please. Don't flatter yourself. We have other things to talk about besides you."

"Good. Keep it that way." She waited until Jenny waved from her car in the parking lot before locking the shelter's doors and heading to her SUV.

Once she reached home, she found a note from Giselle. Dad had eaten—jerk chicken with fried plantains, coconut rice, and kale—one of his favorite meals. There was an extra plate in the fridge for her. At this time of night, the spice would probably keep her awake, so she opted for a peanut butter and jelly sandwich instead. After cleaning up her meager mess, she made her way upstairs.

Noticing the light glowing under Dad's door, she knocked. At his permission, she counted to ten and poked her head inside. "Hey, Dad. I'm home. I'm gonna grab a quick shower and go straight to bed. I'm drained."

He nodded. "Giselle made jerk chicken. Did you eat?"

"Uh-huh." He'd freak if he knew what she ate, so she didn't specify. Instead, she added, "But there's plenty left for you for lunch tomorrow."

"Okay, kiddo. Get some sleep."

"I will. Love you, Dad."

"Love you too, Leah."

"Don't stay up too late."

He nodded again, and she closed the door then padded down the hall to the bathroom. Minutes after she finished her shower, she was in her pajamas and snuggled under the pink and white counterpane hand-knitted by her mother so many years ago. A fresh, cool breeze cleansed the room, thanks to the windows she left open at least a crack year-round. She barely remembered closing her eyes before she fell asleep.

The next two days passed in a blur.

Seven dogs and three cats were adopted over the weekend. The shelter was still at full capacity, thanks to additional dogs rescued from the horror house last week who'd finally received their clean bills of health from the local veterinarian and were transferred to local facilities, including hers.

On Monday, Leah spent the morning with several of the new dogs, Penny among them. The happy pup turned out to be not only sweet-tempered, but smart—a definite therapy dog candidate. A few of the others would need more work, and the Dobey mix she'd named Romeo had some aggression issues. His counterpart, however, Juliet the Labrador, had more patience and would do well in a family with older children. Once she returned the dogs to the kennel, she sat in her office and made notes regarding her observations.

Thanks to all the downtime the previous week, her office was pretty well-organized. Okay, no putting it off any longer. She would have to call Gabe before he called her. With a deep inhale for fortitude, she picked up the phone and dialed his number.

When he answered, she exhaled and plowed into the conversation. "Hi Gabe, it's Leah."

"Leah! It's so good to hear from you. How are you today?"

"Good, thanks. You?"

"Terrific. Have you thought about when you'd like to go to dinner?"

"Umm...yeah, about that. Gabe, I'm sorry. You... umm... caught me off-guard on Friday, and I had someone in my office... and, well...."

"Say no more," he replied, his tone matter-of-fact. "I understand."

No, I doubt you do. She bit her tongue. "I'm sorry. Honestly. I'm sort of...involved with someone, and umm..."

"Leah, relax. It's okay. No hard feelings."

She exhaled a relieved breath. "Thanks. I appreciate you saying that."

"No sweat. I hope it all works out for you. You know I wish you nothing but happiness."

Happiness. She hadn't felt that emotion full-tilt in at least seven years. Oh, sure, there'd been moments of laughter, but they were rare. These days, she faked her smiles, buried her pain, and only found joy in the furry friends surrounding her. Swallowing the bitterness like a nasty pill, she struggled to make small talk for a few minutes. She owed Gabe a chance to regain his dignity, especially considering how graciously he'd taken her rejection. They chatted about the new residents at the shelter, and she thanked him again for his help getting the electricity fixed before finally saying goodbye and hanging up.

Funny, she'd never considered how she'd let her life go to the dogs—literally and figuratively—until Gabe had wished her happiness. Toss in Jenny's comment that she hadn't dated in...forever...and Leah experienced a much-needed wake-up call. She'd mourned her losses too long. When was the last time she took a walk for the fun of it? When was the last time she did anything for fun?

"Time to get back in the game, girl," she told herself and knew exactly where to start. "Shake up your life."

She needed to rediscover the old Leah, the one who laughed too loud, stayed out too late, and just-plain-old had fun. Too bad she'd turned down Gabe's offer. He was funny, kind, good-looking, and they shared a love of animals. There wasn't a definitive spark there, but chalk that up to her less than electric personality these days. Maybe, once Wyatt left town again, she'd call Gabe and ask *him* out. She could always say her other relationship didn't work out. No lie there. Besides, one date wouldn't hurt. She might even have fun.

While this fire still burned in her belly, she was going to make a few changes. Right now, before she lost her nerve and retreated into her shell again. After grabbing her purse and coat, she locked her desk and headed out to the reception area where Jenny and one of their part-time volunteers, Sue, opened crates of supplies.

"I'm out of here for the rest of the day," she announced.

Hard to tell whose jaw dropped lower.

Jenny blinked first. "Did something happen?"

"Yeah," she replied with a big grin. "I just woke up."

As she walked out, Jenny's elated whoop echoed with her. Inhaling the crisp autumn air filled her with buoyancy. For one day, she planned to have fun.

She drove home and went straight to the basement. Among the dated yearbooks, summer clothes, and Christmas decorations, she found the black, fake leather case and pulled it out. She brought the case upstairs to the dining room and went straight to work cleaning the keys, bell, and mouthpiece of her once-beloved sax. With some tender care, she soon had the old girl gleaming and ready for music. She couldn't resist coaxing a few gentle notes from her instrument. Almost immediately, a surge of pure joy jolted her.

Why had she ever stopped playing? Her fingers danced as she performed a familiar tune, a song her mother used to sing. Her heart softened and warmed, filling the cracks that had cut off her roads to happiness for so many years. She lost herself in the song, manipulating each note, drawing out the pleasure the music brought her.

When she finished, she removed the instrument from her mouth, staring in wonder at the magic she'd discovered, until an emotion-packed voice said from behind her, "Your mother used to love that song."

"Dad?"

♋

Wyatt waited until Monday morning to visit the cemetery. The sun shone with a wan light and little warmth as he knelt at the simple marker that indicated the last resting place of Laura Blackthorne. She'd died two weeks after his sixth birthday.

An accident, they all whispered, *a tragic accident. Tripped on the stairs on her way to the laundry room in the basement, hit her head, and died later that day. Her boy found her, you know. Poor child.*

For decades, that image had haunted his dreams—along with another disturbing snapshot: a pair of hands on his mother's back, giving her a quick and powerful push. He never knew if he imagined the second half of the nightmare. Part of him hated to believe his father was that much of a monster. But another part of him, the part that put up with the beatings, the abusive language, and the neglect, understood the possibility couldn't be easily dismissed. Years of therapy had led him to the conclusion his personal experience with his father had colored his memories of that horrible day.

"Hi, Mom. Sorry I've been away so long." Kneeling at the marker, he arranged the bouquet he'd brought with him into one of the plastic cones with the spike bottom. Satisfied, he speared the cone into the ground. He'd brought a special grouping of blooms with him today, mums and daisies. On his mom's last birthday, as a young child with no money of his own, he had gone to the neighbors' and picked flowers from their garden. When the Robinsons had come to the house to complain, his father had grabbed his belt. But Mom stepped between them and had assured the Robinsons Wyatt would pay them back with hard work. That one criminal offense had become his saving grace in childhood. From Mrs. Robinson, he'd learned how to garden, how to cook, and even how to sew a button on his own shirt. From Mr. Robinson, he'd learned about engines and cars, responsibility, and the true measure of a man. Long after he'd paid his debt to society, he'd spent hours with the Robinsons. In those early years after his mother's death, they'd been his sole refuge—until Mr. Robinson passed away and Mrs. Robinson had moved in with her daughter's family, leaving twelve-year-old Wyatt to his father's sole and cruel care.

Wyatt stayed at his mother's gravesite for quite a while, catching her up on his life. He then said his goodbyes, kissed his fingers to her marker, and pulled a diagram from his back pocket. After orienting his position based on the map given him by the cemetery's office, he climbed back into his bright red sports car—an embarrassment in such a somber setting—and drove around the grounds, to an entirely different section.

In contrast to his mother's grave, Mrs. Stewart's site was marked by an elaborate headstone that proclaimed her the "beloved wife of Alan" and "devoted mother to Leah." A wilted bouquet in a similar plastic cone near the marker indicated someone had visited this site recently, perhaps in the last few days. He added his own tribute in a second cone, pink roses wrapped with deep green ivy and snowy lily-of-the-valley.

He still couldn't believe she was gone. He could picture her so clearly in his mind, hear her laughter singing in his ears. If the Robinsons were the saviors of his childhood, the Stewarts became his oasis during his rocky teen years. At the Stewart house, he always found a hot, nourishing meal, a gentle hug, and unquestioned acceptance. So when Mr. and Mrs. Stewart asked for his promise seven-and-a-half years ago, he didn't have the stones to say no. Had he been able to see the future, had he known the twisted roads all their lives would take, he might have dug deep inside himself and come up with the courage, but at the time, denying them such a simple wish would have shown him as ungrateful and proved their point.

Once again, he kissed his fingers and touched them to the headstone. "I'm gonna win her back," he said. "No fame, no money, no success means more than she does. I think that's what you hoped I'd discover, though I disagree with the method you used to teach me."

Having the final say, he left the cemetery and checked off another imaginary box. One more demon to conquer. He shuddered while turning onto the familiar street and gritted his teeth against the urge to turn tail and drive in the opposite direction.

The first thing that caught his eye was the mailbox. A whimsical white cat, a black and yellow butterfly perched on its nose, served in place of the battered utilitarian metal cylinder which had always been crammed full of overdue bills and new credit card offers.

The front lawn, once more dirt and pebbles than grass, was now a lush, green carpet decorated with male and female scarecrows, hay stalks, and fake spider webbing. The house itself was covered in a Federal blue aluminum siding with bright yellow shutters and gleaming windows. On the stairs leading to the porch and front door, a carved jack o'lantern sat sentinel on each step, creating a goofy, orange parade. Over the white vinyl fence, the top of a plastic tree house and green slide peeked out. The house screamed happiness and family harmony.

Wyatt pulled the car to the curb across the street and stepped out onto the sidewalk. Leah had been right. With all the changes, he barely recognized the place where he'd lived for twenty years.

Only one familiar memento remained from his days here. The tool shed he and Mr. Robinson had built still stood on the property's edge, although now it was painted a sunny yellow to match the house's trim. The curtains Leah had sewn no longer decorated the lone window, but he wasn't surprised. The home's current residents probably didn't know this shed was once used as a bedroom when dear old Dad's binges became excessively violent. When he was about seventeen, he lived out here all summer. Leah had insisted on curtains not only so no one would know he was sleeping in the tool shed, but also because she didn't want anyone to know their relationship had become more intense, more *intimate*.

"If your dad doesn't kill you," she'd said, "*my* dad will."

A wistful smile twitched his lips at the memory of those stolen hours. They'd loved each other with a passion too deep, too—

"Can I help you with something?"

The feminine voice jolted him out of the past and brought him face-to-face with a pretty young woman, her hands gripping the handles of an umbrella stroller, her eyes narrowed with suspicion.

"Sorry," he said and pointed to the house. "I used to live there."

The woman's complexion blanched, and she covered her open mouth with a hand. "Oh my God! You're Wyatt Blackthorne!"

He shrugged, his arms spread wide. "Guilty as charged. And you are…?"

"Cynthia Donatelli." She gestured at the stroller where a child, bundled in a blue fleece jacket with a Superman logo on the breast, slumbered. "And this is Danny. The Jansens, who live next door to us, told me it used to be your house, but I didn't believe them. Oh, wow. This is incredible. I'm a big fan."

"Thank you. That's nice of you to say."

"No, I mean it. I first heard *Carry Me Home* on one of those internet streaming radio stations and it hit me so hard. I couldn't wait to download the whole album. See, I'm from upstate—Poughkeepsie—originally. My husband's company transferred him down here, and the first year or so was rough, you know? It's a different world from what I'm used to. Anyway, I was feeling lonesome one day and I heard your song and bam!" She tapped her chest with her fist. "It got me right here."

He smiled at her the way he did for all his fans. "I appreciate that, Cynthia. It was nice meeting you." Pushing the button on his fob, he unlocked his car doors.

"Hey," she said, drawing his attention again. "Do you want a tour of the house? Maybe see the inside? I bet you've got a lot of good memories here."

Wanna bet? "No. Please, I don't want to trouble you. I actually have an appointment to keep. I just happened to be in the neighborhood and thought I'd drive by the old place. I hope you and your family are happy here."

"We are. But…umm…before you go, could I…" She giggled and looked at her feet. "God, this is so embarrassing, but I know I'll kick myself later if I don't ask…I mean, when will I ever get the opportunity…?"

"You want an autograph," he finished for her.

Her blush reddened her cheeks. "Would you mind?"

"Not at all. Do you have a pen and something for me to write on? I'm afraid I don't have anything with me."

"Hang on." She rifled through the diaper bag hanging from the stroller, dug out some kind of shopping receipt and half an orange crayon. "Crap. Let me run inside and get a pen."

"No, honestly, I'm running late." He'd once signed a napkin with a lip gloss, but somehow, didn't think that was appropriate in this case. "I'll tell you what, Cynthia Donatelli. As soon as I get back to the studio, I'll contact my promotions manager. He'll not only send you an autographed photo, I'll make sure you and your husband are added to the guest list for the release party of my new album."

"Oh, my God! Really! Oh, that would be awesome." She dove back into the diaper bag, came out with some kind of mini photo album to lean on and hoisted the orange crayon. "Don't you need my address?"

He rocked on his heels. "Umm…no. I think I can remember that."

She blushed, and another giggle overcame her. "Oh, right. I'm a dolt. Of course, you remember your old address. Gosh, I'm glad Danny got cranky so I had to take him for his walk earlier than normal."

"It was meant to be," he said, his tone smooth and sultry as aged whiskey.

"Wait! Wait!" She whipped a cell phone out of her jacket pocket. "Would it be okay if…?"

"Sure." He wrapped an arm around her waist while she held the phone above their heads. "Good?"

"Perfect. One…two…threeeeee!" She squealed when, on three, he leaned in and kissed her cheek. After surveying the photo on her screen, she bounced with delight. "This is awesome. I can't wait to show my sister. She'll be so jealous. Oh my God, thank you *so* much!"

"You're very welcome. Thanks for being a fan."

While she crossed the street and sprinted toward her home—a world away from his house on that same property—he climbed into his car and headed back to his motel room. The time had come to create some lyrics for *The Girl Who Got Away*. He hoped he was finally ready.

11

Leah didn't know if she should address the thousand-pound gorilla or not.

Before she could decide, Dad seized the opportunity from her. Easing into the chair opposite her—as if he did so every day—he rubbed his hands together. His light eyes twinkled with humor. "Surprised to see me out of my room?"

She settled the sax on her lap and smiled up at him. "Now that you mention it…"

"Well, I was surprised to hear you playing, so that makes us even now. It's been a long time."

"Too long," she admitted and patted the bell. "I really missed this old girl. I should've pulled her out years ago."

With a heavy sigh, he clasped her hand in his. "Aren't we a sorry pair? I think if your mom could see us, she'd probably want to slap us both in the noggin for not coming to terms with all this before now."

All this. Code for "Mom's death." He might have come downstairs, might have finally left his room, but he still couldn't bring himself to say the words that had sent him scurrying into hiding to begin with.

No, this is Fun Day. Don't go there. Keep smiling. Keep the conversation light. Maintain fun. "If I'd known all I had to do to get you to come out of your room was pull out my sax, I would've done it eighteen months ago."

He squeezed her fingers. "No, you wouldn't. You weren't ready. Neither was I. We're both works in progress. Day by day, taking on challenges one at a time. Or maybe, one year at a time."

She chose her words carefully. "Well, I'm ready to put 'all this' behind me and start enjoying my life again. How about you?"

He nodded. "In small steps. I think I'll start by asking the guys to come here for poker. In the den."

"That'd be great. Like old times here again. I can order a hero like Mom used to, and make sure you have plenty of beer and chips, and the guys have sober rides home afterward."

She must have sounded a little too eager, because Dad grimaced. "I've made life rough for you in the last two years, haven't I? First, you wound up skipping vet school to take care of Mom, then instead of registering to attend when she was gone, you had to stay here for me. And how did I react? Selfishly. Making you wait on me hand and foot, having Giselle come over from next door to cook for me and keep an eye on me when you have to work. You should've moved on with your life years ago. Instead, you got stuck taking care of your old man."

She shook her head. "It wasn't so bad. Besides, after all the years you took care of me, how could I not repay the favor?"

"Because you're not supposed to. I'm a grown man, perfectly healthy. I shouldn't need a babysitter. I promise you, things are gonna be different from now on. I'm capable of making my own meals, coming and going out of my room, and taking care of myself without your help or Giselle's. And I'm going to do just that, starting right now. I'll call the guys. If they say yes, I'll order my own hero, arrange all the details, and even clean up afterwards. You've got enough on your plate to worry about. You shouldn't have to worry about your old man, too. I want your promise right now that you'll focus on you from now on."

A sparkle of delight rippled through her. This Fun Day was getting better and better. "Okay. I can do that, as long as that means I can consider the shelter part of focusing on me. I want to reschedule my fundraiser, and that's going to require a lot of attention to detail."

"Before you get to the shelter and the fundraiser, you've still got a few other items on your to-do list that have lingered a lot longer."

The sparkle chilled. "Like what?"

"Did you talk to Wyatt yet?"

So much for Fun Day. She dipped her head to study an invisible bit of dust on the sax's body. "No."

He chucked her under the chin, bringing her gaze level with his. "Leah," he said in that disapproving parental tone she remembered from childhood.

"Dad, don't. Please. Don't judge me. You didn't just come down from the mountain of wisdom with the answers to all of life's problems. You've spent the last year and a half upstairs, never leaving. *A year and a half.* After all that time, are you ready to give up your obsession with that alert device you're trying to create?"

A flush rose in his cheeks. "Well, no, but—"

"How many years will it be before you can actually walk out the front door again?" She lifted their clasped hands to her lips and kissed his knuckles. "I love you, and I understand how much Mom's loss hurt.

I miss her, too. Every day. You and Mom had years together—decades, actually. When you spend that much time with someone, your rules of total honesty and no secrets from each other are vital to staying together. Wyatt and I are over. We're not going to be together ever again. No good can come from him finding out about the miscarriage. What could he possibly say or do to make what happened better?"

"You won't know until you tell him."

She shook her head and stifled the shriek of frustration struggling to erupt. "Telling him will only open up old wounds. He'll feel guilty he left before he knew; I'll become bitter he never gave me a chance to tell him; and we'll be caught in an endless cycle of blame. Meanwhile, nothing will change. He still left, our baby is still dead, and I'm still unable to have any more kids. End of story." Tears sprang to her eyes, a common occurrence whenever she discussed this topic. "I can't do it, Dad. It's not his pain to bear; it's mine. It will stay mine."

"He deserves to know the truth," Dad said, soft but firm.

She frowned. "No, he doesn't."

"You won't ever have peace in your life, sweetheart, until you make peace with what happened in the past. All the saxophone playing, dog rescuing, and fundraiser planning in the world won't soothe your broken heart entirely."

They were never going to see eye-to-eye on this issue. "That's a risk I'll have to take," she said and rose from the chair. She packed the sax back in its case and flipped the locks with twin clicks. "Right now, I've got a hankering for a fried clam strip basket from Captain Jack's down at the docks. You want me to bring you back anything?"

Her father shook his head again, this time with a proud grin on his face. "I'm going to make myself tuna salad. I might even cook dinner for us tonight. My special pork tenderloin with cranberry gravy. How does that sound?"

Since she'd been lying about the fried clams to get him off her back, she didn't have to feign excitement about dinner. "Sounds fabulous. Need me to pick up anything while I'm out?"

He gave her a sheepish look. "Do we *have* a pork tenderloin?"

"I'll stop at the market on my way back and get all the ingredients, to be on the safe side."

"No, you won't. I'll get them."

Her jaw dropped. "You're…you're actually going to leave the house to go food shopping?"

He slapped his hands on his thighs and rose. "Don't be silly. I'm going to call their home delivery service." As he headed into the kitchen to pick up the phone, he said over his shoulder, "Small steps, Leah. You succeed at the hardest journeys by taking small steps."

Uh-huh. In other words, he wasn't about to let her forget about telling Wyatt, no matter what tactics she tried pulling. She almost wished he'd stayed upstairs. Instead, she wished Wyatt would get the hint and leave town soon—never to return.

"Thanks, good to know," she remarked dryly. "I'm bound for Captain Jack's and a dozen deep fried clam strips. I'll be home in a few hours."

She grabbed her coat and her car keys and headed out the door. In the driveway, she stopped. Now what? She didn't dare go back to the shelter. Jenny would never let her live it down if she only took a half-day. She really didn't want to go out for lunch. Most of her friends had fallen by the wayside over the years as she'd become more focused on her mom's illness and then her dad's decline. In fact, the only friend she still had unrelated to the shelter was Giselle. She climbed into the SUV and drove it around the corner, in case Dad peeked out and noticed it was still in the driveway. Then she got out and walked to Giselle's house.

The older woman opened the door and greeted Leah with a warm smile. "Come in, darlin'. Come in. Is everything okay?"

"Actually, everything's better than okay. Dad came out of his room."

Her eyes rounded. "You're kiddin'."

Leah laughed. "Nope. I was playing my sax and—"

Giselle held up her hand, and the gold bangles on her wrist jangled. "Wait a minute. *You* were playing your sax? Since when?"

"I know, I know. It's been a weird day."

"Well, then, this calls for tea and cookies. Take off your coat and let's go in the kitchen." Giselle glided through the cozy den with its warm pomegranate-colored walls and the framed lithographs of art work by fellow Jamaican, Carl Abrahams. She claimed she was somehow loosely related to the late artist and collected copies of all his paintings.

After leaving her coat on a hook near the door, Leah followed Giselle. The houses in their neighborhood were all built at the same time and each was designed to one of four specifications. Leah and her father lived in the center hall colonial: two stories; three bedrooms and two baths upstairs; living room, kitchen, den/study, and half-bath on the main floor. Giselle lived in one of the ranch-style homes: three bedrooms, two baths, living room and kitchen all on one floor. Her kitchen was in the rear of the house, as opposed to Leah's, which was situated to the left of the front door.

In the kitchen with its white cabinets and Caribbean-blue walls, a person could almost hear the sea and taste the salt air. While Giselle filled the kettle and placed it on the stove, Leah sat in one of the swivel chairs at the octagon-shaped table.

Giselle brought over a round tin full of butter cookies and popped the lid to reveal the white-paper cupped sweets inside. The last time Leah had seen a similar tin, her grandmother still hosted holidays at her house in the city. Grandma had been dead for more than twenty years.

"So," Giselle said, choosing a cookie and grabbing a seat, "you started playing the saxophone again. That wouldn't have anything to do with a certain hunky old flame who's come back to town, would it?"

"No!" She realized how loud and fast the denial left her mouth and added a more sedate, "Not the way you're thinking it did, anyway. This morning, I turned down a date with a really nice guy, and afterward, it occurred to me that I've let a lot of my life slip through my fingers over the years. Among the things I missed that used to give me joy, I realized I missed my sax, so I dug it out of the basement. For whatever reason, my dad heard the music and came downstairs." She shrugged. "I guess something about the song I played, which was one of my mom's favorites, led him into considering his own situation and how he'd spent the last two years since Mom died. It wasn't intentional, I swear. I played the first song that popped into my head. I had no idea it would affect Dad the way it did. He's making dinner as we speak and plans to invite his friends over to play poker—in the den."

Giselle bit into her cookie, chewed and swallowed before remarking, "That's good, no? All of this sounds promising to me."

"It is," she replied. "I mean, he's still got a ways to go. He doesn't seem in any rush to leave the house yet. But I'm thrilled he's willing to leave that room. And I have an idea how to bring him the rest of the way."

"You do?" Finished with her first cookie, she reached for a second. "How? And what can I do to help?"

"Nothing yet," Leah said with a wink. "I think I've got this particular plan under control, but I'll let you know if I need you."

♋

Wyatt found Chaz and Angelo in the sitting area of his hotel room, another soccer game blaring from the television. With his arms spread wide, he belted out the words that had whispered in his head all the way back here. "She was music and laughter, meant for happily ever after, but I made her hold on too long."

The two bandmates exchanged thoughtful glances, and their heads bounced as they tried out the lyrics to the music they'd created.

At last, Chaz nodded. "I like it. You got more?"

"Not yet, but I just came up with that much on the car ride. I think I can have the lyrics down by later tonight and then we can play around with them against the backdrop of music in the studio tomorrow."

Chaz clapped. "Okay, so what are you waiting for? Get to it, lyric boy. I'll order Chinese for dinner. What do you want?"

"I'm not hungry," he replied. "I've got words to write."

He left the two men flashing thumbs-up and entered his bedroom. After closing and locking the door, he pulled a notebook from his bag, along with a pen, which he stabbed into his hair behind one ear. He grabbed his guitar from its stand in the corner and settled on the bed. With all his necessities ready, he strummed the bridge and toyed with the words in his head before committing them to paper.

She was music and laughter,
Meant for happily ever after,
But I made her hold on too long.

I swore she would wait for me,
No matter how late for me,
But I made her hold on too long.

Every word of his frustration with Leah poured out onto the page. This was his pain, his loss, his disappointment—just as Chaz had insinuated in the studio.

She hung up before I realized her worth
I'm the loneliest man stuck walking the earth
Some women are too precious to wait on hold.

Now I'm home on bended knee,
Begging her to come back to me,
But I made her hold on too long.

He had no idea how many hours passed while he wrote, rewrote, and wrote again. When he finally left his room to stretch the kinks from his back and grab a bottle of water from the fridge, he found the living area dark. The air was redolent with the pungent seasonings of soy sauce and sesame oil. He flipped on the light and surveyed the debris of white takeout boxes littering the counter and stovetop.

"We saved you some."

He turned to find Chaz on the couch, his arm thrown over Jenny's shoulder. Both looked sleepy and sated.

"What happened to Angelo?"

"He left when Jenny got here. Three on a date makes him uncomfortable."

Crap. Just what he didn't need right now, another reason for Leah to despise him. "Umm…Chaz, can I talk to you for a sec?"

"Who's stopping you?"

He gestured toward Jenny, who was apparently an expert in body language, because she yawned and spread her arms wide.

"Wow," she exclaimed. "I didn't realize how late it is. I've gotta get home and get some sleep. I've got work in the morning. Goodnight, Wyatt. Chaz…" She kissed his cheek, subtle and sweet, but who was she trying to fool? They all knew how the couple had spent the last hour or two. "I'll talk to you tomorrow." She grabbed her coat and purse from the armchair and sashayed out.

"Well, that was embarrassing," Chaz grumbled. "When did you become my dad?"

He gathered up the takeout containers and shoved them in the trash can beneath the counter. "When you decided to play around with a woman directly linked to Leah. For God's sake, couldn't you find someone else? Someone in the next town, or even better, couldn't you have stayed a solo act for a little while? Everywhere we go, it's the same routine with a new girl. We're barely finished playing the last song in one place, when you're onto your next conquest in another."

Chaz's lips drew into a tight line. "This one's different."

"The only difference is, this time, when you break Jenny's heart, I'm gonna be the one to pay for the damage."

Bam! Chaz slammed a fist onto the counter. "First of all, this *is* different. I'm crazy about Jenny, and I think she feels the same way about me. Yeah, I know we've only known each other a week or two, so save your breath. You're no expert on love, Wy. In fact, if your issues with Leah confirm anything, it's that you stink at relationships. No surprise there, really. You were a kid when your ma died and your dad was a no-good cretin, from what you've told me. Therefore, you have little to no experience with how to treat the woman you claim to love."

Wyatt stiffened. He'd already faced enough of the past and didn't want to continue lingering there. "What's your point?"

"My point is, maybe you're holding on to Leah because you've got unfinished business between you. Unfinished business isn't love, my friend." He pointed at Wyatt. "All of the women I met before Jenny knew our trysts were temporary. I never made promises I didn't keep, and I didn't leave them hanging when I walked away. You did both to Leah. Now, you tell me. How many women have you been with over the years? How many did you leave hanging when you walked away? Did you make promises to any of them?"

"Of course not!"

"Right. Of course not. You know, you can sneer all you want at me and point fingers at the ladies I've met over the years, but here's what you're missing. None of them, *not one*, made me feel the way I feel when I'm with Jenny. That's how I know she's different. That's what makes her special. When I'm with her, I feel like Superman, I swear to God. And even crazier? I want to be better. Better than Superman."

"I'm happy for you."

"Thanks. So am I." Either the sarcasm flew over his head, or he purposely ignored the edge in Wyatt's tone. "You, though, you're different. After all the women you've been with over the years, you've come back to Leah. Is that because you truly feel something for her, or is it because you feel guilty about those unkept promises between you? Personally, I think you're really chasing her because it's important to you that Leah still see you as her Superman and not as a villain, even if she's got another man to play her hero role now."

Unused packets of duck sauce and soy sauce followed the other debris into the trash. "Don't be ridiculous."

Chaz said nothing, simply quirked a brow.

That stupid expression on his friend's face pushed Wyatt over the edge. "I've come back to Leah because it's always been about her," he exploded. "I didn't leave her voluntarily. I had no other choice. And I've regretted that decision every single day since I caught the bus out of town."

"Then why wait so long to come back? Why not call her and apologize and ask her to join you on the road?"

"Because I promised." He pushed past his friend, eager to keep moving, to run, to pace, to get the recriminations out of his mind. "Let's drop it, okay? And try not to hurt Jenny too harshly when you dump her."

"I don't intend to 'dump her.' But, you're right. Let's change the subject. You finished the song."

Wyatt relaxed slightly, leaning his hip against the wall of cabinets behind him. Music, they could talk about calmly. Women, not so much. "Yeah. First draft, anyway. You wanna hear it?"

"You bet." Chaz flipped the switch to illuminate the sitting area. "Why don't you get your stuff, and I'll grab mine? We can play around with it together for a few hours. Did you catch any sleep earlier? You want coffee?"

"No, thanks. I'm buzzed enough."

12

Over the next week, Dad kept his promise to start taking care of himself. He not only made dinner most nights, he'd occasionally wake up early enough to surprise her with breakfast. With one yoke of responsibility lifted from Leah's shoulders, she was able to focus on other pressing matters.

She opted for the Saturday night before Valentine's Day as the new date for her shelter fundraiser. It was a big risk, since a lot of frugal couples might use that night for their holiday celebration to avoid crowds, special menus, and higher prices. But February was, aside from the fourteenth, a cheaper time of year for catering and entertainment services, which helped strengthen her bottom line. Plus, if she could pair the concept of love and Valentine's Day with her animals, maybe donors would find a little more generosity in their hearts.

Alone in the reception area on a slow afternoon, Leah and Jenny bounced ideas off each other, trying to come up with a clever theme and plan the festivities accordingly. Each had a unique way of brainstorming. While Leah preferred making lists and writing her ideas down, Jenny liked to tap a pen against the desk's edge, which, to be honest, jangled Leah's nerves more than usual today. She knew why. Whenever she and Wyatt used to do anything creative—songwriting, homework, plans for the future—he would tap whatever he had in his hand: a guitar pick, a pencil, a pair of sunglasses. Until recently, she'd forgotten he also subscribed to the habit. Funny how his return to town had awakened so many memories of earlier days, some good, some not-so-good.

"Puppy Love and Kisses?" Jenny suggested.

Leah considered it. "Maybe. It's cute, but we're raising money for older dogs, cats, and kittens, too. I don't want to leave them out or mislead our donors."

Tap, tap, tap. Tap, tap, tap, tap. Tap, tap. Tap, tap, tap.

Leah had to grit her teeth to keep from lunging across the desk and yanking the pencil from her friend's hand.

Bam! Jenny slammed her palm on the desk. "My Furry Valentine!" she proclaimed.

Leah burst out laughing. "Yes! That's perfect."

"We could even do a bachelor auction kinda thing," Jenny continued. "Put the dogs in tuxedo costumes and tiaras. We can walk them out on stage so guests can bid on them."

Allowing an unfit person to adopt one of their animals, based on the size of his or her donation? She shivered and offered a firm, "No. Way too much stress on the animals. Sensory overload."

"How about speed-date a pet? Prospective adopters could spend a few minutes with different animals to decide which one they like best."

Leah shook her head. "Be serious, please. Picking a pet to adopt is not like picking a date to go to dinner with. This is a lifetime commitment."

Jenny leaned her chair onto its two rear legs and folded her arms over her chest. "Fine, then you come up with something."

"I'm sorry," she said on a sigh. "My mind's leaping light years ahead, and I can't seem to stop it. I've been thinking, maybe we could start putting some money aside for the vet van. Do you have any idea how much we could do if we were mobile? Spay, neuter, vaccinations. Pets who've never seen a vet because their owners can't afford treatment could get much-needed care. We could expand our trap-neuter-release program."

Jenny's tapping increased to double-time. "You're talking major bucks. It's gonna take a lot of fundraisers for everything you want to do."

"I know. Like my dad always says, 'Small steps.' Van first. We'll probably need a bunch of sponsors from different places: the town government, a specialty veterinarian group, veterinary supply companies, pet food and supplies, and money backers. But if we have some brochures and business plans available at this fundraiser, we can show prospective investors the good we could do together. Maybe they'll be more willing to get involved."

"Do you ever stop planning?"

"From what I've heard, not even in her sleep."

Leah jerked up, and Jenny slammed her chair on all four legs again, beaming with some sudden inner light. "Chaz! What are you doing here?"

He lingered near the entrance, all smiles as he gazed at Jenny. The temperature in the room seemed to skyrocket between them. "I've been trying to call you, but you weren't answering your cell. I would've called the office, but didn't want you to get in trouble with your boss."

He waved at Leah. "Hello, boss."

She laughed. How could she not? His openness confirmed he meant no harm. "Hello, Chaz."

"So, what's this I walked in on? What big plan does Leah have now?"

Leah clucked her tongue. "I'd ask you how you know about my penchant for plans, but I think that's obvious. What exactly did Wyatt tell you?"

"That you've been making lists since you could count to five. And that you believe if you write your goals down, as well as your various methods of achieving them, you're more likely to make them a reality. I happen to agree with you. I'm a firm believer in visualization creates realization." He strode to Jenny and planted a hearty kiss on her mouth. "What are you visualizing now?"

"We're brainstorming the next fundraiser," Jenny replied. "And this time, it's not for something like a generator that one or two events will cover. This time, she wants a van outfitted like a mobile veterinary clinic and, eventually, a staff to run it."

"Whew! That's gotta cost a lot."

"Upwards of a hundred fifty thousand dollars for the van itself, then about three to four hundred dollars a day to run," Leah rattled off from memory. These days, the numbers buzzed around her head all the time, even in her sleep.

Chaz's jaw dropped, and his eyes bugged out of their sockets. "How are you going to raise that much cash in one fundraiser?"

Heat rushed into her face. "We're not. It's going to take a good twenty years of fundraisers to put aside enough money to finance this project. I'm not stupid. The van is my long-term dream, and I'll probably die before I ever see it come to fruition. For now, I'll be happy if we make enough money to cover our regular expenses through the year."

He nodded. "What have you come up with so far to rattle the kettles?"

At first, she hesitated but soon reconsidered. What the heck. Another brain in their storm couldn't hurt. "We're scheduled for the Saturday before Valentine's Day. Jenny came up with the theme, 'My Furry Valentine.'"

Chaz tousled Jenny's hair. "You came up with that? Cute."

Jenny beamed at his praise. "I know, right? So, now, we need to come up with cute activities and unique ways to promote the shelter that revolve around our theme." She mock-glared at Leah. "Sadly, none of my ideas for that have been good enough to pass approval so far."

"Because you keep forgetting we're dealing with animals, not humans," Leah retorted.

Chaz held up a hand between them. "Ladies, ladies. Let's not argue. Let's put all our energies into creating a knock-them-out event that people will be talking about all over the state."

"I'd settle for being talked about in *town*." Leah planted a chin on her fist. "Got any ideas on how we can make that happen?"

"Well, yeah," he replied, "I've got a great idea. Who's your entertainment for the evening?"

Shivers of suspicion spidered up her spine. No. No way.

"We have a local deejay we always use," Jenny said. "Ricky Delacruz. He plays a little bit of everything for us: slow dances, fast dances, instrumental during the meal, party stuff, yadda, yadda. He even has two assistants who hand out props for different songs. The crowd loves him."

"*And*," Leah added pointedly, "he's an adopter. From *our* shelter."

Chaz stroked his chin, and his grin took on a wolfish quality. "I happen to know of a pretty famous band currently residing in the area who might be persuaded to play the event. Maybe even for *free*."

Jenny bounced in her chair. "Ohmigod, Chaz, you'd do that for us?"

His gaze stayed locked on Leah when he answered, "It's not up to me. Someone's gonna hafta ask the big guy."

She shot up from her chair and smoothed shaky hands down her jean-clad thighs. "Don't look at me. Not happening. I don't need the 'big guy's' help. I've been doing fine on my own for years now. We're using Ricky, as always. He's loyal to us. We owe him the same."

"But, Leah—"

She cut off Jenny's argument. "You two can bounce around other, more reasonable ideas. No bachelor auctions or famous singers, thank you. Meanwhile, I'm going to work with the new dogs in the yard. Oh! That reminds me. Jen? Put Penny on hold for me."

"On hold?"

"Mmm-hmm. I have something special in mind for her."

"Okay."

She yanked open the door and headed for the kennels, certain she could hear the conversation they'd engage in once she was out of earshot. There'd be comments from Chaz questioning her temperament, with confused but loyal defense arguments from Jenny. She didn't care what either of them said. She had no intention of allowing Wyatt one foot back into her life. She was so distracted by her resentment she bumped into Dr. Shah, their veterinarian, and nearly knocked him into the concrete wall.

"Leah!" He took hold of her arm with one hand while sliding his black-rimmed glasses back up his nose with the other. "Is everything all right? You look flushed."

"I'm fine," she lied. "Just preoccupied. Sorry I bumped into you. How'd Oreo's procedure go?" Oreo, a black and white cat, required dental surgery to remove an infected tooth.

"Patient is doing fine, came through the operation like a champ. Casey told me a few of your newcomers in the dog kennels have developed giardia. I'm just going to check them out, and I'll leave you some meds for them. You know what to do."

She nodded. "I'll take care of it."

He gave her arm a squeeze. "I know you will. You were the best vet tech this shelter ever had. You would make an excellent veterinarian, if you're ever inclined to go back to school..."

"Thanks. I appreciate that." His compliment reminded her of dreams unfulfilled and plans that would never come to fruition. She casually stepped out of his reach. "But I'm happy with where my life has taken me." Those other plans had been made a lifetime ago—by a different Leah. The Leah here and now, irrevocably altered by events that shaped new goals, new plans, barely remembered her. And, she realized, she was happy with where she was and where she wanted to go these days. "Besides," she told Dr. Shah, "this shelter already has an excellent veterinarian. Thanks for taking such good care of our residents here."

With a smile and a nod, he headed up one end of the hallway while she strode down in the opposite direction. She chose Penny, Loki, and Juliet for some exercise and rehab. It was vital to get the dogs accustomed to human interaction before introducing them to the public. Thus, she or another employee would work with them every day, using toys, praise, and reward systems to transform abused or neglected animals into potential family pets.

Some trainers preferred the "alpha dog" method, which often relied on choke chains or electronic collars to correct bad behavior. Leah couldn't disagree entirely with their results, but believed her dogs responded better to positive reinforcement. When she did encounter a dog who required alpha training, she sent him to a local specialist in the field, Joe Marin. Joe often appeared on television reality shows like "My Dog's a Menace."

The three dogs she took from the kennel today had already graduated from the basic commands of sit, come, stay, and down. Now, it was time to begin working on "leave that" before each pet could graduate to one-on-one leash training.

So as not to show favoritism, she took Loki through his paces first. For the new lesson, she held a treat in each fist, but kept one hand behind her back. She held out the other, fist closed tight. Loki sniffed and licked her locked fingers, desperate to get to the biscuit.

"Leave it," she ordered in her firmest tone.

He barked. She ignored him. He sat, tail wagging, expecting her to reward him. When she didn't, he nudged her fist with his nose. She repeated her order that he leave the treat alone. When he finally laid down and placed his head on his paws, she rewarded him with the treat from her other hand. Again and again, she held out the treat in one fist and rewarded good behavior with the treat from the other. Once Loki seemed to grasp the concept, she moved on to teaching Penny, then Juliet.

Several hours had elapsed and dusk had begun to fall before she returned the dogs to their kennels and made her way back to the front office. A large neon pink sticky note adhered to their bulletin board seized her attention.

Hey, Jenny had written. *Chaz is taking me out for dinner. Dr. S. left a vial of pills and a list of dogs with giardia. He said you know what to do. Helen went home sick – nothing major, just some tummy issues, so I closed early. If you need me, text. Otherwise, see you tomorrow.*

Might as well pack it in, she thought. Brainstorming could wait another day. And honest to God, she was down-to-the-bone tired.

When she pulled onto her street, though, the line of cars parked in front of her house suggested her plans for the night were about to change. She spotted the red sports car among those vehicles, and all her hopes for a quiet, peaceful evening were dashed.

♋

Inside the Stewart family's living room and holding a full house, aces over tens, Wyatt sensed the exact moment Leah entered the house. Static charged the air, raising the fine hairs on his nape. Funny, none of the other guys seated at the round poker table set up between the couch and the fireplace seemed to notice.

"Call," Mr. Stewart said, dropping several white chips into the pot.

Her presence surrounded him like an aromatic cloud when she stepped into the den.

"Leah!" Tom Martin greeted her arrival. "How you doin', kiddo?"

Her dad looked up from his cards. "Hey, sweetheart. You're home early."

Early? It was after seven. What time did she usually come home?

"Hi, Daddy." She bent to kiss his cheek then straightened to glance around the table. "Mr. Martin, Mr. Brougham, Mr. Ebert, nice to see you all again."

He noted she didn't include him in her comment. Well, he'd

remedy that. "Hello, Leah."

"Wyatt." Terse. Business-like.

"How are you, sweetcakes?" He laced the pet name with lots of heat and was rewarded with the rosy blush that filled her cheeks, but she made no verbal reply.

"There's pizza in the kitchen," her father offered.

"No, thanks. I'm going upstairs to work on some of the details for the fundraiser for a while. I want to call Julian, but San Francisco's three hours behind us so it's still too early."

Mr. Stewart fanned the cards in his hand and nodded without looking up. "Okay, sweetheart. Don't stay up too late."

"I won't. Goodnight, everyone."

All the men in the circle wished Leah a good night. Wyatt, on the other hand, frowned at her mention of her fiancé. Served him right, he supposed. He'd baited her, and she'd parried back with a perfectly timed thrust that pierced straight to his heart.

She climbed the stairs with a decided saunter in her step. He remembered a time when he loved to watch her bouncing on her toes as she walked away from him, mainly because it meant he'd made her deliriously happy. Now, another man made her happy, and he burned with jealousy.

"Wyatt!" Frank Ebert jabbed him with an elbow. "You gonna play, or do you plan to spend the rest of the night staring at thin air where Leah used to be?"

He shook off the spell she'd cast and glanced at his cards again to refresh his memory. Full house, aces over tens. He placed his hand face-down on the felt tabletop and leaned back in his chair. "I fold."

"Okay, Tom," Mr. Stewart said. "It's between you and me. Whaddya got?"

"A pair of jacks."

"Ha!" Mr. Stewart crowed as he spread out his cards, displaying three queens, a five of clubs and a two of hearts. "Three ladies."

"You're on a lucky streak tonight."

"That I am, Wy." Distracted by his winnings, Mr. Stewart gathered the pool of white and blue chips and sorted them into precise towers at his elbow.

As a poker player, Mr. Stewart wasn't hard to figure out. He grew more intent on staring at his cards whenever the gods of fortune smiled on him. Give the old man a full house, aces over tens like Wyatt just held, and the table could burst into flames without him noticing. If he grew distracted, toyed with his chip towers, nibbled on a slice of pizza, or glanced out the living room's bow window at the streetlight, he had nothing in his hand worth betting on.

For the last hour while they'd played, Wyatt made certain to lose gracefully whenever Mr. Stewart's body language revealed he thought he had a sure thing. He didn't throw every game and took a few small pots to ward off cheating accusations, but he definitely lost more than he should. He could afford it. Unlike Wyatt's bandmates, this crew played for quarters, with no chips valued at higher than a dollar. All told, thus far, Wyatt was down a whopping five bucks.

"Whose deal?" Malcolm Brougham asked.

"Mine," Wyatt replied, burying his aces in the pool of other discarded cards that littered the center of the table. He straightened the deck and shuffled. "Black-eyed face cards wild." As he dealt, he feigned a casual attitude to ask, "Does Leah always work so hard?"

Her father shrugged and picked up his cards. "She's pretty busy these days. The storm threw her off, did some damage to the shelter, and put a kink in her plans, but she'll bounce back. She always does."

Wyatt didn't miss the steel glint in the older man's eye. "Have she and Julian set a date yet?"

Mr. Stewart fanned his cards and rearranged their grouping in his hand, his gaze fixed on what he'd been dealt. "The Saturday before Valentine's Day, I think."

"Wow, that's only four months from now. No wonder she looks so…frazzled."

"Yes, well, the storm screwed up all her plans, and she's had to regroup. She spent the night before the nor'easter on the phone, canceling caterers and entertainers and the venue she'd booked, calling guests to advise them they'd reschedule. Then, bright and early the next day, she was at the shelter to take care of the animals and survey the damage. She's been running ever since and barely gives herself time to eat or sleep. I gotta admit I didn't realize myself how much she's taken on her shoulders over the years until recently. But that'll change now."

"Are we gonna talk or are we gonna play?" Frank grumbled. "If you want to know about Leah, Wyatt, go upstairs and ask her. Otherwise, keep your head in the game."

No need. He'd already learned enough.

Four months. He had four months to change her mind, to change "the girl he'd made hold on too long" into "the girl he'd hold forever."

13

I changed my routine, go out of my way
So you won't think I still care,
If you come home someday.

I box with my shadow, leaving on all the lights
It's practice for fighting my heart
Should you show up at night.

I pray you won't cause me to fall to my knees.
I'll cry if you bring me to tears.
Please stay far away, don't ever return
I can finally bear your loss after all these years.

Leah had taken a tremendous risk, mentioning Julian to her father, but the three queens held in his hand at the time made it a calculated risk. Everyone knew Dad could barely concentrate on anything else when he thought he could win at cards. Like his poker buddies over the years, she used his tell to her advantage. From the glower Wyatt threw in her direction as she scaled the stairs, her bluff had paid off. That ought to convince him to leave town now.

Satisfied, she settled onto her bed with three spiral notebooks. The first held her lyrics, and she'd already scribbled her latest on the page. The second contained phone numbers and contact information for donors, whether private sponsors or businesses who'd donate their services for the February fundraiser. The third was new, unused as of yet, where she would jot down notes tonight.

On the first page of the new notebook, she wrote "My Furry Valentine," and the date of the fundraiser. She then proceeded to detail her conversations with the caterer, the banquet manager, the florist, and

Ricky Delacruz, the deejay. All were on board with the new date. She flipped to another clean page, added another title. "Ideas." For now, she left the page blank and flipped again to write a third list on the next page. "Other Fundraisers to Pay for Mobile Van."

Done with the easy part, she stared at the words on the top line, but they blurred into fuzzy blue bugs on the paper. Her mind had already hurtled into the past to the night before Wyatt left town.

She should've seen something, should have noticed he was distracted or pulling away from her. Obsessed with her own worries, she'd missed the signs.

Last time she saw him, they sat in the makeshift recording studio in the back of Coifs and Cuts hair salon, where she'd just put down lyrics to another of his melodies, creating the song, *Our Love Can See Us Through*. This was a song he'd leave behind when he skipped town like a thief in the night, probably because she'd carried her notebook home with her. Maybe she'd sensed the truth on some deeper level that she refused to acknowledge.

That day, she noticed while he strummed his guitar he'd occasionally pause to roll his shoulders. The rain. On rainy days, or in humid weather, the excess moisture in the air exacerbated the dislocation he'd sustained during one of his father's drunken abuse sessions years ago. While he refused to talk about his home life and all he'd suffered until moving out when he turned twenty, most of their friends and probably half the town knew the truth.

She stifled the feelings of sympathy he always hated and nestled her sax in its velvet-lined case. "Are you coming over for dinner tonight?"

"I don't think so," he said. "I got some stuff to take care of."

Some stuff. At the time, she had no idea "some stuff" translated to packing his bags and slipping out of town in the middle of the night without so much as a goodbye note.

Shaking off the nostalgia, she shoved two of the three notebooks off the bed with force. If he was being honest about not wanting her lyrics, a fact everyone else seemed to believe, why did he come back? What would make him return to a place, to people, he couldn't wait to abandon, except his desperation to cling to his fame and success? After all, he'd found it easy enough to ditch everyone who loved him in pursuit of stardom and the money he desired, to begin with. Not just her.

Their bandmates, Alex and Nancy, had been stunned when they found out, too. A year after Wyatt's departure, they'd married and moved to Colorado. For a while, the couple and the woman left behind stayed in touch, but when Alex and Nancy's second daughter was born,

Leah found it too hard to keep up any pretense of happiness regarding her own barren status. She stopped writing, and eventually, Nancy stopped sending baby pics, stopped emailing, stopped calling, and left Leah alone.

As time passed, she'd chided herself for being so petty as to lose a valuable friendship over jealousy. Even now, that familiar pang of regret made her wince. She'd lost touch with a lot of old friends because she had trouble dealing with her constant pain.

Nowadays, the shelter was her life's work, its residents her babies, its day-to-day operations the music for her injured soul. Wyatt's temporary return to Osprey Cove threw a banana peel in front of her steady stride, but she'd skate by—as long as he left soon!

A sudden knock on her bedroom door jolted her.

"Leah? Sweetheart?"

Hearing her father's voice, she rose and opened her door to his concerned face. "Hey, Dad. Don't tell me the poker game's over already?" She glanced at the clock on her nightstand. 8:05 p.m. The guys usually played 'til at least ten.

He scrubbed a hand over his head. "Wyatt left shortly after you came up here. Since he was the one losing the most pots tonight, once he went home, no one else wanted to continue playing and risk giving up what they'd already won."

"Oh. I'm sorry." She dipped her head, allowing her hair to brush her flaming cheeks.

"I'm happy they agreed to come at all—even Wyatt."

Head still down, she headed back to her bed, settled against the headboard, and hugged one of her pillows to her chest. "Uh-huh."

Dad strode into the room and sat beside her on the edge of the bed. "You haven't made peace with him yet, have you?"

"What makes you say that?"

"Julian, for one thing."

If she were combustible, the mattress would've exploded at that moment. "You caught that?"

"Not at first, but when Wyatt asked about it..." His brow pleated in confusion. "It?"

"Him." Julian was a him. Sort of.

"Him," he amended. "When Wyatt asked about him, I figured you were giving him a not so subtle hint you wanted him gone. Who's Julian?"

"No one." She shrugged and placed the pillow back in its place on the bed.

"Obviously, he's not 'no one.' Who is he?"

"Really. He's no one." At her father's harsh look, she curled up into a ball, her knees against her chest, her chin balanced on her knees, and sighed. "I made him up. He's based on a character in a book I read."

Dad sighed and rubbed his eyes. "Oh, Leah…"

"I know, I know." She held up a hand to stem off the disapproval speech. "I panicked when he first showed up here and made up an invisible boyfriend." Fiancé, but Dad was already disappointed enough in her. "Once I took the cap off that bottle, I couldn't stuff the genie back in, so I've been keeping the story alive ever since."

He frowned. "By lying to him."

"It won't be for much longer. Provided I keep up the pretense, he should be out of here before the end of the month."

"You sure about that?"

"Of course." She shifted her knees, and sat upright to face him. "Why? What exactly did he ask you?"

"He wanted to know if you and Julian set a date."

"What did you tell him?"

"Well, at the time, I was holding two jacks and hoping for the third, so I admit I was a little distracted. I thought he was talking about the fundraiser for the shelter. I said Valentine's Day. It was only after he left that I realized he'd said the name, Julian, but I still wasn't sure what he meant by it. You told him you were engaged?"

So much for keeping that fact to herself. "I told you, I panicked. I wasn't expecting to see him in our house that night. He comes downstairs all clean and classy-looking. And there I was, exhausted, sweaty, covered in dog hair—"

"And still angry because he left."

"I'm not angry. Not anymore. Besides, it doesn't matter. Now that he thinks I'm getting married in four months, he'll leave. Probably in the middle of the night with no warning. That seems to be his standard M.O."

Her father didn't reply. He simply patted her hand, stood, and left the room.

♋

On Halloween weekend each year, employees and volunteers at the shelter all dressed in costume. Even some of the agreeable potential pets became superheroes, food products, or mythical creatures to entice families to adopt during the holiday celebration. This year, Leah opted to be Red Riding Hood. Aside from being a fairly cheap costume to create, the outfit served two additional purposes. It was warm against the chilly autumn weather. And a month and a half from now, after tacking on a bit of white fur, she could re-service the cape for her Mrs. Claus portrayal at the Santa Paws pet adoption festival.

Lots of families attended the event, thanks to the hot cider and cookies, as well as the trick-or-treat stations set up on the grounds outside for local children. A mere two weeks after the devastating storm that had torn through the east coast, she'd managed to clean up most of the damage and return to normal. Almost.

Wyatt still hung around, much to her chagrin. He showed up at their Halloween celebration dressed as the Big Bad Wolf, complete with paws, a tail, and a hood with pointed ears, all covered in fake fur.

The moment she spotted him, she gasped and raced across the lawn, her red cape swirling around her legs with her anger. "Are you crazy?" she demanded, attempting to push him out the gate where he'd entered. "You'll scare the dogs in that getup."

He stood his ground, becoming an impenetrable wall of muscles she couldn't budge. "Oh, come on. They may not understand the concept of Halloween, but they're smart enough to know I'm not a real wolf. Give them some credit."

Almost on cue, Jenny, garbed as the latest Disney princess, strolled by with Romeo, who could not be convinced to wear anything but a collar and leash. Dad would advise her small steps were necessary with this one. The shepherd mix took one look at Wyatt and growled, low and menacing.

"You planned that," Wyatt said with an accusatory finger pointed at Leah.

She laughed. "No, I didn't." Still, she'd have to slip Romeo an extra treat later for his help. "Now, take off that getup before the rest of the dogs become riled at the sight of you."

"But it's my costume! The only one I have."

"You'll just have to come up with something else." She tapped an index finger against her temple. "I know. Why don't you go as a famous musician? That should work. A lot better than that..." She pointed at the fur collar and claws. "...ridiculous outfit."

"I bet you wouldn't throw out Julian, if he showed up in this costume," he muttered.

"Guess again," she retorted. "Bear in mind, though, Julian's smart enough to know better than to show up in fur of any kind."

"I bet." Grumbling to himself, he retreated into the parking lot, much to Leah's satisfaction.

"You should tell him the truth," Jenny remarked in her ear. "About Julian and...whatever else you're hiding."

And admit he'd made her so desperate she'd invented a fake fiancé? "No way."

With a heavy sigh, Jenny shook her head. "You know, you lying to Wyatt means I'm lying to Chaz. And I hate that I can't be a hundred percent honest with him. He's become very special to me."

"Really?" Wrapped up in her own troubles, she hadn't paid much attention to her friend. Sure, Jenny and Chaz were dating, but...was it more than just the occasional dinner and movie between them. A wave of guilt swamped Leah, and she offered Jenny a tremulous smile. "I'm sorry. It won't be for too much longer. I promise. Whatever Wyatt wanted from me, it's obvious by now, even to him, that he's not going to get it."

"I don't think *you* get it." Jenny shoved an accusatory finger into Leah's shoulder.

The anger in Jenny's action took her by surprise. "What do you mean?"

"Never mind. Forget it. But, Leah, I'm warning you. I lied for you when this whole thing started, but if Chaz ever comes out and asks me for more details about Julian, I'm going to tell him the truth. I love you, but he's the best thing to come into my life in a long time. I'm beginning to love him, too, and I don't want to screw that up. Especially not because you can't face whatever it is that's between you and Wyatt." Leah opened her mouth to argue, but Jenny held up a swift hand. "Don't give me some line of bull about a stolen song. There's more in your closet than that skeleton about a bunch of lyrics—lyrics you get a nice royalty check for on a regular basis, I might add. I oughta know; I do the books. I don't particularly want to know what secrets you guys are hiding or what the big deal is that you can't tell him, but don't lie to me and say it's nothing. It's something. Something big. That much I know. You want to screw up your life or risk losing any possible happiness you and he might have coming to you? Be my guest. But don't expect me to follow along on your downward spiral." She yanked on the shepherd's leash. "Come on, Romeo. Let's get you back to your room."

She strode away, the dog speeding up to keep pace with her while Leah stood at the fence, slack-jawed. The angry words buzzed in the air like a nest of hornets, each one armed with a stinging barb. As she paced and rubbed her arms to absorb the pain, Wyatt returned to the gate, this time *sans* fur and claws, in jeans that fit a bit too snug for comfort and a navy hoodie. Her stomach flipped when he grinned at her, spreading his hands wide at hip-level to display his outfit. He should be arrested for looking so good. It was a crime what he did to her every time he got close.

"Better?" he asked.

She took a deep breath to calm her jumpy insides and turned to gaze out at the crowd with her back against the chain link. No, but she couldn't have him wearing the wolf costume just to appease the memories of touching, of laughing together, of being beside him in better days. "Yes, thank you."

"You're welcome. I'm here to help. Where would you like me to start?"

"The adoption booth," Jenny called out from the back door. "Give Chaz a break. He's been stuck there for two hours."

His gaze swerved from Jenny to Leah to the assorted structures set up on the lawn. "The adoption booth?"

Leah's first reaction was a big fat no. The last thing she needed was his fame distracting her potential adopters. Then again, maybe his fame would propel maybes into yeses. Plus, if he were busy with the customers at the booth, she could keep some distance between them. Win, win.

"Why not?" She flipped her hair off her shoulder and pushed off the fence. "Might as well put all that excess charm to good use. Come on. I'll show you what to do."

She strode across the expanse of lawn to the white-tented booth with multi-colored circus flags draping the perimeter. Behind the table stood Chaz, costumed as a ringleader in black top hat and a scarlet jacket with gold embellishments, chatting with a couple who held several of the shelter's brochures.

"Well, well," Chaz drawled. "Looks like my relief is here."

"Oh, my God," the woman exclaimed, her eyes wide with surprise. "You're Wyatt Blackthorne!" She thrust out a brochure, nearly shoving Leah into the table to get closer to the musician. "Could I have your autograph?"

"I'd be delighted," Wyatt replied, smooth as polished glass as he took the brochure and picked up one of the black permanent markers on the table. "Were you planning to adopt one of the pets here today?"

The man with her stood taller and placed a possessive hand on his companion's jacketed shoulder. "Not sure yet. We were just trying to get a feel for—"

"Is there a dog you'd recommend?" the woman cut in, all goo-goo eyes and fluttering lashes. "I'd love to see your choice. I was thinking of that Chihuahua mix, Bonita, but Randall wants a bigger dog." She threw an impatient look at her companion. "Something *manlier*. What do you think, Mr. Blackthorne?"

"Please," he replied. "Call me Wyatt."

Leah caught Chaz's smirk and had to turn away to steel her eyes from rolling in her head. She made another scan around the field where families and couples milled with leashed dogs and costumed employees and volunteers. She noticed the buzz the second it started, a series of excited expressions sweeping over faces, followed by whispers behind hands and pointing fingers. Her adoption booth was about to suffer under a swarm of rabid Wyatt Blackthorne fans. Time for her to make a graceful exit. "Looks like you're all set here. Chaz, show him the ropes and then you can let him fly solo for an hour or two. Jenny wants you with her for a while."

"My lady beckons and I obey," Chaz said with his hand pounding a heartbeat rhythm against his chest.

Leah bit back an indulgent chuckle. The more time she spent with Wyatt's bass player, the more she understood what drew Jenny to him. He was charming, funny, and seemed crazy about her friend. Lucky Jenny. Lucky Chaz.

Wyatt, finished with his autograph, handed the signed brochure back and looked up at Leah. "You're not leaving, are you?"

She nodded at the woman who stared at the signature as if she held the Hope Diamond and fought the acrid taste of bitterness rising in her throat. Over the years, how many women had fawned and flirted and slept with Wyatt while she allowed herself to become mummified in her grief? "Don't worry. You'll do fine out here. You're a natural."

"No, I mean, yeah. I'm sure I can handle the booth. I just want to make sure you'll be here for a while. You're not leaving the event yet, right?"

"No, I'm here for the duration." Why did he care so much?

"Oh, okay. Don't leave until I see you again. I have something to show you. Later."

He did? She narrowed her eyes. "What?"

"You'll see." He chucked her under the chin, and she delicately turned her head to avoid any further touch.

Whatever his surprise was, she wanted no part of it. For the sake of their growing audience, though, she smiled. "Okay. Tyler will relieve you here in a couple of hours. Have fun."

Leaving him with his circle of adoring fans, she climbed uphill toward the back door and headed inside to the front desk where people clamored for tours of the kennels, filled out adoption applications, and argued about why they had to pass a background check—including a reference from a veterinarian—before adopting one of her babies. She was used to that kind of chaos. After viewing the crazy fandom Wyatt engendered, she'd find the usual madness an oasis of peace.

For the next two hours, she helped with paperwork, passed out pens and applications, answered questions, and gently chastised children for putting their hands inside the bars of the pets' pens. By four o'clock, the wan sun had opted to surrender its struggle against the burgeoning clouds, and Leah flipped on the outdoor lights, bathing the grounds in a golden glow that gave off an impression of warmth, but no real heat.

Near dusk, the crowds had dispersed to the occasional straggler. While she sat alone in the front office of the shelter, the fine hairs on her nape danced. Only one reason for that reaction. Sure enough, she swiveled her stool to find Wyatt's silhouette looming in the doorway leading to the yard. As he drew nearer, the fairy lights dancing on the breeze in the trees behind him illuminated him as if he stood on a stage. Once again, her belly flipped at the sight of him.

Impatient with her reaction, she climbed off the chair to stand with her back to the desk, the wooden ledge lending her support and focus. Her gaze trained on the cardboard box the size of a cat carrier he held in his hands. And, she noted with some derision, he'd removed his navy hoodie in favor of a gray one. Did the man need a wardrobe change like he was at some kind of an award ceremony every time he entered a new area?

"Here."

She stood on tiptoe to see the top of the box, but it was taped shut. "What's this?"

"A peace offering. Let me show you."

Dropping back to flat feet, she gave him a disgruntled look. "This better not be a trick."

He quirked a brow. "Why do you always think the worst of me?"

"Because I've *seen* the worst of you." She now looked forward to seeing the *last* of him.

"Then I'm going to have to reintroduce you to the better part of me."

"Uh-huh." *Not gonna happen.*

Once he set the box on the high counter in front of her, he took a few steps back, grinning. "Look."

Again, she arched to her tiptoes, but he stopped her. "No, silly. Look here." He gripped the hem of his sweatshirt, pulling it taut to display her logo and the shelter's name in bold white lettering across the chest.

Her eyes narrowed. "Where'd you get that sweatshirt?"

"I had it printed through a manufacturer." He patted the box. "There are five hundred more in assorted sizes in here. T-shirts are coming, too. I figured you could use them for all the employees to wear and as a fundraising tool."

"Where did you get my logo?" She struggled to hold onto her patience. His high-handedness irked.

"I swiped a business card from the desk here, sent it with the order, and the shirt company took care of the rest." His grin broadened. "Nice, right?"

"You do realize you didn't have authorization to use copyrighted material without the owner's permission, don't you? I mean, I know that's a habit for you, but…"

The accusation hung in the air, a noxious odor, and his face filled with color.

He placed a palm flat against the desk's surface. "Okay, let's clear things up once and for all."

She folded her arms over her chest and stiffened her spine. "I really don't want to hear—"

"Tough." He kicked her chair, propelling it on its wheels toward where she stood. "You're going to sit and you're going to listen to me for once." When she didn't move, he leaned closer and through gritted teeth ordered, "Sit, Leah. Now."

Despite her resentment, her knees weakened, and she sank into the chair.

Once she complied, he said in his more sedate, subtle tone, "Look. I get that you're mad, and I don't blame you."

"Oh, well, gee, thanks for understanding."

His withering look dried the rest of her retort on her lips. "I never intended *Take My Heart Again* to make it on that first album. But it was the one song we'd never performed publicly. Cooper had already heard all our other numbers at Sudzy's Bar that night—"

"There was a reason Cooper never heard that song. The same reason we never performed it in public. It was supposed to be *our* song—yours and mine. Our little secret, something just for the two of us. You stole that secret from me." In a fit of temper, she shoved Jenny's wheeled chair across the narrow space between them and stifled her grunt of satisfaction when he had to dodge the rolling missile. "Oh! And by the way, there were four of us who performed for him and for the rest of the crowd at Sudzy's that night. We were a band, a team. There was no Wyatt Blackthorne, soon-to-be-famous solo rock star. We were 'The LAWN,' and that stood for Leah, Alex, Wyatt, Nancy."

The bell on the front door jangled suddenly, and a family of five walked inside.

"Umm, hi," the father said. "Is this where the Halloween adopt-a-thon is?"

Leah rocketed up from the seat and raced around the desk, a wide welcoming smile on her face. "Hi there! I'm Leah." She pushed past Wyatt, her hand outstretched toward the newcomers. "I'm the owner and manager of Fur-Ever Friends."

"Tom Hurst," the man replied. "And this is my wife, Paula, and our kids, Tommy, Thalia, and Tyler."

"Nice to meet you." She bent to talk to the children in their costumes. "You guys look terrific. Come on. The party's outside in the back." She rose again and gestured the family out the door to walk around to the yard entrance. "Just around the garden there."

"Leah?" Wyatt called after her. "We're not done here."

"Yes, we are. Put the box behind the desk for now." Once assured the family was out of earshot, she leaned in the doorframe and whispered in a harsh tone, "Thanks for the shirts, but if you ever take anything of mine again without permission, I'll press charges. Now, I've gotta get back to work."

With her game face on, she walked out onto the crunchy gravel path, her attention lasered on the Hurst family and all the remaining families shopping for a new pet.

14

October turned to November, and Leah breathed a sigh of relief when Wyatt stopped coming by the shelter. Oh, he was still in town, but she never saw him. According to Jenny and Chaz, Wyatt spent most of his time in a studio in New York City, getting the last of the vocals down for the tracks the band had previously recorded. While he was out of sight, though, he was far from out of mind.

Over the last several days, customers showed up at the shelter in droves to buy the sweatshirts, and Jenny's approval rating for Wyatt skyrocketed to idol status. "At thirty bucks apiece, do you realize once we've sold all the sweatshirts, the shelter will clear close to fifteen thousand dollars?" she asked as she replenished the ever-dwindling supply on the counter behind the reception desk. "And you said he ordered t-shirts, too? That's a heckuva donation."

Looking up from the order forms from the pet supply distributor, Leah quirked a brow at her. "You don't wonder *why* all these people are coming in to buy sweatshirts?"

"Of course not. Besides, what difference does it make? You think anyone else would hand over fifteen grand for this place? With no strings attached?"

"Okay, first of all," Leah replied with a snort, "he didn't spend fifteen grand for the shirts. That's our markup. And secondly, there are always strings attached when it comes to him. I just don't plan to be yanked by them. I'm nobody's puppet—least of all, Wyatt Blackthorne's."

Jenny clucked her tongue in disgust. "Why do you always have to look for ulterior motives with him?"

"Because I know him better than you do. Better than anyone. He's only hanging around here to finagle something out of me. If he's not trying to get his hands on my lyric books, and mind you, I still think that's a strong possibility, he wants something else. Trust me, I learned the hard way. There's always an ulterior motive with him." She grabbed a yellow sticky pad and scribbled the name Julian with a question mark, then tore off the page and stuffed it in her jeans pocket. "I may have to up my game to get him to understand no means no."

"I think you're being way too hard on him."

Leah had to anchor her eyes to keep from showing her impatience. Her tongue had no such impediment. "Oh, please. Quit with the hero worship."

"Why should I? This was an amazing gift *for you*. He didn't do this for the animals or for any lyrics. He did it *for you*."

"Yeah, sure. For me to forget how he left me high and dry seven years ago. To clear his conscience." She tossed her head. "Hmmph! He thinks he can buy my forgiveness. It ain't happening."

Jenny folded her arms over her chest. "I don't think you're giving him his due on this. But then, what else is new? I haven't understood much of anything about you since the storm blew into town."

"This has nothing to do with the nor'easter."

"Who's talking about the nor'easter? Hurricane Wyatt came back to Osprey Cove, and you've been topsy-turvy ever since." When she offered no reply, Jenny slammed a fist on the desk. "Why can't you just say thank you? Show him some appreciation? Cut him a little slack? Whatever happened between you, he's obviously trying his hardest to make amends. Look at the crowds he's brought into this place. We placed twelve pets at our Halloween event. Twelve! Double what we normally do. And that happened 'cuz he ran the adoption booth. This is supposed to be about the animals, isn't it? Who cares how we make our goals in seeing these guys adopted—as long as they get placed in loving homes."

A guilty flush heated her throat. Jenny had a point. Maybe Wyatt bought the shirts as a peace offering. Accepting something that would benefit her pets didn't obligate her to go running back into his arms. Maybe she could be grateful and still keep her distance. Maybe—

"Excuse me?" A young woman, perhaps in her late twenties, walked into the shelter's reception area, breaking through Leah's musings. "Umm...hi. You guys are open, right?"

"Mmm-hmm. 'Til five." Leah glanced at the clock. "Which gives you about a half hour or so. How can we help you?"

"Oh, I don't think I need that much time," the woman replied. "At least, I hope not. I've got a party to go to tonight, and I was hoping you still had one of those sweatshirts left."

Jenny flashed Leah a triumphant smile. "Sure. What size do you need?"

"I'll take whatever you've got, no matter what size. I just need a sweatshirt fast so I can get to the mall before five-thirty."

Suspicion raised Leah's trouble antennae. "What's the rush?"

"You know, the promotion you guys are running."

"Promotion?"

"On the radio. Didn't you hear it?"

"No."

The woman's cheery expression dimmed. "Oh, God, don't tell me it was a joke. I faked sick at work to get out early so I could get here and to the mall before the deadline."

"What deadline?" Leah asked.

"The deadline for Wyatt Blackthorne to sign my sweatshirt. The radio ad said if I came over here, bought a sweatshirt, and got on line near the center meeting area in the mall before five-thirty, he'd autograph the shirt, take a photo with me, *and*...I'd be in the running for an all-expense paid trip to L.A., including front row seats to his concert in March!" Her eyes sparkled with her excitement, and her speech became rapid as she continued, "It's all true, isn't it? This is how he's promoting his new album, right?"

Jenny's jaw slackened, and Leah stifled the urge to say I-told-you-so. Instead, she grabbed her jacket and a leash from the hook behind her. "I'm gonna go work with Penny for a while. You've got this, right, Jen?"

"Uh-huh." Her friend shook off the invisible residue from her burst bubble with a series of eye blinks.

Empathy warred with temper as Leah headed for the kennel door. She, more than anyone, understood the pain of disappointment when it came to placing confidence in anything Wyatt Blackthorne did or said. Discovering Wyatt's true nature in no way resembled his public persona always dealt a vicious blow.

As she strode down the narrow hall, a boisterous round of barks greeted her entrance. "Easy, guys. I can't take all of you out right now. I promise, we're gonna find you nice homes. Eventually. In the meantime, please enjoy our hospitality." She stopped outside Penny's room—she refused to call the areas cells or cages—and bent to slide her hand into one of the chain link diamonds. "Hey, girl. Wanna go outside for a while?"

Penny leaped up from her bed in the corner, tail wagging and tongue lolling. In the few weeks she'd been here, the red-haired dog had improved dramatically. Her coat was thicker and shinier, her eyes bright. When Leah engaged her, she responded eagerly. A few more weeks, a month at most, and Penny would be ready to start training for her new life. Leah hoped the dog's potential owner would recover with the same speed when he finally saw her.

Leah opened the door, and when Penny loped out, she slipped the leash around her neck. "Come on, baby. Let's go play some games." She needed the distraction from thoughts of Wyatt and the past.

Linking her shelter to his new album release and upcoming concert tour? What would he do next? Change the name of the album from "Homecoming" to "Fur-Ever Friends?"

And what if he did, a saner part of her asked. Why not use him the way he'd used her? They could convince him to pose with a bunch of her adoptable dogs and cats on his album cover, concert posters, and all sorts of marketing ventures. An image of a bare-chested Wyatt cuddling a sweet kitten or fluffy puppy on a glossy calendar page sent an unexpected wave of heat through her. Impatient with her own reaction, she fanned herself and focused on trying to be more mercenary in her assessment. Fame like his was a virtual unlimited revenue stream. Not only could she find homes for her animals in no time, she'd probably raise enough money to finance her mobile van, too.

So, why not let him help?

Simple. Because getting his help with promoting meant getting closer to him, keeping him in town, spending more time with him, and she couldn't risk that. Sure, her fake fiancé weighed on her shoulders, but Julian was a feather, compared to the weight her heart strained under whenever Wyatt was within visual distance. Even thinking of him warmed her skin and sent her stomach into freefall.

Which reminded her...

She pulled her cell from her pocket, along with a blue rubber squeaky ball. After tossing the toy and watching Penny bound down the hill after it, she activated her phone and scrolled to the number she'd saved to her contacts just last night. On a quick, deep inhale and long exhale, she dialed.

For the next three rings, she panicked. This idea was insanity. Could she really go through with it? What choice did she have? Nothing else had worked. Penny sprinted back to her side, the ball clamped in her jaws. While cradling the cell awkwardly between her jacketed shoulder and collar, she pried the soggy ball from the dog. Penny turned and stiffened, gaze on the sloping grass field, poised to spring into action again.

Leah didn't disappoint. She hurled the ball, farther this time, and Penny took off, a streak of red against the brown and green landscape.

At that precise moment, a man's voice said from the other end of the phone, "Sawyer Theater Company. How may I direct your call?"

She fumbled, recovered, and rushed out, "Umm...hi." Her voice croaked like a frog with laryngitis on a foggy night. She swallowed and tried again. "I was wondering how I might hire one of your actors for a temporary...umm..." She couldn't think of a single appropriate term for what she was about to do. The best she could come up with was "…gig."

"What kind of gig?"

Her cheeks flamed, and her throat dried to dust. She took another swallow, another inhale and exhale, and a quick stroll to the tree line, far away from the building where Jenny hawked sweatshirts and fawned over Wyatt's generosity. Cupping the phone against her mouth, she whispered, "This is gonna sound so stupid. See, the thing is, there's this guy."

God, could she sound any more idiotic? This was a mistake. A big one. But she forced herself to plow ahead. Nothing ventured, nothing gained.

"We used to date a long time ago. And now, he's come back to town. But, see, it's not the typical I-just-want-to-make-him-jealous-thing. He's…like…famous now, and he seems to think I've spent the last eight years of my life waiting for him to return and sweep me away. So, I told him I was engaged. And I'm not even dating anyone! It's stupid, I know, but I freaked out when I saw him because I don't want him to know that…" Tears welled in her eyes, and she sniffed them back. "When he left… It was the worst time of my life. I lost my baby. Then I lost my mom. I lost almost everything that mattered to me. And he wasn't here. I can't forgive him for leaving me just when I was about to need him most."

Something cold and wet nudged her hand, and she looked down into Penny's big brown eyes. The dam broke, and the tears fell, unhindered.

Her speech was met with silence, and Leah feared the guy on the other end of the phone had become disgusted with her soap opera plot and hung up. Maybe that was for the best. This whole idea was too crazy for anyone to take seriously. She was about to disconnect when a low rustle crackled in her earpiece. "Umm… Hello? Are you still there?"

His voice was soft and sorrowful. "Oh, honey, that's just the saddest thing I ever heard. Tell me what you need, and we'll find the right man for your gig."

♍

At four-thirty, Wyatt and Chaz were hustled into the mall through an underground security entrance.

"You should see the crowd out there," the young guard in the ill-fitting uniform said. His nametag pinned him as Officer Frealey. "There must be a coupla hundred people on line."

Good. If even half of them had followed instructions and stopped at the shelter first to buy a sweatshirt, that would translate into a quick, tidy injection of much-needed cash for Leah's plans. *I wonder if Prince Julian ever came through with such a generous gift.*

"What'd you say?" Chaz asked.

Well, crap. He hadn't realized he'd spoken the thought aloud. Waving a dismissive hand, he muttered, "Nothing."

Chaz snorted. "You really think she's gonna show up, all impressed with your huge sacrifice for her benefit? Dude, you're delusional."

"Shut up."

"Yeah, it's pretty crowded out there," the kid said, apparently unaware of the underlying tension between the two men. "All the other guards are needed to keep people inside the queue we set up. We actually had to borrow a bunch of those red velvet rope thingies from the movie theater."

"No kidding?" Chaz replied, pretending to be impressed. "Wow. Did you hear that, Wyatt? We've got those red velvet rope thingies. Isn't that great?"

"Let it go, Chaz."

"You must be soooo proud," Chaz continued, disregarding Wyatt's demand. Sarcasm dripped from every syllable. "Yes, sir, you sure are *the* man. I can't imagine why Leah isn't throwing herself at your feet right now. After all, you're *rich and famous.*"

"Knock it off!"

"I will if you will, pal."

Wyatt didn't need to ask Chaz what he meant; he knew. They'd done nothing but argue since Wyatt had placed the order for the sweatshirts.

"She's not gonna like this, man," Chaz had said. "From what I know about Leah, she's someone who needs to be on top of things, a stickler for details, who can't stand surprises. So you're gonna prove you still care about her by doing everything she hates? How exactly do you think this will play out?"

As the days passed, and Chaz proved to be right about Leah's less-than-enthusiastic reaction to his donation, Wyatt had doubled his efforts to make the whole situation better, winding up with this autograph gig at the mall, to push sweatshirt sales. He knew it was a mistake, even when pitching the idea to Cooper, but his producer had loved it and advertised it as the first promo for the new album. Once he heard the spot on the radio, he realized he'd gone too far to back down. And now, Chaz had insisted upon coming along to the event to watch his downfall. His only saving grace was the realization that Leah, angry as she probably was, wouldn't appear.

"Let's just get this over with," he growled as Officer Frealey opened the door leading out to the center of the mall.

The low murmur of the crowd increased to a roar when he appeared. Cooper, already on the makeshift stage, shouted into a microphone. "Ladies and gentlemen, Water Soul Records is proud to present Wyatt Blackthorne!"

Cheers and shrieks erupted.

"Think this'll be enough to feed your enormous ego?" Chaz asked. "Or will you have to come up with another way to raise funds for the shelter while promoting yourself at the same time? Hey! Maybe you could get your autograph on a branding iron and sear your signature on the rump of every dog and cat the shelter puts up for adoption."

"You've made your point, Chaz. That's enough."

Chaz hung back, loitering on the side of the stage, but offered one parting shot. "It won't be enough until you stop acting like some superior jackass. Cripes, I thought you were past this phase. Had I known the jerk would return as soon as you got here, I would've told you to stuff the new contract and the new album."

Wyatt muttered a quick expletive and strode to the center of the stage. Forcing a broad smile, he waved to the crowd with both hands. The cheers grew louder. He took the microphone Cooper offered and shouted, "Hello, Osprey Cove! How's everybody doing tonight?"

Hoots and howls came from the people below him.

"Did everyone bring their sweatshirts from Fur-Ever Friends Animal Shelter?"

On another series of shouts, the throng waved their shirts in the air like gray banners.

"That's great! You're all contributing to a worthy cause, so on behalf of the shelter and all its animals in residence, thank you. Let's get started with the signing."

He passed the microphone back to Cooper and took his seat at the table prepared for him at the rear of the stage near a set of steel stairs. While waiting for the guards to hand the first fan a raffle ticket and unclip the red velvet rope before ushering her up onto the stage, he cast a glance at Chaz. His friend stood glowering in the opposite corner, arms folded over his chest, his posture stiff. As Wyatt watched, Jenny appeared on Chaz's side of the stage and caught his attention. Chaz gestured her to join him and, with the help of the boyish Officer Frealey, she climbed up. Once there, she kissed him then covered her mouth with the flat of her hand to say something to him. He glanced at Wyatt and burst into lunatic laughter.

"Hi," a young blond woman said from his right, diverting his attention before he could figure out what the couple found so amusing.

"Hi there," he replied and wreathed his face in a wide, welcoming smile while picking up the black Sharpie Cooper had conveniently placed near his right hand. "Thanks for coming."

"Ohmigod, I wouldn't miss this for anything! I'm a huge fan."

He uncapped the marker, spread out the front of the shirt, and scrawled his name. "Thank you. That's nice to hear. Good luck in the drawing."

Before the conversation could continue, another guard ushered the blonde away to make room for the next person in line. And so it went for the next two hours. As the flood of people on line trickled down to a remaining few, the guards allowed the fans a little extra time with him as a reward for waiting so long. He chatted, accepted the accolades and adoration with grace, but felt nothing.

Despite her initial reaction to his gift and the copyright accusation, a tiny spark of hope had resided inside him, a wish she'd come here tonight, see the throng of people, and understand he'd done all of this for her. When the last gaggle of teenage girls insisted on coming up together, he nodded to let the guards know he was amenable. While signing their shirts, he said, "Thanks so much for donating to the shelter. It means a lot to me."

"Oh, we didn't donate," one of the girls replied. The others clustered around her giggled and jostled one another.

"You didn't?" He frowned. "Where did you get the shirts?"

A gangly girl with braces grinned, the overhead lights sparking against the metal in her mouth. "There's a lady outside the mall with a big box of them. She's giving them away to everyone who enters and telling them to be sure to come over here and get them signed to enter the raffle for the free tickets."

That was when he remembered Jenny talking to Chaz and Chaz bursting into laughter. His gaze swerved toward where they stood, cuddled up together in the corner of the stage, watching him.

With a smug air, Chaz tossed him a curt nod. "You were right. Leah showed up after all."

"Leah said to tell you that you're even now," Jenny added.

She gave them away? How many of the shirts he'd bought in order to help her and her shelter had she given to shoppers at the mall tonight for free? He had no way of knowing. Judging by what she was doing now, he doubted she'd kept sales receipts for any of the ones purchased earlier, either. She did it to spite him. Of all the stubborn, pig-headed, obstinate...

Why would she turn down a hefty donation so readily? Because it came from him? *Leah said to tell you that you're even now.*

Their private joke, borne of their first meeting when he'd squicked out over the frog dissection and she'd taken the scalpel into her very capable hands. Whenever he underestimated her ability on anything, whether it was biology or fishing or good old-fashioned sarcasm, she'd turn around and excel at the task, then tell him her one-upmanship made them even now.

Did she really see his gift as a dig that she couldn't raise the funds on her own? Was everything with her a competition? Did she compete the same way with her fiancé? Only one thing to do. He pushed away from the table.

"Whoa, Wy, where you going?" Cooper put a hand on his shoulder to keep him in the seat. "You can't leave yet. You have to pull the winning raffle ticket."

Crap. "You do it." He pushed Cooper's hand away and shot to his feet. "Or have Chaz do it. I've got something else to take care of."

"Right now?"

"Right now." He didn't bother to grab his jacket from the back of the chair, only paused to ask the girl with the braces, "The lady with the sweatshirts. She's at which entrance?"

The girl pointed toward the major department store anchoring the north end of the mall. "The front doors over there."

With a quick nod of thanks, he fled, down the stairs, past the arms that reached out to touch him, leaving a confused Cooper, a chuckling Chaz, and a gaggle of goggle-eyed spectators in his wake. While he raced through the security scanners and into the well-lit store, he hoped she was still there. He dodged around two women in the shoe department, leapfrogged over a fallen stack of socks near hosiery, and barely glanced at the headless mannequin sporting the latest in neon Lycra workout gear.

She had to still be here. He knew how she thought, always had. She would expect him to loiter with his fans, to bask in their adulation, and delay the ticket drawing, giving her plenty of time to escape before he found out she was here at all.

As he reached the set of glass doors, he spotted the bounce of her telltale hair as she hefted a cardboard box onto one hip. In one smooth dive, he pushed through the exit and clamped a hand on her arm. "Need help with that?"

Her sudden gasp pierced the night air and gave him some small satisfaction. So did the guilty flush staining her cheeks a dusty pink beneath the sodium parking lot lights.

"No, thank you. I've got this. Don't you have a thousand autographs to sign inside?"

"At most, I'd have five hundred, give or take whatever you still have in that box."

She glanced down at the package in her arms and cradled it closer to her chest. "I've got plenty left. I guess you're not as popular as you thought."

"Then that box must be awfully heavy for you. Maybe I should help you take it to your car."

She took a step backward. "That's not necessary. I'm fine."

"Oh, I insist."

"I don't need you, Wyatt. I never did, did I?"

"No, you didn't." He closed the distance between them. "I needed you."

He would have sworn tears glistened in her eyes, or perhaps it was a trick of the lights reflecting on the glass doors.

"Not enough." Her voice was a husky whisper, full of sorrow and regret.

He'd give everything, every dime he had, every scintilla of fame, if he could erase her disappointment in him. He placed his hands under hers to take the box and wasn't the least surprised when he discovered it wasn't nearly as heavy as she wanted him to believe. Still, she yanked it from his grasp, jostling the contents, which let out a series of pitiable meows.

Kittens. Of course, while plotting revenge on him, she still found the time to rescue kittens. He burst into laughter.

"Go back to your fans, Wyatt," she said and sped into the parking lot with her box of kittens.

"That's how I'm gonna win you back, you know," he called after her. "You've always had too soft a heart, sweetcakes. No one knows you better than me."

"Fat chance," she shouted back and kept running.

15

Leah sat at the table in the coffee shop in the quaint historic village of Coleman Harbor and tried to calm her jangled nerves while pretending to sip the caramel latte she had no intention of drinking. She was fifteen miles from home, she reminded herself over the rim of her cup. No one would know her here. Still, every time the café door opened, her heart leaped in her chest. Wyatt's parting shot last night had run through her head, even in her sleep. She only hoped she wasn't about to be disappointed—or make a bigger idiot of herself.

When the tall, blond Adonis walked in and scanned the room's occupants, her heart bounced against her rib cage. Her cup fell back on the saucer with a loud clink. It was him. Had to be. He wore a black jacket and dark jeans, and even from across the room, the electric blue of his eyes jolted her. Every stride was bold and confident, yet graceful. His gaze connected with hers and locked as he smiled and approached her table. The closer he got, the better he looked. And God, he smelled great, too, like a cleansing ocean breeze. At last, he stood in front of the empty chair beside her.

"Leah?" She nodded, and he sat. "Hi, there. I'm Tim. But you can call me Julian."

She sucked in a sharp breath. *This is insane. What am I doing?* Panic overwhelmed her, and she shot to her feet, the words tumbling from her lips, unleashed. "I'm sorry. This was a mistake. I'm really sorry. I should go. I never should've done this."

He didn't flinch, but his hand cradled hers, steady and warm, and when he spoke, his tone was gentle, with no pressure or anxiety. "Easy, Leah. Relax. Sit. Let's talk. Just talk. If you decide you don't want to go through with your initial idea, no worries. We'll come out of this as two friends who met under unusual circumstances. Okay?"

She stood, hesitant, until his sense of calm became contagious.

Her heartrate returned to normal, and she rediscovered her sense of humor. Maybe he had a point. Maybe all she needed was to talk this out with someone who knew neither of them. Who couldn't use another friend? Finally, she sank back into her faux leather chair. She'd started this charade; she might as well see it through, whether that meant over the next hour or the next month.

"Welcome back. You okay now?" Tim—*Julian* asked.

"I think so."

"Good." He unzipped his jacket and ran his hand through his thick hair.

Beneath the stark overhead lights, she studied his beautiful face, his eyes without a wrinkle, the fullness of his hair, his utter perfection. He was too good to be true, and she had a feeling she knew why. "How old are you?" she blurted.

He flashed another disarming grin. "Thirty-two."

"Really?" No way. "You look...I dunno...ten years younger than that. If not more."

"Ah, right." He tugged on a length of the coiffed gold that skimmed his collar. "The hair, right?"

"Among other things."

"I don't usually wear it this long. And I've got contacts in my eyes."

Some of her discomfort faded. "Colored contacts?"

"Absolutely. I mean, my eyes are blue, but not *this* blue. I don't think any human naturally has eyes like these."

"Then why wear them?"

"Part of the job. Not *your* job. My regular job. I'm currently working in a stage production. We're doing 'Bye, Bye Birdie' over at the Sawyer."

"Oh! I didn't realize. I'm sorry. Michael didn't tell me he'd be pulling you away from a legitimate role to play boyfriend for me."

He touched her hand again, clasped her fingertips, and a tiny thrill zipped through her bloodstream. "He didn't pull me away from anything important. I'm the understudy for the lead, so unless the star gets sick, I'm stuck in the chorus Wednesdays for two shows and weekend matinees. Here. Give me a second. I'll show you the real me." He rose from his seat. "Promise you won't go anywhere 'til I get back?"

"Mmm-hmm." She pointed to her cup. "Can I order you something?"

"Just a bottled water, thanks." He reached into his jeans pocket, but she stopped him with an outstretched hand.

"This is on me."

"Unh-unh." He pulled a ten dollar bill out of his pocket and dropped it in the center of the table. "Julian does not allow his fiancée to pay his way."

"He doesn't?"

He quirked a brow at her. "You know him better than I do. Would he?"

"No, I guess he wouldn't."

With a curt nod, he replied, "There you go." He leaned down and slid his lips across her cheeks, soft and sweet. "Don't go away. I'll be right back."

A sigh rose inside her, and she shivered at the surprise show of affection. How long had it been since a man had shown affection for her—even if it was hired affection? *Earth to Leah! This is no time for a pity party. Get a grip.* While he headed for the restroom, she signaled the waitress and ordered his water.

When he returned a few minutes later, he'd slicked back his hair and put on a pair of wire-rimmed glasses that obscured the watery blue color of his real eyes. Leah gasped. He still had the same aura of confidence, the same self-assured stride, but now, with a maturity to match. Good God, he was the perfect image for her fake fiancé!

"How's that? Better?"

She blinked several times while her mind reeled. "I-I'm stunned. You're exactly what I would have pictured Julian to look like."

"Well, if something doesn't fit what you had in mind, this is your chance. Tell me about your ideas for Julian. And give me all the dirt on the guy you're trying to forget."

Her teeth chewed her lower lip. "I wasn't sure how this was going to go so I… umm… I brought the book." While her cheeks blazed, she dug into her purse.

"The book?"

She raised her gaze to him. "Uh-huh. See, when I first saw Wyatt again, I panicked and told him I was engaged. He asked for details—"

"Wait, hold up," he interjected. "Wyatt. You mean Wyatt Blackthorne? The singer? That's the guy who's kinda famous you're trying to make jealous?"

She grimaced. Well, he would have found out eventually anyway. This way, at least he wouldn't become starstruck the first time they met. *If* they met… "Yup," she confirmed. "The one and only. And I'm not trying to make him jealous. I'm trying to make him *gone*."

Somehow, he managed to keep his expression blank otherwise. "Okay. Sorry about interrupting you. You said he asked for details?"

"Yeah." She dove into her purse again and pulled out the romance novel that had started her on this lunatic path. "I based *my* Julian on the Julian in this book: same name, same career, same background."

He slid the book closer and peered at the cover, which displayed a male torso, nude from the waist up, and a woman's finely manicured hand against his tan six-pack. Without a hint of ridicule on his face, he tapped the cover. "That's going to be a real benefit for me. Okay if I take this to read?"

Her eyebrows arced. "You're willing to do that?"

"Sure. It's research, part of the job. Tell me. Is the heroine in this story anything like you?"

"No, not at all." A smile twitched her lips. She liked him. Tim was a genuinely nice man, quickly becoming a friend. Maybe this could work out after all. "I needed a fiancé to talk about at a moment's notice, and he popped into my head, fully formed and ready to rescue me."

"He must be a complex character to be so memorable." He placed the book next to his untouched water bottle. "This will give me a lot of information to enrich my portrayal. And since we're dealing with Wyatt Blackthorne, I can do enough research on the internet to be more familiar with how to handle him. Now, all I need is to know about you." He took her hand again, raised it to his lips, and kissed her fingertips. "And us."

A lump rose in her throat, and she swallowed. "Us?"

"Uh-huh. How we met, pet names for each other, that kinda stuff."

"Oh. Right." She picked up a wooden stirrer from her saucer and swirled the now-cold latte. "I should probably tell you right now, I'm not a very good liar."

"That's probably better. You should just be yourself. I'll do the rest."

She swallowed again, dug up a nugget of courage from somewhere in her gut. "Can I ask you something?"

"Absolutely. That's the only way this will work, if you and I are clear with each other from the start."

"Why are you doing this?"

He shrugged. "It's good practice. And Michael told me what happened to you. At least, as much as you told him." His eyes grew misty, and his timbre lowered to sympathetic condolence. "About what you lost, the baby and all."

Congratulations, idiot. You just won the pity prize. Happy now?

He kept the same sorrowful tone when he spoke again. "So, what do you think? Do you wanna go through with this?"

Wyatt's remarks from last night thundered in her head. *That's how I'm gonna win you back, you know. You've always had too soft a heart, sweetcakes. No one knows you better than me.*

Fat chance. Straightening in her chair, she hardened her heart and gave him her brightest smile. "Yeah. I do."

"Excellent. Let's get started."

ॐ

The next few weeks passed in a blur for Wyatt, who spent more time in the Manhattan recording studio with Cooper and the rest of the band than in Osprey Cove. In fact, he and the band celebrated the wrap with takeout Chinese food in Cooper's SoHo loft while listening, yet again, to the final cut of the album's first single. Ironically, the record company had chosen *I Made Her Hold On Too Long* for that honor. At least, this time, Cooper didn't insist on changing any of the lyrics.

"This is the most depressing celebration ever," Wyatt grumbled while munching on Kung Pao chicken and pork lo mein.

"We always get Chinese for the wrap party," Cooper remarked. "You never wanted to deal with crowds or special menus. You always said it was no big deal. That you hadn't had a big celebratory dinner since your mom died. What makes this time any different?"

"This year, he finally remembered the girl *he* left on hold too long," Chaz replied. "Smart girl got tired of waiting and disconnected, but our buddy, Wyatt, can't deal with losing."

One of the other band members snorted, and when Wyatt's furious gaze scanned the room, all but Chaz and Cooper focused their full attention on their plates. Wyatt's friendship with Chaz had soured considerably after the sweatshirt debacle, and the two spent more time butting heads than creating music.

Cooper's expression was blank. "What girl?"

"You know." Chaz smirked. "The girl from the animal shelter. The one he held that autograph-slash-free-ticket-contest for a coupla weeks ago. Hard to believe she wasn't bowled over by that indulgent ego-fest. Unfortunately, Wyatt figured promoting the new album by using her shelter to drum up interest would wow her into erasing all the past offenses he subjected her to."

"Shut up, Chaz," Wyatt growled.

"Whatsamatter, Wy? Can't handle the truth?"

"Wait. What girl are we talking about?" Cooper waved his clear plastic fork between them. "Not that Kira from years ago, is it?"

"*Leah*," Wyatt corrected automatically then added a hasty, "but she has nothing to do with anything."

"Bull. She's the reason we're here and the whole reason for this album." Chaz slammed a palm on the table, and two of their bandmates flinched. "Jeez, haven't any of you guys put it together yet? Think of the songs he's written this time around. There's no rocking cut like *Down at the Riverside* or *We've Got Something Good.* They're all ballads. *I Made Her Hold On Too Long, Forgiveness is a Gift, I've Never Loved Another, The Reasons You Don't Know, Forever My Girl, Even Now.* Every song is one long, boring apology to the girl who got away."

The room grew silent, broken only by the sound of plastic utensils scraping against cardboard boxes and paper plates. No one would look Wyatt in the eye, which told him they all agreed with Chaz's assessment. After all, they'd seen his arrogance go into overdrive once before. They knew what a jerk he could be. But this time was different. This was Leah. He couldn't lose her.

"The problem is," Chaz added, "the girl who got away wants him to *stay* away. No song, no autograph signing, no sweatshirt bonanza is gonna change that fact. She's moved on. She got engaged, for God's sake. He's the only one hanging onto a past that doesn't want him anymore. It would be comical if it weren't so pathetic. Do us all a favor, Wy. Let. Her. Go.

"Why can't you just shut up already?" Wyatt demanded.

"Why can't you just accept defeat?" Chaz shot back.

"Come on, guys," Kenny interjected, leaning between the two combatants. "Let's drop it, okay?"

Wyatt poked at the fried rice on his plate and said nothing more. He couldn't accept defeat because the tears he'd seen from Leah that night at the mall said she still cared. If she hadn't given up on him entirely yet, a slim chance existed he could win her back. Slim was better than none. Time, however, ticked against him. He had no idea when her fiancé would come back to town, and he had a national tour coming up, starting in the Pacific Northwest in March—and Leah's wedding was slated for the month before.

Maybe he *had* left her on hold too long, thinking that, despite the deal he'd made, she'd know the truth and wait for him. He hadn't counted on the other party in their agreement up and dying before the mess could be sorted out. Now, he had no one to back up his side of the story—and he didn't know if Leah would believe him without a corroborating witness.

On one aspect of this whole mess, though, Chaz was right. Using his fame would never impress Leah or convince her he'd never stopped loving her. He needed more than a grand gesture, something bigger than the actions he'd already taken. In other words, he needed to tell her the truth. Once and for all.

16

Another Friday, another visit to the St. Ignatius Nursing Home. This time, Leah brought Tim with her and a few kittens of assorted ages and colors. Once again, Charlotte met her at the door. When the older woman spotted the man walking beside Leah, she smoothed a hand over her hair and straightened the hem on her blouse. Leah had noted the handsome actor had that effect on a lot of people, particularly women.

"Who's this?" Charlotte asked, her hand outstretched.

"This is Julian." She tried to give Charlotte one of the dog's leads, but the woman ignored her in order to shake hands with Tim. Leah shrugged it off. "He's helping me out today. Julian, this is Charlotte Coulter." After greetings were exchanged, she asked, "Are we all set in there?"

Charlotte might have answered Leah, but her gaze stayed fixed on Tim. "Absolutely. A full house, too. When I said you were bringing kittens, a lot of the residents who rarely come out decided they wanted to attend today."

"Terrific!" Another switch, today she'd included Penny for her debut. She allowed the dogs to parade in first. Leah jerked her head in Tim's direction, indicating he should fall in line behind her. After putting on her brightest smile, she strode inside to at least two dozen residents. Standing room only. "Good morning, ladies and gentlemen. Once again, it's Fur-Ever Friday, and today, I've brought some old friends and new friends to visit."

She introduced the dogs first, ending with, "Penny's a newbie to our group. She was rescued from a local house filled with starving and abused dogs a little over a month ago and has been recuperating nicely at our facility. This is her first foray into the public spotlight so everyone, please give her a warm welcome."

A soft round of applause broke out, and she led Penny into a canine version of a curtsy, front paws crossed with a dip of her head.

When the room quieted again, a snide voice erupted from somewhere in the back. "Leah Stewart. Still lying down with all the dogs, I see."

Leah stiffened. It couldn't be. Yet, she knew it was. Wyatt's father had always delighted in insulting her, first to get a rise out of her, then to rankle Wyatt. The uglier the names, the more enjoyment the old man took from their reactions.

She scanned the faces around her, noted sympathy and discomfort mirrored in the other residents' expressions.

"Now, Mr. Blackthorne, if you can't be civil to our guests," Charlotte chastised, her Scottish brogue thick with her umbrage, "you'll hafta return to your room." She placed a hand on Leah's shoulder and gave a comforting squeeze. "Pay him no mind. He's just an angry old man who fights with everyone. He promised he'd behave today, said he only wanted to see the animals, but if he gets more sour, I'll have him rolled out of here at once."

"If you think my son came back here so you can get your hooks into my money," Ezra growled, "you better think again. I'll tell him the truth about you. Tell him about that rumor that was going around a few years ago."

Fighting back shivers, she forced herself to look up and locate where the vile, poisonous threats came from. It didn't take long. He sat in a wheelchair in the far corner, a shrunken version of the man she remembered—except for the eyes. Those black, soulless eyes glared at her with the same hate-filled intensity he'd always reserved for her. A chill rushed through her, freezing her in place.

"Leah?" Tim's prompt came from beside her, but sounded miles away. His touch on her arm was gentle, warm, and soothing. "Are you all right? Do you need me to get you out of here?"

"No." She shook off the old man's threat with effort, and focused on the other residents. These were the people she came to see, to entertain. She wouldn't let him see he could still affect her. She had a job to do, and she'd do it. The others here deserved the joy her pets could instill in their lives—even for an hour or so. "Mr. Blackthorne doesn't bother me," she said loud enough to reach the back of the room. "He has always been a difficult man."

"Hmmph!" Charlotte added in a whisper. "That's putting it mildly. I swear he's still alive 'cuz the devil refuses to take him."

Leah snorted back a half-laugh, half-gasp. Truer words were probably never spoken. Stronger now, and determined not to let the old man get under her skin, she removed all the dogs but Penny from their leads. Penny would stay by her side as they walked from chair to chair, from person to person.

"And by special request, my friend, Julian here, has brought us a few smaller, cuddlier furry friends."

With a flourish, he unzipped the top of the multi-cat carrier and pulled out an orange and white tabby kitten.

"Meet Cincinnati," Leah said, "and his friends, Cleveland…" He placed the orange tabby on the floor, took out a pure black long-haired kitten, and held him up for the crowd. A series of oohs and ahs erupted from the residents."…and Columbus." The third cat, a calico, joined the two on the rug. "Based on their names, can you guess where these beauties all came from?"

"That's easy," Mrs. Lippman said in her booming cackle. "Ohio."

"That's right," she replied, pointing at the old woman. "They were residents in a high-kill shelter, and we were fortunate to get them out to save their lives."

"Bring the black one to me," Millie Lippman called. When Charlotte bent to reach for the kitten, she added, "Not you. Let that young hunk bring me the cat. Nothing finer for these old eyes to behold than a good-looking man holding a good-looking kitty."

"Happy to oblige," Tim said with a wink and scooped up Cleveland. "Come along, Cleve, my friend. You and I have a command performance to attend."

Charlotte picked up the other two cats, placed one on the lap of an old man with an afghan tucked around his knees. Columbus immediately curled into a ball and went to sleep. Cincinnati climbed up the chest of another man and licked his earlobe.

"He kissed me!" the man exclaimed with a chuckle. "This little guy just kissed me!"

A woman seated beside the man reached out to rub Cincy under his chin. "He's adorable. They *all* are."

While her animals charmed the residents in their usual manner, Leah walked the room with Penny, allowing the residents to pet the pooch, croon to her, and marvel at her lovely red coat. As she drew closer to that dark corner, her stomach churned. She wanted desperately to avoid him, but knew that would only delight him more. On a deep inhale, she strode confidently toward his wheelchair. "Mr. Blackthorne, nice to see you again."

His thin lips twisted into a macabre smile. "No, it ain't. Not for me, not for you. Don't lie, girl. You were never any good at it. I always saw right through you. Still can. You thought you and your family were better than us. Tried to make my son a prissy boy you could drag around by some ring in his nose. He showed you, though, didn't he? Skipped town in the middle of the night, rather than take on some other man's kid. Wy and I spent a lot of nights laughing at how you mooned over him."

The words sliced into her, death by a thousand paper cuts, and each one made her bleed. "That's not true," she whispered. "None of what you say is true."

Tim appeared and wrapped an arm around her shoulders. "Come on, Leah. Let's go."

"Who's this?" Ezra pointed a bony finger at Tim. "Be careful, my boy. She's not as pure as she looks. I oughta know. I used to see her out in the tool shed cavorting naked with my son." His expression turned malevolent. "Didn't know I watched, didja?"

The room had gone deathly silent, and Leah wished the floor would open up and swallow her.

"That does it!" Charlotte stomped to the hallway. "Derek! Get Mr. Blackthorne out of here. Take him back to his room, please."

A burly bald orderly in pale blue scrubs appeared and strode straight to the old man's wheelchair. "Let's go, Mr. B. Looks like you've worn out your welcome again."

Charlotte approached Leah where she stood, with Tim still hugging her close. "I am so sorry, Leah. I promise you, I won't have him here again."

She nodded. "It's okay," she replied, her voice shaking on each syllable. "Like I said, he's always been a difficult man."

But it wasn't okay. It was excruciating. Somehow, she managed to pretend she wasn't dying inside while her pets entertained the residents for their full hour.

♋

"Your old girlfriend was here the other day."

Wyatt stiffened in the chair at the old man's bedside. "Leah? Here? Why?"

Why on earth would she come anywhere near this spawn of Satan? She didn't have to. *He* had no choice, since he was the spawn of the spawn of Satan.

"She comes here every week with those dogs of hers. I don't usually bother to leave my room to see her—she ain't worth my time—but since you've come back to town, I wanted her to know she still wouldn't get her claws on my money, no matter how she bats her eyes at you."

His stomach rolled over. Good God. He was going to have to talk to Mrs. Coulter, find out exactly what happened between Leah and his father.

"I don't know why I bothered," Ezra continued ranting. "You two deserve each other. I should just cut you out of my will and let her have

131

you as you are, poor and useless. Joke'd be on both of you. You don't respect your old man, you don't deserve to inherit. She thinks she's gonna get the big payout and gets nothing." He cackled. "Serve you both right."

Wyatt rose from the chair and leaned over the bedrail until he was eye to jaundiced eye with the devil. "Listen to me, old man, and listen good. Leah has made it very plain she wants nothing to do with me, so you can leave her alone. I didn't treat her the way I should have, and somebody else scooped her up, somebody who saw her value and knew how to treat her. That's *my* fault, not hers. I took off without a word, never called, never got in touch, and she got tired of waiting."

"Of course she did. She couldn't go for long without a man panting after her. She was probably cheating on you the whole time you were dating her anyway. You were a sap to trust her. You can't trust any woman. They're all the same—just after a man for his money. Like black widow spiders. They'll drain you dry and when there's nothing left but your hollowed out carcass, they move on to their next victim. You wanna know the stories I heard about your precious Leah once you were gone? All the nasty stuff I told her I was going to tell you when you came to visit again? I bet if you know the truth, that your pretty little girlfriend isn't as pure as you thought, you'd stop mooning after her. You'll see. Give me ten minutes and you'll be thanking God you dumped her when you did. Only smart thing you ever did, if you ask me."

"No one asked you." He grabbed his jacket from the back of his chair with a snap. "I'm out of here. I won't be back—unless I hear you've come near Leah again. She's no longer part of my life so you have no reason to continue harassing her, you hear me? Let her be. She's put up with enough from you."

His father coughed, dry and hacking. "I'd spit in your face, boy, if I could muster up enough moisture. Good riddance to both of you."

Wyatt left his father to his hateful raving and went in search of the home's administrator. He found Mrs. Coulter in her office, alone, with the door open. He knocked twice and leaned his head in. "Got a minute?"

She looked up from her cell phone and smiled in welcome. "Wyatt. Of course. Come in, come in." She waved him inside and gestured to the chair on the other side of her desk. "Sorry. I finally had an hour to myself to check up on personal emails."

He turned to leave. "Oh, well, I don't want to bother you."

"Nonsense. You're never a bother. Come in. Sit down." Once he complied and sat across from her, she placed her cell phone face-down on the corner of the desk and focused her full attention on him, hands folded together on the desktop. "How are you, dear boy?"

"I just came from my father's room."

Her face fell, and she twisted her hands. "Oh, dear."

"No, no. There's nothing wrong with him or his situation here. I'm not here to complain." He offered her a self-deprecating grin. "Believe me, I'm grateful you're willing to keep him at all."

"Yes, well, he is rather difficult, but like many bullies, he's mostly bluff. Call him on it and he generally folds."

He leaned back in the chair, keeping his posture fluid, non-confrontational. "That's what I wanted to talk to you about. He mentioned he had some words with Leah Stewart the other day."

She frowned. "Last Friday. He never comes out of his room when she brings the pets here, but last week, for some reason, he insisted. I had no legitimate reason to tell him no, so I allowed it. But I did warn him he would have to behave, or he'd find himself back in his room right quick."

"What happened?"

She squirmed in her chair. "Oh, dear. It…didn't go well. He was unforgivably rude to her. I had to have Derek escort him out within five minutes of her arrival."

"What did he say?" Mrs. Coulter looked away to stare out the window at the gray sky and thick clouds. "Mrs. Coulter, I know better than anyone what the man is like. Please, don't hold back on my account. Tell me the truth. What did he say to her?"

"He was horrid to her," she murmured. "I don't know how she stood his insults as long as she did. He started in on her the moment she walked in. He made some kind of crack about her still lying with dogs."

Wyatt stifled a curse. "Then what?"

"I don't remember word-for-word. He said how she wasn't a good liar, he always saw right through her, and she'd never get his money. At first, she did her best to ignore him. She was introducing a new dog to the rest of the group, and I guess she thought she couldn't go right by him so when it was his turn, she addressed him directly, just as she had all the others. That's when he went for her jugular." The woman's cheeks flushed scarlet, and she returned her gaze to the window. "There were comments about her making you a prissy boy, how you taught her a lesson by skipping town in the middle of the night, and some particularly nasty comments about you and Leah in your tool shed."

"Son of a—" He stopped himself, but his hands gripped the arms of the leather chair tight enough to crush the steel frame. "Sorry." She waved off the apology. "How did Leah take it?"

"I admit I was distracted and didn't see most of what happened, though I heard it. Everyone heard it. He was loud, and ugly, and insulting. Thank God for that young man of hers, Julian."

Wyatt sat straight up, all thoughts of strangling his father temporarily forgotten. "Julian was with her?"

"Yes, and I'm so glad he was. By the time I realized what was going on, he was by her side, bolstering her, and glaring daggers at your father. That's when I had Derek escort your father back to his room."

A ball of ice formed in his stomach. "Umm…what do you think of Julian?"

She smiled wistfully. "Oh, he's such a nice young man. And handsome as they come. Why, he even charmed Mrs. Lippman within minutes of meeting her. And you know what a dragon she can be. He charmed all the ladies. He's a very nice young man."

Wyatt nodded, but inside his brain scrambled to deal with this new information. Julian was back in town. For good, or just for the holidays? No way to know. Not without showing everyone how much the idea bothered him.

So, Wy, my boy, what do you plan to do about it?

Simple. He was going to do whatever it took to win her back. Julian or no Julian.

17

Leah found herself enjoying most of her time with Tim, aka Julian. They got to know each other in an attempt to become comfortable using simple romantic gestures like holding hands and displaying affection in public. The art of kissing with any pretense of love and commitment, however, eluded Leah's acting skill level.

"I'm sorry," she said when he leaned in too fast and she flinched—again. "I'm way out of practice."

He sat back in his chair at the same coffee shop where they'd met a few weeks earlier. "It's okay. How long has it been for you?"

Her cheeks heated to the temperature of the noon sun, and she gulped from the straw sticking out of her iced latte until her brain froze. "Not since Wyatt…"

He stared at her, agape. "But that was…what? Five years ago?"

"Seven," she corrected.

"He hurt you that badly?"

The pain sliced through her yet again, and she placed a palm over her stomach. "You have no idea."

"Tell me." When she hesitated, he reached across the table and cupped her hand. "Please? We're friends, right? You know I'd never betray your trust. It might help you get past this hurdle. Besides, I know plenty of acting exercises you can use to get out of your own head." She must have given him some kind of signal she was considering his offer because he pressed his advantage. "Start with the highlights. I don't need to know all the dark and dirty stuff."

"You already know the dark and dirty stuff. I got pregnant, he skipped town, I miscarried, and now can't have any more children."

He gave her hand a gentle squeeze. "So, back up. How'd you meet?"

"High school. Ninth grade biology class…" She answered all his questions, charting her romance with Wyatt from that first day

135

forward. She bypassed the tales of Wyatt's father since that was *his* dark and dirty stuff, and she had no right to reveal it to anyone without his permission, no matter what the old man had said to her at the nursing home.

"In the spring of our senior year, we formed a band with a couple of our friends, Alex and Nancy." A wistful smile tugged at her lips at the memory. "You know how it is. We all thought we'd be rich and famous in no time. The first few years we played together, we performed covers of the current rock hits like all the other local bar bands. Then, when we were sophomores in college, Wy and I started collaborating on original music. He handled the melodies, and I wrote the lyrics. We came up with several songs that we interspersed with the rock hits we covered, until we garnered a good-sized following, then we switched to playing all original music. We were good. So good, about a year after we went all-original, Cooper Milburn came to hear us play one night. We'd created a demo that we sold after our shows, and he actually bought a copy. We all went home stoked that night, thinking this was it. We finally got our big break."

"But it wasn't *your* big break. It was his."

She nodded. "I guess you see that happen in your line of work, too."

He sipped from his water bottle. "From time to time."

"I knew something was up with Wyatt almost immediately, but I didn't know what. He'd go off for a few hours by himself and when I asked where he was, he'd give me some lame excuse. He had a flat tire. He fell asleep and lost track of time. He got stuck working overtime at the current construction site. He'd get phone calls in front of me and tell the caller he'd call back later. At the time, I was already pretty sure I was pregnant. I assumed he figured it out, too, and was pulling away to avoid me." She ducked her head. "Not my best moment, considering we'd been together for four years at that point."

Julian grunted. "Not his best moment, either, considering how it all turned out."

She lifted her cup to point the straw in his direction. "Exactly!" How nice to have someone understand *her* side of the story without questioning if she overreacted, maybe even a little, when she doubted Wyatt's actions and intentions. "One day, Wyatt was just…gone. No note, no phone call, nothing. For a few days, I did nothing. Then, finally, I took a pregnancy test, and of course, it was positive. I had to go to my mother and tell her I was pregnant. This was a month before I was supposed to start veterinary school, and instead, I was going to have a baby whose father had ditched me in the middle of the night. God, I will never forget the disappointment in her eyes and how that made me feel. I broke my mother's heart that day. I don't think she ever recovered from her daughter's fall from grace."

His tone didn't lose its empathetic timbre. "That's not true. I'm sure of it. You might have surprised her, and she probably wasn't thrilled at the circumstances at first, but I bet she doesn't think any less of you now."

Tears stung her eyes, and she blinked them back. "She passed away a few years ago. Complications of bladder cancer."

Another hand squeeze. "I'm sorry."

Nodding, she allowed the tears to fall. "Thank you. I miscarried about six weeks later, due to an abnormally large blood clot that burst and bled into my abdomen. The doctors had to perform an emergency hysterectomy to save my life, and I wound up spending ten days in the hospital. I came home, recuperated, tried to regroup, but I just couldn't deal with anything. Until Mom got sick. Then all my focus fell on her and her battle. Another year went by. One day, I remember driving her home from one of her chemo appointments and this song came on the radio. I recognized it immediately. How could I not? I wrote it. *Take My Heart Again.*"

"You wrote that song?" His empathy turned to surprise.

"Uh-huh. It was supposed to be between the two of us, a song I'd hoped we'd one day hear performed in public for the first time at our wedding." She scowled into her cup. "Wyatt put it to another use instead."

"You mean, he took it without your permission?"

"Yup. It wasn't on our demo. I don't think Nancy and Alex ever knew it existed. If they did, they'd never heard it in its entirety. That song was meant to be ours alone, mine and Wyatt's. Then suddenly, without my knowledge, it belonged to him and his fans. Imagine that. *My* wedding song became the official first dance choice for thousands of brides and grooms all over the country for the next five years."

"What'd you do that day? When you first heard it?"

"Honestly, I went numb. I just remember gripping the steering wheel so hard I was lucky I didn't break my fingers. The voice was Wyatt's, so he hadn't sold it to someone else. Instead, he'd stolen it for himself. I suddenly realized why he left so secretively. Cooper Milburn didn't want the band; he wanted Wyatt. And he got him, but he also got a huge piece of me—my words. Meanwhile, I lost the only piece of *us* Wyatt had left behind." The old feelings of shame and resentment stirred inside her, but she tamped them down by curling her hands into fists and digging her nails into her palms. "A few months later, I got a big envelope from some hotshot California law firm. Inside, I found the first royalty check, along with a legal letter telling me Wyatt had listed me as the lyricist of record for *Take My Heart Again*, and I could expect regular checks of varying amounts, based on sales. I still get checks, though they're a lot smaller these days."

"He never contacted you?"

"Not until he showed up here last month, looking to romance me." She took another sip of the cool coffee drink to ease her aching throat. "That's the whole ugly story." His rounded eyes and slack jaw told her what he thought. "Not exactly a fairy tale, is it?"

"Life isn't supposed to be a fairy tale. Right now, I'm still digesting the fact you wrote *Take My Heart Again*. That song." He stared up at the ceiling and sighed. "God, the words punch me in the gut every time I hear them. For you, it must be a million times worse. You wrote it."

She pursed her lips at him. "I'm pretty sure we established I'm the lyricist of record."

His gaze returned to her, steady, curious. "Have you written any other songs?"

"Not for sale. I have notebooks full of lyrics, but they're just for me. My thoughts, my experiences, my emotions."

"Would you ever consider writing something for a specific project?"

A shiver of suspicion slithered up her spine. "I've never been asked. Why?"

"A while back, I wrote a stage production. I can't seem to sell it. My agent thinks it needs to be a musical, but I'm not good at composing. Do you think you could write a score?"

She pushed her chair back from the table, gaining some distance between them, and held her hands up toward him. "No, you misunderstand. I don't have songs. I have a lot of little poems that could one day be worked into songs, if I wanted them to be, which I don't. I wouldn't know how to begin anything as ambitious as a musical score."

"Don't you think it's time you tried? Maybe, this is what you need to get over the hurt of Wyatt's betrayal. Total control over who gets to use your songs, songs that reflect a fictional character's life, not yours or his. And the chance to win over your own audience, without Wyatt Blackthorne."

Her mind flipped over the possibilities. She wouldn't use the words in her notebooks. These would be new words, words based on someone else's story. A tingle of excitement rippled her spine. This could be the start of something new, something that would allow her to release the words always screaming in her skull. "I might be willing to try. What's the production?"

"Oscar Wilde, Lord of the Vampires."

Her jaw dropped. "You're kidding."

He flashed her a grin that lit up his too-handsome face into stunningly beautiful. "No. I know how it sounds, and you're right. It's meant to be campy and over-the-top and fun. And that brings me to something else I need to tell you. You do know I'm gay, right?"

She blinked at the non-sequitur. "Huh?"

"I could be wrong, but I think the reason you can't relax enough around me to kiss me with any credibility is that you're afraid I might become romantically interested in you." He shrugged. "I figured it might help if you knew."

"Oh." No other words came to mind.

♋

Wyatt chose Monday morning to visit the shelter, expecting fewer staff members and customers. The bells jangled when he opened the front door. Sure enough, only two people stood inside. Leah and Jenny, both manning the reception desk, looked up. One smiled, one frowned.

"Hi, Wyatt," Jenny said with her usual cheer. "Nice to see you again."

"Hey, Jenny." He nodded at Leah. She glowered in an attempt to look formidable, but failed big time. He found her expression adorable and bit back an indulgent smile. In her pale blue sweatshirt and stonewashed jeans, with her hair loose and tousled around her shoulders, she still resembled the high school girl he fell in love with.

Never taking his eyes from her, he addressed Jenny. "Could you give us a few minutes alone, please?"

Jenny swerved her attention from him to Leah, who made a cutting gesture across her neck. In reply, Jenny nodded with so much enthusiasm, he worried she'd snap her spine. "You got it." Before leaving, she moved closer to Leah and said in a stage whisper, "Play nice." With one last carefree wave in Wyatt's direction, she opened the side door and disappeared into the shelter's inner sanctum.

Now that he'd dispatched her support system, he assumed Leah would finally have no choice but to face him. Instead, she dropped her gaze away from him. For all he knew, she was staring at her shoes. "What do you want now, Wyatt? I'm working."

He took a step closer, and she shuffled papers on the other side of the desk. "I wanted to apologize to you."

"Okay, fine. Apology accepted. Bye, now." She picked up a pen, wrote something on something, never looking up.

"Don't you want to know what I'm apologizing for?"

At last, she glanced toward where he stood. "It's not a blanket apology for the last seven years? Okay, fine, I'll play." She returned her attention to whatever she wrote. "What are you apologizing for?"

He strode to the desk and leaned over the edge to see her list of pet supplies scribbled on an order form. "I'm sorry about what my father did the other day."

On a gasp, she dropped the pen, and her head shot up, eyes wide with surprise. He had no idea whether he'd startled her with his nearness or the mention of good ol' Ezra.

"Why? What'd your father do?"

It was his turn to frown. "Don't play games now, Leah. I'm sorry for what happened at St. Ignatius the other day. He had no right to speak to you at all, much less the way he did."

Her cheeks suffused with pink. "H-how'd you find out about that?"

"How else? The old man couldn't wait to tell me."

She blinked several times, and her lips parted as she pondered his revelation. "You saw him?"

"I saw him." It took all his self-control not to lunge across the barrier separating them and pull her into his arms. *He* should have been the one to protect her from the monster, not Julian. Was this what Chaz had meant by being better than Superman? Because, right now, he'd settle for being better than Julian. "I won't be visiting him again until he's in a coffin."

"I'm sorry." She dipped her head again, allowing her hair to fall like a curtain over her eyes, a trick she pulled whenever she didn't want anyone to see the emotions always so visible on her face.

"Why are *you* sorry?"

"I never wanted to be the one who came between you and your father for good."

He chucked her under the chin. She drew back, out of reach, but kept her eyes level with his. "You had nothing to do with it. I realized long ago he would never change. No Ghost of Christmas Past was going to show him the error of his ways. I'm only sorry he dragged you into his miserable existence one last time, but I *do* promise it will be the last time. I spoke to Charlotte Coulter at the home. She's assured me my father will no longer be allowed to attend your…what do you call it…? Fur-Ever Fridays?"

She nodded. "You didn't have to do that."

"Yeah, I did." He shifted on his feet before addressing the next part of their conversation. "I…umm…I hear Julian was with you when my father insulted you. I hope that didn't make things uncomfortable for you."

"A little," she admitted with a wan smile. "I never told him...I mean, even afterwards I still didn't explain about..." Her eyes went blank, as if she looked through him. "What I mean is Julian doesn't know about your dad. I mean, after what happened on Friday, he knows how mean he can be, but not how *mean* he can be."

In other words, she hadn't told her fiancé about the abuse he'd suffered in his childhood. "Thank you for that."

"You're welcome."

He swallowed his pride, a bitter pill. "I'd like to thank Julian for being there for you when I wasn't. Will I get the chance?"

Her smile became more confident. "I'm sure we can work that out. I'll talk to him. How's the album coming along?"

"Great. We're in post-production, finally." Cripes, this was awkward. The two of them shouldn't have to struggle with small talk. "Maybe you and Julian can attend the release party." If she hadn't kicked the interloper to the curb by then. Charlotte Coulter's voice rang in his head. *Oh, he's such a nice young man. And handsome as they come. He charmed all the ladies.*

Charming, as in con man charming? Or just a decent fellow? Wyatt still didn't know, but he'd gauge the man's worth first chance he got.

A teenaged boy, his head obscured by a dark hoodie that did nothing to hide the silver hoop piercings in his lip and nose, strode in through the front door. "Hey, Leah," he shouted as he tossed off the hood and yanked a pair of white headphones from his ears. Even from across the room, the thunderous boom-boom of his music smacked the walls.

"Indoor voice, Robbie," she chastised him.

"Right." He pulled his phone from his jacket pocket, pressed a button, and the music silenced. "Sorry." Despite his clueless appearance, he must have sensed the electricity crackling in the air because he tilted his head to ask, "Everything okay?"

"Everything's fine." She turned back to Wyatt. "Mr. Blackthorne was just leaving."

That easily, she dismissed him.

18

Black Friday was always a hectic day at the shelter. Since many families preferred to avoid the shopping malls and crazy crowds, especially while suffering from a turkey hangover, and the kids were often bored from too many hours stuck indoors the day before, the shelter became a welcome diversion. Too bad, this decision often devolved into tears and tantrums when the kids were told they couldn't bring a new pet home. By ten o'clock that morning, the shelter buzzed with people.

To help control the chaos, Leah had a full staff on hand, including her latest volunteer from the county's Youthful Offender program, a mid-teen boy named Robbie who'd wound up in the system after punching his stepfather for threatening his mother. So many of the kids in the system reminded her of Wyatt, which was why she'd become involved in the first place. Always touched by the story of the older couple who'd taught him how to be a real man, Leah honored Wyatt and the Robinsons every time she took on another child who'd scraped against the law. She hoped she might change the circumstances they found themselves in before it was too late. Maybe, someday, one of her offenders would become governor or a teacher or just a really good parent.

Wyatt's visit on Monday had left her restless, but today, Leah was nervous for another reason. This afternoon, she would introduce "Julian" to Jenny and the rest of the staff. Throughout the morning, her jitters kept her bouncing from front desk to kennel to yard and back to the front desk.

As luck would have it, she stood near the main entrance, pinning photos of recent new adoptive families on the corkboard, when he arrived. She stood on tiptoe, stretching beyond her reach. Warm fingers curled around hers, and his becoming-familiar voice crooned, "Need help?"

"Hey, you," she said with a wide grin.

He wrapped his arms around her waist and pulled her against his chest. "Hey, yourself."

His mouth came down on hers, and thank God, she didn't flinch or recoil. She even managed to wind her arms around his neck and pull him closer. She didn't know whether her new comfort level came from familiarity or knowing he was gay. For her purposes, the reason didn't matter, only the results were important. His kiss looked more passionate than it was. In truth, she felt nothing: no sparks, no sudden surge of heat, none of the dizzying sensations Wyatt's kisses had always evoked in her. Still, to their spectators, they looked like a madly-in-love couple. When they pulled apart after one last starry-eyed look at each other, Leah noted the shocked expressions and slack jaws of all the employees in the office around them—including Jenny.

"Leah?" her friend asked while casting her gaze from Leah to Julian and back again.

Leah turned so that Julian's arm continued to circle her waist and she stood nestled inside his hold. "Everybody," she said, "I want you all to meet my fiancé, Julian."

The younger staff members burst into gasps of happy surprise and one or two clapped. Robbie shrugged off the news as inconsequential and returned to sweeping up the pet hair that accumulated on the floor. But Jenny...

Jenny stood too fast, sending the wheeled stool she sat on to career against the wall with an reverberating thud. When she finally spoke, the words came out through gritted teeth. "Leah, I need you to sign some papers in your office. Come with me now, if you can tear yourself away from...*Julian* long enough."

"Sure." She whirled to look up at the man holding her. "I'll be right back."

"What can I do in the meantime?"

She shoved the pile of pics still held in her hand into his and dug in her sweater pocket for the case of pushpins. "Would you hang these on the corkboard for me?"

"Of course, angel."

"Thanks, honey." She had to speed up to keep pace with Jenny's long-legged stomps through the side door to her cramped office with its cluttered desk and cot. Once inside, she took her seat while Jenny slammed the door shut and turned on her.

"Have you lost your mind?"

"Nope," she replied without a modicum of worry.

Jenny's brow pleated in worry lines. "No? Leah, what have you done now?"

"I've brought in reinforcements." She folded her hands on the desk blotter and beamed. "Isn't he perfect?"

"Who is he?"

"An actor from the Sawyer Theater. Don't worry, I did my research. He's going to give Wyatt fits." She spun her chair left to right, right to left, in a seated shimmy of delight.

"Are you out of your mind? Don't you think you're taking this too far now?"

"I haven't gone far enough until Wyatt's far gone from Osprey Cove, with no intention of coming back."

"Did it ever occur to you he has other ties that would make him come home? That maybe, it's not just about you?"

"What other ties?" She couldn't stifle the bitterness in her tone, and had to stop the chair dance as the memories shrouded her happiness. "He lost all his friends when he ditched us without a backward glance."

Jenny planted her hands on her hips. "How about his family ties?"

She blew exasperated air through pursed lips, rustling her bangs. "Pffft. The only family he has here is his father, and he doesn't want anything more to do with the old cretin."

"Maybe yes, maybe no. Maybe he's been looking for a way to reconnect with the old cretin."

Leah shook her head before memories of their last interaction could lodge in her thoughts. "Not willingly. Ezra Blackthorne is the meanest excuse for a father since Darth Vader."

"Maybe he's mellowed in his old age."

"Hmmph! Trust me. I have better chances of winning the lottery without ever buying a ticket."

"Look, I really don't care what his relationship is with his father or you or why he's really here at all. All I care about is that you don't get hurt, and I have to say I'm worried. I'm beginning to think you've gone off the deep end." Jenny wagged a finger. "You can't just use that poor man out there for your own agenda and then dump him when you're done, you know."

"Don't be ridiculous. He knows all about Wyatt and me. And I'm paying him for his services. This is a business arrangement, not a real romance. He's an *actor*. This is what he does. We're already becoming good friends, and guess what?" She rolled her chair forward until the desk's edge nudged her abdomen and lowered her voice to an excited whisper. "He and I are collaborating on a musical."

Jenny blinked, but her face was otherwise a blank canvas. "A musical what?"

Duh. "A musical *play*. You know, like a Broadway show."

"What do you know about producing a Broadway show?"

Disbelief sharpened the edge in Jenny's tone.

"I'm not producing it, I'm writing the score."

"The score?"

"The music and lyrics."

"Oh." Jenny picked up a pen from the desk organizer and bounced it between her fingertips. "You might actually be good at that."

"Gee, thanks for the vote of confidence. I'll try not to let you down."

"You already have."

She winced with a dramatic flair that would make Tim proud. "Ouch."

"This Julian thing isn't going to end well, Leah. And I'm not sure I'll be around to pick up the pieces when it all falls apart."

She sobered. "Why? What do you mean? Where are you going?"

"Nowhere, at the moment." Leah exhaled her relief, but Jenny's expression turned smug. "Then again, who knows? Chaz and I have been talking about the future. *Our* future. I have a feeling he's going to ask me to go on tour with them. If he does, by the way, I plan to say yes. You might want to start interviewing someone else to take over my position here."

"Wow. That's…fast." Too fast, which made Leah question her friend's motives. Was Jenny threatening to leave to get Leah to give up this Julian thing? Or did she really intend to fly away, regardless of how this all played out?

"All I can say is that it feels right for both of us." Jenny finally sank into the chair on the other side of the desk. "I already told you, Lee. I don't like lying to him. You bringing in this guy to play Julian puts me in a delicate position."

Guilt dried her throat and warmed her cheeks. "You're absolutely right. I'm sorry. I hadn't considered how my actions might affect you. That was selfish of me, and I'm sorry. But I'm in a delicate position, too."

Slapping her hand on the desk, Jenny shot to her feet. "No, you're *not!* All you and Wyatt have to do is talk to each other—*really* talk. I swear to God, if I thought it would do any good I'd—" She stopped short.

"What? You'd what?"

An unholy light filled Jenny's eyes, but she waved off Leah's question. "Nothing. Forget it. Come on. Let's get back out there before something blows up."

Leah pushed down the feeling of unease Jenny's sly expression instigated in her belly. "I promise, I'll do my best to keep you and Chaz out of my game with Wyatt. Okay?"

"It's gonna have to be. You better hope you can keep all these lies straight. I won't come to your rescue when this all goes ka-blooey in your face." Without another word, Jenny left the office in as much of a huff as when she'd entered.

She'd said *when*, not if. Wasn't that a rousing cheer for success? So much for her best friend's unwavering support. On a sigh, Leah got up from her chair to follow. Bringing in Julian had better push Wyatt out of town for good. She didn't want her friendship with Jenny to become a casualty in this war.

She returned to the front office to find Julian and Jenny talking quietly, heads bent conspiratorially toward each other while Casey welcomed a couple with three kids, all under the age of six, who'd wandered inside. "Okay, gang, break it up. Julian, honey, let me show you that thing I want to upgrade."

"Of course."

Okay, so there was no "thing" to upgrade, but no one on the staff dared to question her. Not even Jenny. After donning her jacket and gloves, she led him out the back door into the yard, where several families clustered with dogs held by other staff members. The day was chilly but bright with a platinum sun providing little heat against a steely sky.

"You've got quite a crowd here," he said as they strolled hand-in-hand around the grounds.

"Don't read too much into the number of people," she replied. "Traditionally, we don't do a lot of adoptions this weekend. Or the next several weeks, for that matter."

"Circumstances change. I mean, some of these people look pretty happy. You might have had bad years in the past, but I say your luck's about to flip for the better. Who knows? This weekend could find you adopting out so many dogs you have to bring them in from other shelters to fill the demand. That'd be great, right?"

"Not really." She waved her hand, encompassing the clusters of humans and dogs scattered over the lawn. "These people aren't shopping for a long-term pet right now. They're thinking about the holidays. They want new décor for their guests, or pricey presents to put under the tree. And the last thing they want to take on is a dog or cat who'll have accidents on the new rug or scratch the furniture or chew up all those plastic toys."

"What about the parents who want a new puppy or kitty under the tree for their kids?"

"I turn them down." Her gaze locked on a young African-American couple standing with Helen and nuzzling Bowser, an eight-year-old bulldog mix. Humans and dog seemed in love with each other. In fact, while she watched, the gentleman rubbed the dog's belly with genuine affection. In that moment, the couple won over both Bowser and Leah. For that couple, if they passed the application process, she'd probably make an exception to her "no adoptions around the holidays" rule.

"You do? Why?"

"Because too many of those puppies wind up right back here a few days later. Holidays aren't a good time to adopt. If a family asks to adopt for Christmas, I ask them to come back after New Year's. I'll even put a dog on hold, if I think the family is serious. Sometimes they do come back. A lot of times, they don't. I'd rather not put my pets through the stress of 'I'm adopted, no I'm not' just to satisfy a kid's Santa fantasy for a few days."

"What's to stop them from going to some other shelter and adopting there?"

She heaved a disappointed sigh. "Absolutely nothing. I can't save them all, but at least, *my* babies won't suffer through the trauma of another temporary home, if I can help it."

"Your babies." He drew a finger across her cheek. "You've got too soft a heart, Leah. Guard that softness, or you'll wind up hurt time after time."

Once again, Wyatt's taunt mocked her. *You've always had too soft a heart, sweetcakes. No one knows you better than me.*

She stifled a shiver of apprehension and abruptly changed the topic. "What were you and Jenny talking about when I came back into reception?"

"Nothing. Just getting acquainted and making sure we have our stories straight."

Odd. After the issues she'd raised in the office, Leah would've bet her last dime Jenny would want nothing to do with the Julian plan. Then again, maybe she wanted Leah to believe she felt that way to scare her into giving up. Whatever the reason, she was grateful for the cooperation.

Now, all she needed was a reasonable scenario to bring Wyatt face-to-face with Julian. The sooner, the better.

♡

Leah sat at the kitchen table in Tim's tiny apartment in Coleman Harbor with a cup of tea on one side, a manila folder full of notes and papers on the other. "I loved the storyline."

He took a sip of his ever-present bottle of water—she'd learned he never drank anything else because alcohol and caffeine put lines on a person's face—before leaning forward to peer at her with excitement.

"You did? Really?"

She'd read through the script over the last few days and, despite her initial reticence when he'd told her the title, she found the plot witty and engaging, not at all the farce she'd expected. "It's like a social satire about modern political issues set against the backdrop of nineteenth century England, told by two people desperately in love who aren't allowed to go public with their feelings for each other. It was sad and romantic, the whole star-crossed lovers angle..."

He pointed his index finger in her direction, a satisfied grin on his pretty-boy, lineless face. "Yes! Exactly! But with the added benefit of vampires to give it an edge." He shrugged. "I figure, if zombies worked for Jane Austen, why not vampires for good ol' Oscar?"

She laughed. "Oh, it works. In the oddest way, but still. And I actually had fun with the paranormal aspect while working up a few songs. They're still in the first draft stage, but I wanted to run them by you to make sure they match your vision of the story." She frowned as she pulled out the pages of notes she'd created. "Bear in mind, there's no melody yet. I was thinking rather than relying on heavy organ music, which would make it sound clunky and campy, we might be better off using some modern guitar and a bass. A bassoon to represent Oscar. Sax for Bosie. The sax can be such a sad instrument, when it's played right. Do you have someone in mind to do the music?"

A flush stained his cheeks. "I thought you'd do it."

Her? "Tim, I'm a lyricist. I don't write music."

"You wrote *Take My Heart Again.*"

"I wrote the lyrics." When he cocked his head and his eyes narrowed in scrutiny, she squirmed on the chair. "And a little bit of the music. But that's not like writing a full musical score."

He clasped her hand in his and gave her a gentle squeeze. "You can do it. I have faith in you. Anyone who can write something as magnificent as *Take My Heart Again* has a gift in her soul. Maybe right now, your gift is sleeping. So all we have to do is wake it up and bring it to the surface."

She shook her head and removed her hand from his to toy with the sheaf of papers on the table. "I hate to disillusion you, but Wyatt was the one who made that song sing—figuratively speaking. It's why we made such a good team. He's always been the melody behind my words. In that song, I just poured out my heart to *him*, detailing all the things he made me feel, what our life was like and what I hoped it would be like when we finally married and lived our happily ever after. I set it to a simple tune, but he enhanced what I gave him. He understood what I was trying to say and made it into something perfect for us." Which explained why his thievery still hurt so freakin' much.

"Maybe, but a lot of other couples identified with the song, too. Thanks to both the music and the lyrics. Probably the lyrics more than the music, if you ask me. And *you* wrote it. Do you have any idea how amazing that is? No, more than that. It's…pure magic. You know what's my favorite part? 'With your arms around me, your love surrounds me…'"

She finished the rest of the chorus automatically. "'…I want to take away all your sorrow, all your pain. That's why I'm begging you to take my heart again.'" She sighed. There were so many lines in that song about the joy they only experienced when they were together and how nothing else mattered to her but him. All her love had been his for the taking in those days. He could've asked her for anything and she'd have given it gladly. She had always assumed he felt the same way about her. How could she have been so wrong about the man she thought she knew? The man she'd begged to take her heart again. And again, and again, and again. Ad infinitum.

"God, that's such powerful stuff," he exclaimed with a delicate shudder. "You must really love him."

Distracted by the memories, she answered without thinking. "I do." She jerked out of the past and crashed back to reality with a muffled thud. "I mean, I *did*. That was a long time ago and I was a stupid kid who didn't know any better. Let's get back to the play. You're going to have to hire someone to write the music. Words, I can handle, but melodies aren't my strong suit. I mean, I'll be happy to make recommendations, but the major work should fall on someone else's shoulders. I'm not experienced enough."

"I have faith in you, but we can tackle that dilemma later. For now, just show me what you've written so far."

"Okay." An exhale of blessed relief escaped her lips. She thought for sure he would continue to press her about her comment regarding loving Wyatt. Jenny would have. Thank God, though, Jenny wasn't here, and Tim wasn't obsessed enough about her relationship with Wyatt to care. For him, her love life was simply backstory to make his role as Julian more credible. "I wrote this bit for the opening number."

After another sip of water, he waved a dismissive hand. "Forget the opening number. You said in your email you had a great idea for a song in the scene after the dinner party with Bosie. Something about *The Pain of Love*, I think you called it?"

"Right." Flustered, she flipped through the pages with trembling fingers, crinkling the paper and dogearing the corners as she tried to find that particular song in the pile of partials. "Here it is."

He took the page from her and scanned the words, his lips moving to the rhythm of each line. Her heart thudded against her ribcage. She hadn't shared her lyrics with anyone since Wyatt. All the uncertainties and self-doubts littered her senses as she studied his expression, looking for some indication of condemnation or disgust.

Instead, his eyes widened, and his mouth formed a perfect o. "This is good, Leah." His tone took on a hushed whisper, as if he were in awe. "Really good."

A heated blush warmed her cheeks, and she gazed down at the table's surface. "Thanks."

"I'm serious. It's like…you managed to crawl inside Oscar's heart and flesh out all the hurt Bosie's betrayal caused him. The anger, the emptiness, the devastating pain. It's all in these words." He slapped his hand on the paper, then brushed a finger across his eye. "This is going to make audiences weep. I don't know how you came up with so much emotion."

She shrugged. "I've got a lot of experience with betrayal." Crap. She hadn't meant to say that out loud.

"Aw, sweetie." Tim cupped her hand inside his again. "It's okay. We're gonna fix that, right? I promise. In no time at all, you'll be happy again."

Emotions clogged her throat, rendering her mute. She offered a meek smile and squeezed his fingers to let him know she believed him. Inside, though, she knew it was a lie.

19

With the album finally in post-production, Wyatt was able to refocus his attention on Leah. First step: reconnaissance. Oh, not the way Chaz had originally insisted they do it, like some teenage stalkers hiding in a car. And he didn't target Leah, either. No, this time, his attention was on the new guy in her life. Julian. If he planned to win her back to his side, he had to know exactly what he was up against, besides a nice, charming man. He started with a basic internet search and came up empty.

It would probably help if he knew the name of the guy's architectural firm. Still, he found it odd Julian Lannier didn't appear in any kind of article in the local or San Francisco press. Nor did it pop up on any social media site—including Leah's and the shelter's—or any of the career networking sites. Maybe he spelled the name wrong? How else could Lannier be spelled? One n? He tried the new version.

Nope. Still nothing.

This was ridiculous. What kind of architect didn't have an online profile anywhere on the internet? A sleazy one, he told himself. Or one with secrets. Dark secrets? He'd have to dig deeper.

He linked Leah's name to Julian's. Still nothing. Not even a wedding or engagement announcement. He added the shelter's name and expanded his search to include images. Plenty of photos of Leah appeared, mostly at different fundraising events, but still nothing on the mystery man.

"Hey!" Chaz's interruption forced his head up from the laptop. "What's got you so riveted? You watching a movie or something?"

"Just looking something up." He closed the laptop before his searches could be discovered. "I'm curious what kind of promo they're doing for the new album."

"You know they have a pretty good publicity department to take care of that, right?" He clapped a hand on Wyatt's shoulder. "You should get out of your own head for a while. Jenny and I are headed to Annie's Diner for something to eat. You wanna join us?"

After the last time they ate there? When he became the unnecessary three's-a-crowd? "No, thanks. I've got some stuff to take care of here." He put his hand on the laptop, prepared to open it again, when Chaz sat at the table next to him and pushed the computer out of reach.

"What stuff? Come on, man. Let Cooper and his minions take care of the album. The music's good. Exceptionally good. Probably some of the best work you've done in a long time."

"Even if it's all one, long drawn-out apology to Leah?"

A ruddy flush colored Chaz's unshaven face. "You know I didn't mean that. I was tired, frustrated, and missing Jenny something fierce."

"Don't apologize. You were right."

"Well, so what if I was? You tapped into something deep, something meaningful, and the public's gonna love you for it. Especially the ladies. Maybe you should write all your songs for Leah. She seems to bring out the best in you, talent-wise." Wyatt accepted the praise with a curt nod. "Human-wise, that whole relationship is doomed." Wyatt glowered. Chaz slapped his hands on the sides of his thighs and emitted an exasperated sigh. "Come on, man. Come out with us. As far as I know, you haven't left this motel since we wrapped. Except to visit your father. And that always leaves you more miserable than you were beforehand. Come on. It would do you good to get out and socialize a little."

He quirked a brow. "At Annie's Diner?"

"No, but you gotta start somewhere. Feed your stomach first, and then we'll tape up your broken heart, now that you and Leah are officially done. Unless..." Chaz leaned closer to stare at Wyatt's face. "Oh. You're *not* done, are you? Dude, seriously. What's it gonna take?"

Wyatt ran a hand through the hair at his temple. "The truth. I have to tell her everything."

Chaz pulled out his phone. "Tell you what. I'm going to call Jenny and cancel our plans tonight. You and I will order a pizza, and you can run this 'truth' argument past me first. I'll let you know if it's worth chasing her over."

"Just leave it—"

"Nope. I know you too well. You need to either win or lose. For good and forever. So, tonight, you're gonna tell me the whole story, start to finish. As a matter of fact, I'll ask Jenny to join us."

"No!"

"Why not?" He hit a button before placing his phone to his ear. "She knows Leah better than either of us. And she's got the added benefit of knowing Julian, too. She can tell you better than anyone if you've got a shot by telling Leah the full truth."

Before Wyatt could protest, Chaz's attention went to the phone. "Jenny? Change in plans, sweetheart."

♋

After another crazy weekend, on Monday afternoon while Leah reviewed the latest adoption application at her desk in her office, Tim called to ask her to dinner and another brainstorming session for *Oscar Wilde, Vampire Lord.*

"Umm...sure. Where and when?"

"Tonight. I'll pick you up at the shelter right after work."

She looked down at her getup and snorted. "Only if you're taking me to a stable. If we're going anywhere in public, I'll need to go home and shower first."

"Not necessary."

"Oh, believe me, it's totally necessary. I'm covered in pet hair, I smell like a thousand wet dogs, I'm dressed in sweats—"

"You'll be perfect just the way you are, trust me. I'll see you in about ninety minutes."

He hung up before she could argue. Crap. She couldn't let him see her like this. So what if their romance was make-believe? She still had her pride. In a mild panic, she grabbed her purse and left her office, speeding to the front entrance where she found Casey manning the desk. "Where's Jenny?"

He jerked his head. "In the cat house with a customer."

Leah didn't even bother with a coat. She raced outside to the yard and the gray outbuilding decorated with hundreds of black paw prints. When she pulled open the door to the feline sanctuary, a tall woman in a neon pink ski parka stood in front of Jenny with Spooky, the female Russian blue cat, cradled in her arms.

Leah leaned against the door to catch her breath while sweat popped out on her forehead. She probably looked like she'd just finished a marathon.

"Leah?" Jenny said with alarm. "Is something wrong?"

"I've gotta run home. Can you hold down the fort while I'm gone?"

"Yeah, sure, of course. What's wrong? Is it your dad?"

"No, it's Julian." She shook her head rapidly. "Never mind. It's not bad news. I'll explain when I get back. Thanks. I owe you one." She didn't return to the office, but went straight to the car, and peeled out of the driveway, spitting gravel in her tracks.

When she ran through the front door of the house, her dad sat in the living room with Giselle—holding hands? She had no time to ponder that sight, merely took in the coffee cups on the table and Dad's flustered face.

"Leah? What's wrong? You're home early. And where's your coat? You'll catch pneumonia if you don't—"

"Can't talk," she replied as she tramped up the staircase. "Nothing's wrong. I just need a quick shower and change of clothes. Date after work."

"With Wyatt?"

She didn't have the time to indulge his wistful tone at the moment. "No. Not tonight. Not ever again. That's done, Dad. Let it go."

An hour later, she returned to the shelter, scrubbed, with a little blush on her face, mascara elongating her lashes, and a gold cable knit sweater atop a pair of clean jeans to replace her shoddier wardrobe choices from earlier.

"Hot date tonight?" Jenny asked with a hint of sarcasm.

"Julian's meeting me here after work," she said.

"Ah."

Thank God Casey hadn't heard Jenny, or he might have read a whole bunch of meanings into Jenny's single syllable reply—many of them accurate. "Where's Casey?"

She jerked her head toward the side door. "Feeding the dogs."

"Oh. Good."

"You didn't miss much here," Jenny said with a casual air. "That lady in the cat house was the only potential adopter we had, and she passed because we didn't have a gray cat with green eyes for her."

"What was wrong with Spooky?"

"Spooky has *brown* eyes. Miss Particular is going to shop around and 'might...'" She used her fingers to curl quotation marks around the word. "'...check back with us another time. Like we're gonna order her a cat that fits her wants out of a catalog or something." She rolled her eyes like a teenager annoyed with her mom. "Jeez, what a dope."

Leah sighed. "In that case, you and Casey might as well go home. I'll finish the shift here." She intended to head to her office, but Jenny stopped her.

"Umm...listen, about Julian."

She stiffened. "What?"

"You know I just want you to be happy, right?"

"Who says I'm not happy?"

"Nobody. What I mean is...I don't know..." Jenny picked up a pencil and tapped it, rapid-fire, against the counter. *Rat-a-tat-tat, rat-a-tat-tat.* "I guess, it's just that...God, how do I put this?"

Leah's patience, dancing on the high end of simmer, boiled over.

"What? Spit it out, Jenny."

Rat-a-tat-tat, rat-a-tat-tat. "Well, you know how I told you about me and Chaz?"

"Uh-huh."

"See, that's a different kind of happy than how I used to feel when I thought I was happy. I mean, I never realized how insignificant my life was—no, wait. Not insignificant. More like…boring. No, that's not it, either. Purposeless. Is that a word?"

"It is." Tossing her purse on top of the reception desk, Leah folded her arms over her chest. "Can we get to the point? And quickly, since I can pretty much guess where you're headed with this discussion and I want a chance to blister you with my reply?"

Jenny's gaze flew past her, to the doors leading to the kennels, no doubt making sure Casey stayed out of earshot while she lectured their boss. "That won't be necessary." *Rat-a-tat-tat, rat-a-tat-tat.* "Look, I know you feel fulfilled with the help you give all these animals."

"But…?"

"But, think back, Leah. Think back to how you felt when you and Wyatt were in love."

A flame of temper ignited in Leah. "That was a long time ago, and anyway, it wasn't real."

Rat-a-tat-tat, rat-a-tat-tat. "Be that as it may, don't you want to find 'real' for yourself?"

"Not every woman needs a man to feel whole."

A flush filled Jenny's cheeks. "No, that's true. But everyone needs to experience true, deep, abiding love at least once to feel alive."

"Ah, but, see. You've already said I had that with Wyatt. So I'm good. I've hit my quota. Goodnight, Jen." She glanced at the clock behind her. "You might want to grab your coat. You stay here talking to me any longer, and you'll lose the benefit of the extra time I gave you to leave early tonight."

"That's okay. Chaz is picking me up anyway. Looks like we're both waiting around for our men to come get us."

Leah cocked a brow. "You don't want to go home and shower before you see him?"

She shrugged, and her cheeks tinted pink to the tips of her ears. "I'll shower at his place. I keep a bag there with some stuff in it."

"Wow. You guys really are moving fast." She was prepared to let it go at that point, but another thought struck her. "Wait. Aren't he and Wyatt roommates?"

"Not anymore. They had a disagreement so Chaz got his own motel room. It's only temporary either way. I think, eventually, he and I will get a place together."

"Here? In Osprey Cove?"

"Maybe. Maybe not. That's why I want to see you happy—in case I'm not around."

"You'd give up your career for a guy?"

Jenny's laugh was bitter and harsh. "This isn't a career; it's a job. I love you, Lee, and I don't want to leave here, but if Chaz asks me to go with him, I'm gone. My place is with him. I think, deep down, you understand why I say that. He and I fit. We're connected, even when we're apart. I see something that makes me smile, and it automatically reminds me of Chaz. When something upsets me, I know as soon as I see him, it'll all be better. Every day of my life is sweeter because he's there. And I know he feels the same way about me. Can you understand that? Can you remember what that was like for you?"

For the first time in seven years, she let the warm memories blanket her: the way she'd run across the high school parking lot to launch herself into Wyatt's open arms, how his smile could set butterflies free in her stomach and soda bubbles in her veins, the soothing sound of his heartbeat against hers, the calm and peaceful world they created when locked in a loving embrace. She remembered that all her lyrics in those days were about the happiness of love and its eternal promise. *Take My Heart Again* had been a way for her to put into words all the passion, devotion, and romance Wyatt brought into her life, and she brought to his. The fact that he had commercialized those words for his own benefit didn't diminish their power or make her feelings at the time a lie.

"I do remember," she admitted on a harsh whisper as she took Jenny's hand and squeezed reassuringly. "And I'm happy for you. Really and truly. I hope Chaz realizes what a treasure he has in you and that he always treats you that way."

Any response Jenny would have made was interrupted by Casey's appearance in the room. "All set, Jen," he said.

Her somber expression flipped to that of satisfaction. "Great. The boss and I are giving you the rest of the night off. Scram."

"Cool! Thanks."

He grabbed his jacket from a hook on the rack behind the desk and left, bumping into Chaz on the way in. "Hey, take it easy, pal. Where's the fire?"

"Sorry," the teen said as he hustled out, holding the door for whoever stood behind Chaz.

Julian, Leah assumed. "You're early," she said, "but no biggie. We can probably close up shop now anyway. I'm anxious to get started."

"Good," Wyatt said as he stepped into the room. "So am I."

ℭ

"No one's waiting for you, Wyatt." Her booted heels clicking on the linoleum, Leah strode away from the desk, toward the door that would lead to her office and escape—or so she thought.

Wyatt loved seeing her angry, the sparks in her eyes, the determination in her set jaw. He loved seeing her strong and hard and challenging him. He also loved seeing her soft and vulnerable and open to him. He loved every facet of her. He loved her—period. She was his air, his sunlight, his universe. The last seven years without her had been dark and dismal, but now, now he felt the scattered pieces of his heart pulling together, and his world was brighter, warmer, happier. He loved her, and he knew, though she might not be ready to admit it yet, she still loved him.

"Although," she said, shaking him back to reality, "on second thought, maybe this is perfect timing. Julian's on his way, and we're going out tonight. You'll finally get the chance to meet him. But unless you want to be the awkward fifth wheel, I'd suggest that after you've met, you find something else to do and go away."

"He knows, Leah," Jenny said softly.

Her face paled. "He knows what?"

"About us," another voice chimed in. Tim's. When Leah's fake fiancé strolled into the office, she gasped sharp enough to cut glass. "I guess now's as good a time as any to tell you we've been found out."

Wyatt had met Tim on Friday night, at Jenny's insistence, after he'd confessed why he'd left Osprey Cove seven years ago. The four of them had then hatched the plot unfolding now. He had to admit, he liked the guy, particularly after he learned there was nothing between Tim and Leah. "You hired an actor to play your fiancé? I don't know whether to laugh at your commitment to the lie or shake my head at your desperation. Oh, Leah, you did have me going there for a while. Do you know I even looked him up online? I was terrified he was some kind of con artist or criminal meant to do you harm."

Leah's stunned gaze swerved from Tim to Jenny. "You *told* him? How could you do that to me?" She straightened her spine and tossed her head. "You know what? It doesn't matter. Get out. All of you." She yanked open the side door and fled.

Jenny made a move to go after her, but Chaz stopped her with a hand and nodded at Wyatt. "Now's your chance, Romeo. Go get her."

Offering a grateful nod to the trio who lingered behind, he followed his heart into her office.

She sat at her desk, her head buried in her hands, but looked up at his entrance. Her eyes brimmed with unshed tears. "I don't want to talk to you."

He closed her door with a soft snick and leaned against it. He kept his voice soft and even when he spoke. "Good. I'd rather you listened anyway. I love you, Leah. I never stopped loving you. I'm sorry I left that night without telling you why. You have no idea how sorry I am. If I could do it all over again, I never would have gone, but at the time, I had no choice."

"You think it matters? You think you can just walk in here with your money and your fancy red sports car and your fame, and fool me into believing you? That if you tell me you're sorry, I'll forget all about how you deserted me and I'll fall in love with you all over again?" With a loud sniff, she shook her head. "It won't happen, Wy. Face it. You want us to go back to the way things were so you can feel better about us before you fly out of here for another seven years. Or would it be for good this time?"

"Neither." He took a tentative step closer, careful not to spook her into running again, though, in truth, she'd never get past the desk before he stopped her. "I'm asking you to come with me. To be by my side for *all* time."

Leah waved a hand, dismissing him and his declaration of love. "Forget it. I've got a life here, and it doesn't include you anymore."

Stubborn fool. "So, that's it? You're not even gonna consider giving us another chance to make this work?"

"No." She dropped her gaze to a pile of folders on her cluttered desk. "I guess that makes us even now, huh?"

"Not by a long shot, sweetheart." He pounded on the door twice, and within seconds, the doorknob rattled and voices rang out from the other side of the wall.

Her head shot up. "What's going on?"

He flashed a victorious grin her way. "We're locked in, Leah. You and me. I'm finally going to get a chance to talk to you without worrying you'll run away or someone will pop up to interrupt us. You've got nowhere left to hide. Chaz won't open the door until I tell him to."

Her eyes rounded, and all the color drained from her face. "You can't keep me in here. That's kidnapping."

"I prefer to think of it as a mandatory meeting."

She picked up the phone. "I'll call the police."

His grin grew broader, and he gave her a curt nod. "Go ahead."

She put the phone to her ear, and her eyes blazed fire when she realized there was no dial tone. He watched the emotions play across her face as she scanned the room with frantic determination, followed by the utter defeat when she remembered she left her purse—and her cell phone—on top of the reception desk. Her surrender didn't come easy, which only made him more determined to make everything right between them.

She raked her fingers through her hair and then folded her hands on the pile of papers atop her desk. "You think you've won. But you're wrong." She seemed to reclaim some of her outrage and leveled a steely gaze at him. "Eventually, you'll have to leave or we'll both starve to death."

"Not likely. Your employee, Casey? He moved the mini-fridge from the dispensary, the microwave from the office kitchen, and a few other necessities in here while you went home to get ready for your 'date.' You look beautiful, by the way." Ignoring his compliment, she turned her chair to view the room as a panorama. He wondered what buzzed in her head when she noted how completely she'd fallen for their trap. Along with all the appliances, Casey had brought in a case of bottled water, a carton of microwaveable meals, and the office drip pot with its requisite filters and can of coffee. "We've got enough supplies in here to keep us going for weeks. Surrender, Leah. We outmaneuvered you."

"I guess you did," she murmured. "Congratulations. How much did it cost you to get my friends to turn on me? What'd you promise them? I hope to God Jenny held out for more than a pair of concert tickets."

He bit back a smile. He'd always loved her quick wit. "I simply gave them the same thing I want to give you, the truth."

"Uh-huh. Right. Some sob story where you're the victim, and I'm the big, bad villain determined to tie my anchor around your neck? How you had to get away from here before I doomed you into staying in a town you hated forever with a woman you could barely tolerate and responsibilities you weren't ready for?"

Anchor? Doom? Responsibilities? What was she rambling about? "Nothing so dramatic, sweetheart. I was a dumb kid, scared out of my mind—"

She slapped a palm on her desk, and her head shot up, eyes filled with fury. "And what was I? You don't think I was scared?"

"You? You had nothing to be scared of."

The fiery light left her eyes, and she sagged in her chair. She looked tired. Beaten. She sighed and scrubbed a hand over her cheek. "What do you want from me, Wyatt?"

At last, he approached her in three long strides, stopping at the side of her desk. "A chance. One chance to find out where we went wrong."

"We know where we went wrong. You left me when I needed you the most. You saw the opportunity to get away from the town you hated, the father you hated, and the girlfriend you hated, all before the truth got out, and you took it."

He knelt beside her chair and took her icy hands in his warm ones. "I loved you. I left because I loved you and I didn't want to drag you down. You were about to go to vet school, you had plans, a bright future ahead of you—"

"I was pregnant!" The outburst flew out of her, and she yanked her hands away to cover her mouth.

Thunderstruck, Wyatt stumbled, landing on his backside on the floor. His mouth dried to dust. "Pregnant? You were...pregnant when I left?" The idea had never occurred to him. A thousand questions floated through his mind, only a few tangible enough to be vocalized. "How...? When...? What...? Where...?"

She calmed enough to give him some answers, but tears streamed down her cheeks. "How? The normal way. When? I was about seven weeks along when you left. So I'm guessing we conceived on...the night Cooper came to the club? Give or take." Her words sped up, becoming almost gibberish in her haste. "What? I assume you mean boy or girl, and the truth is I don't know. I lost the baby in the first trimester, which I guess answers where, too. Gone. Just like you. *Gone.*" The last word came out a croak, and she collapsed into the desk, burying her head in her arms.

He wanted to reach for her, to hold her close and beg her forgiveness, but couldn't move. Numbness stole over him. Leah had been pregnant when he left. Pregnant.

She moved first, lifting her head to rest her chin on her forearm and look down at where he huddled, a mindless mess. "You didn't know," she stated, as if the idea had only now been confirmed for her.

"No!" he managed to say through his tight throat. "I swear I had no idea."

"I always thought that was why you left."

"God, Leah, I would never...you can't possibly think I...but you *did*, didn't you? When you told me a medical problem kept you out of veterinary school, that's what you were referring to? Our baby?"

She shook her head and sniffed, then wiped her fists across her cheeks. "When I miscarried, I had a complication. I needed emergency surgery to save my life."

"You almost died?" Because of his baby. Because of him. And where was he when she was alone, fighting for her life? In a studio? Silencing the pangs of his conscience while he stole her last gift to him? Laughing at one of Cooper's lame jokes? Shoving her memory far into the back of his head where she couldn't haunt him night and day? He gauged her face now, the hard stony look to her expression, and dared to state the obvious. "There's more, isn't there? What else don't I know?"

She clutched her stomach. "The surgery I had was a hysterectomy."

The air left his lungs. She hated him—with good reason. While he'd reached for the stars, she'd clawed and scrabbled just to survive. "I didn't know, Leah. I swear, I didn't know."

"Yeah, well," she replied, firm and frigid, "now, you do."

20

Leah managed to push away from the desk and stand, although her legs were like Jell-O, wobbling uncontrollably. "We're done now, right? No reason to continue this charming stroll down Memory Lane. For what it's worth, I don't blame you for what happened. I'm over it. It might be a shock for you right now, but I would imagine you'll get over it faster than I did. So, I'd appreciate it if you'd do whatever voodoo you have to with Chaz to get us out of here. I want to go home."

She wished the words would have come out stronger, without the audible shudders that conveyed she was emotionally wrung out. Still, she took a deep breath, steeled herself on her unsteady legs, and waited for him to place the order to unlock the door. The sooner she got out of here, the sooner she could fall apart in private.

With clumsy motions, he scrambled to his knees, then got to his feet. Facing her, he folded his arms over his chest. "No."

She blinked, but managed to keep her jaw from gaping. "No? Did you just say no?"

"No. It's my turn."

Her nerves, stretched taut by the last half hour, snapped and crackled with white-hot anger, and she let the sarcasm fly. "Are you *kidding* me? Do you think, after what I just told you, anything you tell me about what you've done in the last seven years is going to make a difference? What kind of story could you possibly have? How you couldn't get your favorite table at some swanky Hollywood restaurant? That your last album didn't sell as well as you'd hoped? Oh, how my heart breaks for you."

He shook his head. "This wasn't meant to be a contest, Leah."

"Darn right! Because if it had been, you would've lost."

"I already lost. Maybe not as much as you, but I lost, too."

His tone was forlorn, and her soft heart melted slightly. The news had to have devastated him—no! Who cared if what happened to her upset him? She'd lived it, survived it. He would, too. She curled her hands into fists, hoping to strengthen her fortitude. "Yeah, well, like you said, it's not a contest."

"I still want to tell you what happened."

Oh, for crying out loud! She leaned against the door, feigning indifference. "Fine. Go for it. Make it quick though. It's been a long week, and I'm tired."

"Sit down, Leah." He rolled her chair around the desk and pushed it toward her.

"If you don't mind, I'd rather stand."

"I'm asking for a few minutes of your full attention. I think you can give me that." She stared at the chair and glared up at him. "The faster you sit, the faster you can get out of here."

She sat. "Happy now?"

"Not particularly. Look, I admit, what you just told me…" He leaned a hip against her desk and raked a hand through his hair. "I never saw it coming. And once we've gotten past this, I'm going to want to talk to you in more detail about what happened. I want to spend the rest of my life making it up to you however I can—"

"That's not necessary—"

"Let me finish, please. I love you, Leah. I never stopped loving you." She opened her mouth to object, but he placed his index finger to his lips, and she bit back her retort. "Thank you. When Cooper first told me the record deal only included me, I turned him down. I had no intention of going without you. Or the rest of the band, for that matter."

"Funny how quickly your resolve crumbled." He cocked his head at her, and she squirmed in the chair. "Right. Your turn. Go on."

"Like I said, I had no intention of going without you. Not without strong persuasion."

"What kind of persuasion?"

"My father, for one. He was getting worse by the day. You know that. He didn't have me to pound on with his fists anymore, so he used his words instead. Every time I went to that house, it was like he'd been storing up all his hatred and vitriol to spew at me. The day after I turned down Cooper's offer, Dad and I got into another battle. This time, I really lost my cool. He said something that had me seeing red, and the next thing I knew, I had him pushed up against the wall with my elbow rammed in his throat. I swear to God, I could've killed him. I almost did."

"What stopped you?"

"You."

Her hand rose to her chest. "Me? I wasn't even there!"

"You called. When the phone rang, it shook off whatever…rage I was experiencing, and I jumped back. Once the old man caught his breath, he started shouting about calling the cops and pressing assault charges."

"I heard him that day," she recalled. "And you rushed me off the phone so quick..." At the time, she thought he suspected the reason she was calling, to tell him she was pregnant. His "Can't talk now, I'll call you later" were the last words exchanged between them. She shook off the bitterness and focused on the details of his story. "Your father always threatened to call the police on you. He never did, though, because he knew they'd find out he'd been beating you for years."

"Yeah, but this time, I *did* assault him. And I wasn't a kid anymore. I was a grown man. He knew what he was doing that day. He deliberately taunted me. I don't know whether having me arrested was the end game, or if he'd done it just to prove his violent blood ran as strongly in me as it did in him. Either way, he won that day. After years of beatings and insults and neglect, he'd finally succeeded. He turned me into a monster. He knew it, and he made sure I knew it, too. "

Compassion stirred inside her, and she placed a hand on his thigh. "That's not true, Wyatt. You were never like him. Never. You should've come to me."

"I did. Or, at least, I tried. Your mother came to the door before I even made it to the porch, asked me to go for a walk with her."

A queasiness roiled her stomach. "My...mother?"

"Uh-huh."

"What did she say to you?"

"She made me promise that I'd leave you alone."

Leah leaped from the chair so fast it tilted backward and landed on the floor with a clatter. "What?!"

"She and your dad wanted you to go to veterinary school, get your degree. And they thought as long as I was in the picture, you wouldn't do your best. You'd focus on me and the band, your grades might falter, and you'd lose the scholarship. I had to promise her I'd leave you alone until you got your degree. She even offered me money to leave town."

Leah's stomach somersaulted, and she wanted to retch. Mom? Mom made Wyatt leave? Offered to *pay* him to leave? How could she?

"I-I don't understand," she murmured. "Why did my mother do that? And why on earth would you agree?"

He bowed his head to stare at his hand. "Your parents wanted better for you, better than some lowlife son of a drunk with anger issues. So did I. How could I say no?"

She gripped the arms of the chair and bounced with so much resentment, the wheels skidded on the floor. "How could you say yes? Why didn't you fight for me? For *us*? I would've."

When he looked up again, the anguish etched onto his face made her feel two inches tall. "I'd just fought my father for us and lost. I was facing possible arrest, I had a dead-end job, I was living in a one-room closet in the back of a hair salon, and now I was supposed to face off against your parents?"

"Wait. What do you mean you fought your father for us?"

Wyatt waved her off. "He was drunk, it was ugly. Leave it at that."

A deep heat flared in her cheeks and spread to her ears. She knew what he refused to say. Over the years, Ezra Blackthorne had reserved some of his most heinous and vicious innuendo to insult her—as a way of provoking a violent reaction out of Wyatt. If he wouldn't tell her what was said, after so many years, it had to have devastated him. The old man always accused her of cheating on Wyatt—*all* women cheated, he claimed. It wasn't in their nature to be loyal. Had he suspected she was pregnant? Did he taunt Wyatt with the idea the baby wasn't his? He'd pretty much insinuated as much at the nursing home. Was that what had enraged Wyatt?

A ball of bile scorched her throat, but the question burned hotter, and she swallowed with distaste. "What did he say about me?"

Wyatt grimaced. "Words I would never repeat to anyone. Vile filth. I don't want to talk about him, not now or ever again. He has nothing to do with us." He knelt at her chair again. "I'm sorry, Leah. I'm so sorry. I was scared and stupid and I thought I was being noble by leaving you behind. If I'd known about the baby, I would've told your parents to forget it and taken you *both* with me that night."

The enormity of his words lay squarely across her shoulders, weighing her deeper into the chair. She wanted to curl into a ball, protect herself from the pain of the past, but Wyatt had suffered, too. Was her pain so much greater than his? No. Not by a long shot.

She laid her palm on his cheek. "Would you have known what to do when I started bleeding? I didn't. I was scared and stupid, too. If it wasn't for my mother insisting I go to the hospital…" A sudden thought occurred to her and lit a new spark of outrage. "My dad kept pushing me to talk to you, to tell you about the baby." To clear his conscience? Were his constant allusions about not keeping secrets meant to atone for the secrets he kept from *her?*

"Don't," he said, giving her hand a squeeze. "Don't blame your mother—or your father." Amazing how he could still read her mind, after all these years. "They wanted what was best for you. You said it yourself. You almost died. We were two stupid kids, in way over our heads. Besides, it was your dad who made me come home."

She thought nothing else he said could surprise her. She was wrong. "My father?" Wyatt nodded. "How?"

"He emailed me through my website. Not once, but a dozen times. He must have realized I had people who handled my publicity, so when he didn't get a reply to his first two or three messages, he sent a copy of your mother's obituary notice, along with a photo of the four of us from some family picnic when you and I were in eleventh grade. He wrote, 'Please let Wyatt know the woman he considered his second mother has passed.' It got the desired attention. I really was in Europe when the email was forwarded to me. I called from my hotel in Berlin and spoke to your dad. He told me it was time I come home and figure out what you and I planned to do with the rest of our lives. I already knew what I wanted. What I always wanted. You."

A shallow cry escaped her lips, and the tears began again in earnest. She couldn't speak, could barely breathe.

Wyatt took advantage of her temporary disability. "I finished the tour, started work on the new album, and had Cooper make the arrangements for us to come here."

She sniffed, leveling a tear-filled gaze at him. "You called my father, but in all those arrangements, you couldn't call me?"

"I called the house that night. It would have been…I don't know…three in the afternoon here? You were at work at the time, and your dad thought it best I come home and speak with you in person, rather than over the phone or through email. I've been trying ever since." He brought her to her feet and held her against his chest. His head dipped to her shoulder, nestled in her hair. "I love you, Leah. I never stopped loving you. I'm so sorry. I'm here for good, if you'll have me. Can you ever forgive me?"

She placed her hands against his chest and pushed away, allowing a wide gap of space between them. "I don't know. I want to, really. My life would be a whole lot easier if I could just let go, you know?" At his nod, she sighed. "But you have no idea how much pain I went through when I realized you were gone. Thinking you'd left me because I was pregnant, and God, Wy, I was so scared. I will never forget how my mom looked at me when I told her. Like I'd shattered her world. I thought she hated me."

"I doubt she could ever hate you." He touched her hand, light and hesitant. "She probably had some choice words for me, though."

She offered him a wan smile. "Oh, most definitely. After a few weeks, we both got used to the idea, and I started considering names. David for a boy, or Laura for a girl."

"My middle name and my mother's name," he murmured, his tone tinged with awe. "Even then, you still loved me."

No surprise he figured that much out. "Even now, I still love you," she admitted. The weight fell off her shoulders, leaving her lighter, yet still burdened by the past. She gave him a stern look. "Before I can move forward with us, I have to make you understand where my life has gone since you went away."

He nodded. "By all means, tell me. I want to understand."

"Like I said, Mom and I got used to the idea, and I started making plans. I picked out a crib, figured out a way I could juggle a baby and part-time school, made a hundred lists of things to do, to prepare for, to worry about. I was actually getting excited, you know? I was going to be a mom." The pain sliced through her anew, and she clutched her empty belly, as she always did when talking about her loss. "I woke up one morning, the sheets soaked with blood, and I knew. God help me, I knew, but I couldn't move. I was...stuck. And I wanted to die. Right then and there, I thought, 'If I don't say anything, if I don't call for help, all the hurt and the anger and the missing Wyatt will end.' I don't know why I did, because I honestly thought I'd be better off dead, but some self-preservation instinct forced me to scream, and Mom came running. She called 9-1-1, and I woke up a bunch of hours later, empty. Totally and completely *empty*."

The last word came out as an emotional croak, and she collapsed, wavering on her unsteady legs. Wyatt pulled her into his arms again. This time, she didn't fight. After years of standing on her own, she relished in allowing him to brace her against the memories. "When I got out of the hospital, it was too late to go to vet school, and I floated around for about three or four months, unable to do more than remember to breathe once in a while, going through the motions of life, not feeling anything. I couldn't function. Thinking about tomorrow or yesterday hurt too much. Once again, Mom came to my rescue. She told me about Mr. Brooks looking for someone to help out at his new shelter. The moment I walked in and saw the dogs shaking in fear, their sad eyes looking at me for some kind of affection, I realized, in my self-pity party, I had forgotten that I still had so much love to give. I asked for a job, and Mr. Brooks hired me on the spot. And once again, I got used to a new normal, only to have the rug yanked out from under me." A block of tears clogged her throat, and she sobbed.

"Your mom got sick," he surmised. When she nodded, he ran his hand down her back, soothing her, rocking her in a slow motion that offered security and love.

The rest of the story poured out of her in a flood of words. "Dad couldn't deal. I never realized how strong Mom was until she wasn't strong anymore. The worse she got, the more he fell apart. When she passed away, he lost it. Worse than I did when I lost the baby—I guess because they'd been together so much longer. I mean, I barely had time to get used to being pregnant and I wasn't anymore. But Mom and Dad had been together for twenty-five years. Dad went from being part of a set to being a solo, and he went off the deep end. He obsessed over what happened, questioned the doctors and the hospital staff about how they could have missed her aneurysm. When he learned there was no easy way to prevent the possibility for many surgical patients, he decided he'd find one. He locked himself in their bedroom and wouldn't come out. Years went by with him up there, and me handling the house, the bills, the shelter. I did all the work, faced every challenge, while he hid from reality. The only joy I've experienced since you left town is in this shelter, with these pets." She took a shuddering breath and confessed her darkest sin in a whisper filled with remorse. "I wanted to hate the very thought of you. I'd hear your new song on the radio, or see your latest video, and I'd tell myself I hated you. I hated you for leaving me, I hated you for having achieved your dream while I was stuck here with a life so different from what I'd planned, and I hated you for never coming back—not even for Mom's funeral." A bitter laugh escaped. "I don't know what I expected. Like, through some kind of mental voodoo, you'd know about her death and show up to be there with me. I sat in the front row in the funeral parlor those three days and nights, and every time a shadow crossed over me, I'd look up, expecting to see you standing there with your arms open for me. But it was never you. You didn't come. Not for my miscarriage, not for Mom's funeral, not for seven years."

He groaned, low and deep in his throat, and the sound rumbled through his chest. "I'm sorry. You're right. I can never say it enough for it to mean what I want it to. You have every right to hate me."

"But I don't. I never hated you." She clung to him, and years of loneliness, of sorrow, of hidden resentment melted away. "I love you, Wyatt. I never stopped loving you. No matter how hard I tried to convince myself otherwise, I love you. I'm sorry, too. And yes, I'll forgive you if you'll forgive me. Stay. Always. Please."

His mouth came down on hers, seeking all she had to offer, and she gave to him gladly. His familiar scent and taste, long lost to the years, evoked memories of happier times, of laughter and love. She lost herself in the sensations, in the feel of this man who'd come home to her at last.

When he pulled away, he touched his index finger to her cheek, tracing the lone tear that slid from her eye. "I guess I can tell Chaz to let us out now."

She stood on tiptoe, wrapped her arms around his neck, and drew his mouth back to hers. "What's the rush?"

21

The release party for Wyatt Blackthorne and the Ungrateful's new album, *Homecoming*, took place at the My Furry Valentine event to raise funds for Fur-Ever Friends Animal Shelter. Ricky Delacruz took the stage first, spinning all the crowd's favorite songs, and getting everyone up on the dance floor. Blissful in Wyatt's arms and basking in rediscovered love, Leah danced and greeted their many guests with undisguised joy. Cupid had shot a lot of arrows in the last few months. Chaz and Jenny glowed with their own aura of romance. She only wished she could've convinced her father to leave the house and come to tonight's event. Giselle had volunteered to stay with Dad, but Leah suspected she would've arm-wrestled anyone who dared to tell her no. There was a definite spark of something between those two, as well.

After dinner, Ricky packed up his booth and his props, and Wyatt's crew set up a lone microphone and stool on the stage. Just before his introduction, Wyatt pulled Leah into a dark corner behind the curtain.

"What are you doing?"

"Blackmailing you," he said as he nuzzled her neck.

She giggled, his lips nibbling shivers down her spine. "Be serious."

"I am. You are the most beautiful woman here tonight."

"And yet I'll never be as pretty as you."

"God, I'm going to miss that smart mouth of yours when I'm on tour! By next week, I'll be in Seattle."

She sighed, half-delight and half-despair. "I know. Then Portland, Spokane, Boise, San Francisco and Sacramento." She'd memorized his itinerary for the next six weeks and rattled them off with little enthusiasm. "Los Angeles, San Diego, Carson City, Cedar City, Phoenix, Tucson."

He chucked her under the chin. "Then home for a week before I head to the mountain states. A few weeks there, and home again before the central states. And so on…" He kissed her just below her earlobe. "And so on…" He kissed her eyelids. "And so on." He kissed her lips until she swayed on her feet and her brain took off to Venus. When he pulled away again, he took both her hands in his. "I can't ask you to go with me because I know you'll never leave your shelter. I'm willing to share you with your dogs and cats, but I want to make sure you know I'm coming home to you—no matter where I go, I'm always coming home to you as soon as I can."

"I know that, silly."

"No. I need to make it official." He knelt in front of her, a mere inch from the hem of her silver gown. "I loved you yesterday with all my heart. I love you today with all my soul. I'll love you for all my tomorrows. Marry me, Leah? So I'll always know you're waiting for me when I come home."

She gasped, too stunned to speak.

"Say yes, or I'll leave your guests out there hanging without after-dinner entertainment."

Her heart flew, and she would have sworn the sun burst inside her chest with her happiness. "I would've said yes without the threat, and you know that. Yes. With all my heart, with all my soul, for all my tomorrows, too. I love you. Yes."

From the stage, Chaz's voice boomed, "Ladies and gentlemen, my good friend, Wyatt Blackthorne."

"To be continued." He rose to his full height and kissed her again, quick and hard. While she tried to catch her breath, he picked up his guitar from the stand at the edge of the stage and walked out to the applause of the crowds. Leah remained in the wings, her smile too big to contain.

"Thank you," he said, his voice subdued as he took the microphone. "First of all, I want to thank you for your generosity tonight and let you know that we raised more than ten thousand dollars for the Fur-Ever Friends Mobile Veterinary Van project." The audience clapped with enthusiasm. "And because you've been so forthcoming with your donations, I'm going to be forthcoming in my own way and fill you all in on what happened backstage only a minute ago. I just asked the owner of Fur-Ever Friends, Leah Stewart, to marry me, and don't ask me why because she could do so much better, but she said yes." While the crowd cheered and applauded even harder, he added, "Years ago, Leah wrote the perfect love song. It was supposed to be our song, and while we now share it with a lot of other couples…" Uncomfortable laughter twittered from the crowd. "…*Take My Heart*

Again will always be *our* song. For the first time ever, tonight, to celebrate our engagement, I'm going to ask her to come out here and sing it with me."

Leah's smile evaporated, and panic set in. The audience hooted and whistled. Wyatt waved her onstage, but she shook her head in a frantic attempt to get him to take the words back.

Chaz appeared at her side. "Congratulations. Welcome to Wyatt's world. Come on. I'll walk you out there."

She clutched at his tuxedo lapels. "No, Chaz, I can't. I haven't sung in years, and I haven't sung that song in…forever. I can't go out there now and sing it for all those people."

He removed her hands and took her by the arms. "Look at me, Leah." When she complied, he asked, "Do you love him?"

What kind of question was that? His timing was awful. "You know I do."

"Then don't sing it to all those people. Sing it to *him.* The way you did when you first wrote it. He's giving you the chance to take the song back from him and make it yours again."

She stared at him, agog, and allowed what he said to sink in.

"Come on." He offered his arm again. "You ready?"

"I've been ready for seven years," she replied and, alone, walked out onto the stage to the applause and cheers of the crowd.

♈

Leah pulled into the driveway and turned to her passenger. "Ready?"

Penny flashed her canine grin, tail wagging, and tongue lolling.

"Okay, then. Let's do this." She turned off the engine, unbuckled her seatbelt and made sure Penny's leash wasn't hooked on anything. "Stay. I'm coming around to get you."

The star graduate of the most recent canine companionship program sat up, paws straight, eyes bright.

Leah walked around to the passenger side and led Penny out of the car and up the walkway.

At her approach, her father opened the door and peered outside. "Who's this? What's going on, Leah?"

"Dad, meet Penny. Penny, this is your new companion." She handed the leash to her father. Her engagement ring, a diamond surrounded by amethysts—the real symbol of deep, abiding love in the gem world—caught the spring sunlight and sparkled, reminding Leah yet again how much she was loved by the man who owned her heart.

After taking the leash, he bent to pet the dog between her ears.

"Hello, Penny." He glanced back to Leah. "Look at her eyes."

"I know. It might sound ridiculous, but they remind me of Mom's."

He smiled. "They're the same color, and she seems to have that same compassion shining in them."

"Penny's been through a lot of hardship. I thought you and she could heal together. She's a good girl, very affectionate, and she's eager to please. She'll need to be walked—outside—a few times a day. Don't worry. She'll show you the way."

A flash of fear lit up her father's face, and Leah waited a beat, silently praying he'd take the lifeline she was throwing to him. He cleared his expression and nodded. "When should we get started?"

"If you'd like to grab your coat, we can go right now."

"Okay."

Okay. While she took the leash again, he returned inside. Leah crouched on the porch and nuzzled Penny's face. "Good girl."

Dad returned, wearing a lightweight tan jacket with dust on the shoulders. Leah fought the urge to brush it away. This was a big step for Dad, and she didn't want to give him any reason to balk. They headed for the sidewalk, her father tilting his face toward the sun and smiling. She inhaled and took his hand in hers.

"Wyatt comes home tomorrow, huh?" he said.

"Uh-huh." Her heart skipped a beat or two at the thought. The new album was a success and demanded concert stops all over the country, but he always came home to her. They'd bought a house in a nearby town, close to the shelter and their friends, but in a place where they could build new memories, a new life. Together.

"What are you doing 'til then?"

"Tim's coming over this afternoon to work on the score for his play. It's really starting to come together. He ran the opening number past a director friend, and he says we might have a hit on our hands, if the rest of the songs are of the same caliber."

"That's great! I'm so proud of you, sweetheart." He stopped when Penny paused to smell a forsythia bush just beginning to bud. "I'd ask you to dinner, but I already have a guest tonight."

"No kidding? Giselle's coming over again?"

"Yup. She's a nice lady. I enjoy her company, and after all the dinners she cooked for me in the last two years, it feels good to be able to cook for her for a change."

She linked her arm through her dad's and tilted her head to his shoulder. "Should I be planning a double wedding instead of a single?" she joked.

He chuckled. "Small steps, Leah. Small steps."

ABOUT THE AUTHOR

Gina Ardito is the award-winning author of more than twenty romances in contemporary, historical, and paranormal sub-genres. She's a hybrid author, currently published by Montlake Romance, The Wild Rose Press, and independently. In 2012, she launched her freelance editing business, Excellence in Editing. She's hosted workshops around the world for writing conferences, author organization meetings, and library events.

To her everlasting shame, despite all her accomplishments, she'll never be more famous than her dog, who starred in commercials for 2015's Puppy Bowl. For more information, to sign up for her newsletter, and to learn about all things Gina, visit her website at https://ginaardito.com.

OTHER BOOKS BY GINA ARDITO

THE MONEY SERIES
The Bonds of Matri-money
A Run for the Money
♦

A Little Slice of Heaven
♦

THE NOBODY SERIES
Nobody's Darling
Nobody's Business
Nobody's Perfect
♦

Chasing Adonis
Duping Cupid
♦

THE AFTERLIFE SERIES
Eternally Yours
In Your Dreams
Waiting in the Wings
♦

THE CALENDAR GIRLS SERIES
Charming for Mother's Day
Duet in September
Reunion in October
Homecoming in November
Memories in December
♦

A Love to Keep Me Warm
Lightning in a Bottle

www.ingramcontent.com/pod-product-compliance
Lightning Source LLC
Chambersburg PA
CBHW060943180626
46817CB00004B/1689